A Dream Transformed

Stella's Story

Barbara Beck Lovelace

ISBN 978-1-0980-3169-5 (paperback)
ISBN 978-1-0980-3170-1 (digital)

Christian Faith Publishing, Inc.
832 Park Avenue
Meadville, PA 16335
www.christianfaithpublishing.com

Cover photograph used by gracious permission of Geoff Caulton of Norfolk, England, Photodetective.co.uk, who owns the original image and copyright.

Printed in the United States of America

With everlasting gratitude for those who have gone before,
abiding love for those whose lives I share,
and unceasing prayer for those who will follow,
I share the joy of telling this story.

CHAPTER 1

Stella almost ducked as the heavy blanket of fog rolled over her head and seemed to find a resting place in her small space as she held fast to the ship's railing. "Just like Dublin when we left," she murmured to herself. The several days of sunshine during the past weeks of her life aboard *Destiny*, as it ploughed the North Atlantic toward America, had failed to lift the heaviness from her heart or heal her wounded spirit. She was sure nothing would.

"Stella, Stella, do come away from the railing and queue up with the rest of the family," came a warning voice out of the somber gray blanket. Josephine, dear Jo, her older sister by two years. Now nineteen, Jo seemed to always take a special interest in reeling in Stella.

By not responding, Stella earned a firm hand on her arm and received a whispered "Papa will be worried if we're not all together when it's time to disembark." *Papa, always Papa*, thought Stella. This was his dream, this coming to America to start a new life. It certainly wasn't hers. Her dream, left behind in Ireland, was likely shattered forever. How she resented Papa!

But here they all were, nearing the new Ellis Island Inspection Station, and seemingly at the doorstep of New

5

York City: Papa and Mama, and also Jo and Alice, and Michael and small Alfred. Her entire family, all born and reared in Ireland, was now and forever cast faraway from her beloved Dublin.

Stella reflected again on Jo's words as they fell asleep last night in the close quarters of their second-class cabin, "Really, Stella, you might as well determine to make the most of it." Stella sighed heavily and reluctantly released her grip on the railing to rejoin her family.

Dublin, October 1891

It had been a perfect day, Stella mused as she nibbled on orange cake and sipped a gentle Irish tea while smiling with Rose and Mavis, her two dearest friends. She let the exotic aroma of the sweet tea and sugar saturate her senses as she relaxed into the late afternoon with the young ladies of the Poetry Society.

Meeting in Miss Mary Dowling's parlor, the group had just finished reading aloud Yeats' "The Stolen Child," and Stella had been selected to read the last verse. She had read it, according to Miss Dowling, with excellent elocution and feeling. Rose and Mavis thought so too, and Stella was pleased that her long hours spent practicing her elocution skills had earned her some praise. Elocution, Stella knew, was the skill of clear and expressive speech, with distinct pronunciation and articulation. She aimed to excel at it.

The young ladies of the Poetry Society met twice a month to share their keen interest in and recitation of classic poetry of bygone eras and to consider the literary merits of the poetry of living Irish poets. Miss Dowling, a spinster devotee of the written and spoken arts, selected the poets and the readings from her family's extensive home library of literature and poetry. She ever so carefully also judged the offerings of contemporary poets for reading at Society meetings to ensure a good match to the young ladies' sensibilities.

Miss Dowling chose as members of the Society daughters of Dublin's well-known tradesmen who had prospered by serving the needs of the barons of the Dublin textile, brewing, shipbuilding, milling, and other industries. She had chosen Stella Manning because her father owned a much-in-demand watchmaking business, whereas Rose Kelley had gained an invitation because her father traded extensively in printing and publishing. Mavis Sullivan had been invited because her family was well-respected in the business of furniture making.

"Miss D," as her girls called her, believed that these tradesmen's daughters were denied exposure to the gentle arts of poetry and literature that girls from wealthy families enjoyed, and yet their lives afforded enough leisure to benefit from such exposure. Awakening the expressive "souls" of these young ladies from these families was the mission in life she had embraced, having been denied husband and daughters of her own through happenstance and ill luck.

Miss Dowling chose not to dwell on her life this fine afternoon, however, as she bid a cheerful farewell to Stella and the other girls — six in all today — and encouraged each to meditate on poetry and the arts and also to perfect critical reading and elocution talents.

For her part, Stella was prepared to do so but only after enjoying a stroll through Dublin's South City Market with Rose and Mavis, who were on their way to the tram for home. Stella loved living closer than her friends to the welcoming doors of the market's shops, and especially the open stalls that sold everything a modern young Dubliner lady could wish for, from books to millinery, to the finest fabrics for new dresses.

But as Rose and Mavis lingered, today was not a shopping day for Stella. Mama had asked her to hurry home after the Society meeting to help Jo tend to young Alice and

Alfred as she and Papa had an important meeting with their solicitor. Although Stella was curious about this meeting, because Mama rarely attended Papa's business meetings, she thought it best not to pry. Instead, she would try to finagle any available information out of Jo when she reached home. More content to stay home than Stella, her older sister usually had the pulse of family dynamics closer in hand.

Stella didn't mean to snoop. But late in the evening as she walked back to the room she shared with Jo, returning from the kitchen with some rice pudding for a late-night snack, her parents' voices raised in mild contention drew her attention. She paused outside their room, thought better of it and continued, then stopped, turned around, walked back, and decided to listen.

Reflecting on her decision later, she rather wished she hadn't because her whole world tilted in the space of a few minutes.

Papa, sounding patient but urgent, said, "But you see, Esther, this opportunity is made in heaven for our family. Nicholas has prepared the way so well for us. We'll have a shop on the ground floor with ample living quarters above, in a neighborhood frequented by wealthy gentlemen, or at least their servants, for every manner of well-made commodity, but lacking a watchmaker.

"We are well-situated to leave Dublin, with our apprentice Rob eager to take over the shop, and we've been wise with our earnings and savings, so our finances will allow us to make the journey and get established in New York."

New York? Stella was riveted to the closed door.

"But, John," her mama's quieter voice caused Stella to lean in closer to the door, "there are dangers crossing the ocean, even with steamships, and I fear for our family's safety."

"They are safer, larger, sturdier, and faster now, Esther," Papa replied. "And we will cross in the spring when weather is at its best for Atlantic crossings. God will be with us."

Stella caught her breath. *Cross? The Atlantic?* She pressed closer, feeling guilty but irresistibly drawn to the conversation.

"I know you trust your brother, and Nicholas is a reliable man," Mama continued. "But how do you know all will be as he has arranged and written? Will your craft be welcome in New York?"

Stella could hear the excitement in Papa's voice as he said, "More than welcome! A watchmaker's guild has been active since 1866, the first one in America, and they have just celebrated their twenty-fifth anniversary this very year in March with an elaborate banquet.

"Esther, German watchmakers, from fine German families I know, and have corresponded with, founded this guild. It's called the New Yorker Uhrmacher Verein, or Watchmaker's Union of New York. Demand for fine watchmaking has grown apace as the city has expanded in these past decades, even with factory-made watches now available. Many families have become wealthy and seek fine watchmaking. Nicolas says the Union welcomes new members, and he will introduce me to their leaders."

Stella waited quietly for her mother's reply, and it seemed an eternity until Mama spoke, but finally she heard: "John, we have marriageable daughters, and sons to get established in life. How will we accomplish these considerable tasks in a new land without our own Irish people surrounding us?"

"Esther, dear Esther," Papa replied, "there are many, many Irish people in America, especially in New York. And they are our ilk of people too, not just the poor ones who have had to flee from the famines of past years. Many are successful in businesses and trades and have a community of alliances, both personal and professional. Nicholas' family is well-settled, and our children will have cousins nearby.

"And, Esther, our girls will find fine young men, and our sons will have many doors open to them."

Stella heard her mother say softly, "I heed your enthusiasm and yearning, dear one." A pause. "But may we pray about this thing, John, and perhaps talk to the priest?"

"Yes, my darling, we may," Stella heard Papa say gently, "but let's pray without delay and chart our course soon so that if we be of one mind, we may prepare the children, plan all the many details, and let the solicitor know of our decision."

Stella stood stock still, her mind reeling from the import of the private conversation and possible new path in her family's life—in her life. Shock, sorrow—a sense of loss—found their places in her heart, and she slowly turned, then padded quickly down the hall to her room and a sleeping Jo. She wanted to wake Jo and tell her about what she had heard, what might be happening. But it wasn't a sure thing, it wasn't, and she had listened in on a conversation not meant for her ears. Still, tears came without planning.

The pudding abandoned on the bedside table, Stella climbed into bed next to her sister and remembered the last line of Yeats' poem she had read so beautifully—was that just today?—"for the world's more full of weeping..."

October's brisk winds pushed the linden tree branches briskly against Stella's bedroom window, creating a loud scratching sound, which awakened her just after dawn. She lay still, remembering her parents' conversation and saddened by the possibility of great change in her life. *Papa wouldn't do this to them, would he?*

She was not quite ready to get out of the warm bed. Yet, she was eager to begin her day and learn more about

Papa's Grand Plan, as she had just decided to call it. Jo slept soundly still, so Stella eased out of their bed.

A few splashes of the laver's cold water on her face felt refreshing, but a glance in her dressing table's mirror in the early morning's dim light showed her thick brown hair in complete disarray. Quickly scooping up the curly locks into a bun at the nape of her neck, she also pinned back a few errant tendrils around her brow. She dressed in a soft green day dress, securing its bodice's many buttons, and then adding a bright green cloth belt, which Papa always claimed matched the green of her eyes. *Papa*, thought Stella, *dear Papa. Will he be in his shop below stairs or already out and about the city on some errand?*

Papa rose early and always had a meticulous list of tasks to be accomplished and customer demands to be fulfilled, yet managed to take most meals with all of them, save breakfast. As she found her shoes and secured them up to her ankles, Stella smiled as she remembered Papa's kind heart. He found room in each day's busy schedule to listen to each child's questions and conversations, and to show concern for their childish dilemmas. He often worked into the evening to make up for time spent with his family during the day. Surely, he would not uproot their happy family life. Of course, he wouldn't.

Stella stopped to gather some thoughts. Hadn't Papa proved his devotion to all of them—and especially to her? He was ever keen on her studies at the national school she attended for eight years, asking her to read aloud to him, correcting her pronunciation, and encouraging her to reach higher and higher in her quest for knowledge of the language arts, in addition to helping her with her sums.

As she grew into a young lady, Stella considered, he allowed a music teacher, although Stella never did excel in piano, and also a voice teacher. This particular teacher declared Stella's voice range to be extraordinary but not in musical notes. Rather, she encouraged elocution, and thus began Stella's training in that spoken art.

And Papa, she recounted quietly to herself, gave her freedoms, within his rules, of course, to spend time with her friends in worthwhile pursuits such as the Poetry Society, and to explore Dublin's museums and parks. Was it not he who had taken her to the new Museum of Science and Art on Kildare Street after its opening just last year? And when she fell in love with the most ancient of artifacts there, the Tara Brooch from the eighth century, he had gifted her with a truly beautiful replica of it on her sixteenth birthday. She treasured this gift above all her worldly possessions.

Papa. She truly loved and trusted him. Other girls among her circle of friends had pleasant fathers, or at least somewhat pleasant, but hers was the best, she knew. He allowed her, and her sisters, opportunities for learning and adventure other girls only dreamed of, opportunities available only to their brothers.

He had welcomed her into his watchmaking shop too, instructing her first how to wind the numerous beautiful clocks there, and then given her responsibility for helping him care for his creations. Because of her friendly, outgoing and engaging personality, he had encouraged her to spend time with him, to greet customers and speak with them. She was also tasked from time to time with the delicate mission of wrapping and packaging customers' purchases. She loved helping in the downstairs shop and was pleased to be a part of Papa's livelihood.

Yet, though often Stella felt his favorite, he showed great love and attachment to each member of his family, reminding her of the Good Shepherd she had read about in the Bible. She didn't know much about the Bible, but she had heard that story.

Yes, she was blessed with a wonderful father—and a loving mother too, who taught her ladylike manners and habits, plus the womanly art of fine sewing—and she knew

Papa and Mama would always take care of her. Yes, she knew Papa and Mama loved them all dearly.

So Stella asked herself, why was she frightened and feeling so unsettled by Papa's Grand Plan? Why should she feel that way? She resolved to not feel such emotions but rather to trust her future to her parents and to God, whom she didn't know very well in spite of going to Mass every Sunday, but whom her parents said was trustworthy and faithful.

Gaining some peace after her silent but thorough talk with herself, Stella opened her door and stepped into the light of the morning as it sent golden streaks from the high windows onto the highly polished wood of the upstairs hallway.

Descending to the floor below, Stella heard Mama's happy voice in the kitchen, laughing into the day with young Alfred, soon to turn three. The hearty aroma of porridge cooking drew Stella through the parlor and into the warm kitchen, which reigned as the center of family life.

Another childish voice filled the air too, and Stella heard young Michael teasing his little brother. At twelve years old, her oldest brother was up early too, ready for school and a full day of lessons and watchmaking instruction from Papa after lessons were complete. Michael loved learning the trade, Stella knew, but Papa believed in a strict balance between education and trade learning, so young Michael's day was busy with both.

"Stella, you're up early today," Michael commented at her appearance in the kitchen. "To what do we owe this honor?"

A quick hug around his sturdy neck and a kiss on tiptoe to Mama's cheek, then, "To send you off into the world to do great things," she replied, returning the tease.

Regarding little Alfred, Stella smiled at his angelic face, still surrounded by blond baby curls, which Mama begged Papa to let her keep for just a little while longer.

Stella remembered the sadness of years past when Mama had lost another son to fever, baby George, born two years before Alfred, and then the joy of Mama's "last little one" when they welcomed Alfred into the world. Now a chubby and robust small fellow, Mama doted on this sweet boy while trying not to spoil him.

Missing from Mama's brood this morning were only Alice and Jo, but not for long. Jo was tasked with getting eight-year-old Alice up and ready for school, while Mama prepared breakfast and started Alfred on his day. Soon, morning laughter filled the kitchen as Jo followed close behind Alice into the bright and cheerful room, tugging at Alice's braids to apply two saucy ribbons.

With everyone in place, Mama offered a quick blessing over the porridge and her children, as she spooned the creamy offering into bowls for all. Stella watched the steam rise from her bowl as she looked around the small table and helped herself to milk, savoring the early morning moment of camaraderie with those she held most dear. A small voice in her head said, "This is my life, and it's just a normal morning, but how joyful I feel with my dear ones in this happy room. Nothing must change. Ever."

The thought shattered into dozens of pieces as Alfred's attempt to eat quickly caused porridge to fly through the air and land on Alice's dress, which was followed by a shriek from Alice, and then Jo's rush to remove the offending mush before the dress became unpresentable for school. All laughed at Alfred's error, including the small lad himself, except Alice. But her good humor soon returned, and Mama engaged them all in conversation about activities of the day ahead.

"After you see Alice safely into her classroom" — Mama directed at Michael — "do take care to deliver this letter to the postbox before your opening recitations," as she handed him a small envelope with an address in her elaborately written script. Stella craned her neck to see the name of the letter's recipient and caught a glimpse of Mama's sister's name. She wondered if Mama was writing to her of the Grand Plan Papa had proposed. Surely not because she herself and the others were not privy to it, except for her inadvertent knowledge gained late last evening.

Her family was never one to harbor secrets, and she didn't like it one bit that one might be happening beneath her very eyes.

After dishes were done and the kitchen put in order, Mama suggested to Stella and Jo a morning of sewing in the parlor while Alfred played nearby. Never content to sit still, Alfred first climbed on his rocking horse, a beloved toy enjoyed by each Manning child in turn over the years. Made of solid mahogany and hand-carved, it sported saddles and bridles made of leather, all mounted on a sturdy rocker.

As she settled down with her sewing, Stella delighted in hearing Alfred's enthusiastic cries of "giddy-up, giddy-up," as he enjoyed his ride for some minutes, and then a "whoa" as he slowed. Dismounting, he surrounded himself with his wooden trains and building blocks, while the ladies sewed.

Mama was an expert seamstress, and she had taught Jo and Stella well. To her, sewing was both an art and a science, and she made many of the family's day-to-day clothes. Papa's shirts were nicely tailored and fitted although they were practical workaday garments, and blouses and skirts for the girls were stylish and pretty, even if they did have large hems for "letting out" as the girls grew.

Stella enjoyed sewing and had gained considerable skill over the years. Right now, she was working on a school dress for Alice of soft blue woolen. She had cut this

15

garment from a bolt of fabric secured by Papa in exchange for rebuilding and restoring a badly damaged watch for his friend Mr. Murray, who owned a textile business. Papa had come by several such bolts over the years, some of fine Irish linen, as he did a thriving business with many families in the close-knit tradesmen community.

Pleasant chatter filled the morning about everyday things of interest to the three women: friends from church who were ill, news from neighbors who had visited, and opinions about the new portrait of Queen Victoria by the German-born British painter von Herkomer. Stella, although a great admirer of the aging queen, soon grew bored, however, and put her sewing aside to peruse a copy of the latest edition of *Peterson's Magazine* sitting on a nearby table.

She adored this magazine's short stories, poetry, and serialized fiction tales, and she loved the pictures and descriptions of the latest fashions. "Look, Mama and Jo," she exclaimed, turning a new page, "here is a French fashion plate that features a dress just perfect for afternoon visiting, and we can send for the pattern to make it ourselves."

Mama took a look and pronounced the gown too ostentatious but agreed it could be modified to suit with a pattern in hand. Jo, much more focused on sedentary pastimes, which fit well with her quieter, more reclusive habits and preferences, announced, "Really, Stella, I cannot see you in that French gown, but do turn to the pages with the embroidery patterns and puzzles."

Mama smiled to herself as she thought about how her firstborn and second-born daughters were so very different from each other. Whereas Jo was quiet, unassuming, and prone to peaceful, solitary, and meditative pursuits, Stella was outgoing in the extreme, exceptionally curious, and forever seeking new experiences and adventures. Sometimes Mama wished Jo were a little more active, and Stella a little less so, but she loved them both for who they were, and she nurtured each one's personality accordingly.

"Must you always be so boorish, Jo?" asked Stella. "Why would you wish to do puzzles when *Peterson's* short stories are so fascinating and the fashion pages are so interesting? Look at the accessories that go with this gown. So very enchanting!" At which, Jo rolled her eyes at Stella and picked up her sewing again with a "harrumph," which caused Stella to glare at her and prepare another barb.

But Mama spoke up to intervene in the potential conflict she saw brewing with her daughters, and interjected, "Stella, dear, do find the pages with recipes and housekeeping advice. *Peterson's* always has some clever new dish or nugget of household idea that I can put to use."

Alfred suddenly called an end to the sewing and perusing activities with a loud wail signaling hunger, and all three women turned to see Papa hurrying upstairs from his shop below with an expression that, as Stella recalled later, could only be considered incredulous.

CHAPTER 2

Dublin
October to December 1891

Papa collapsed in a heap in the nearest chair, quite unlike him, and paused a moment to collect his thoughts. "An extraordinary thing has happened, dear ones." Mama picked up Alfred and quieted him as Papa sat up straight in the chair and leaned forward to speak. "I've had a most unusual visitor. A Mr. O'Malley from the Guinness establishment."

"Guinness," exclaimed Mama. "What business would they have with a watchmaker shop?"

"Exactly my thought as Mr. O'Malley handed me his card," said Papa. "He explained that he is in charge of the company's many welfare schemes—the many exceptional benefits they offer their employees. As it turns out, Guinness is about to celebrate its fifth year of enormous growth after going public, and he wishes to give a special gift to the supervisors in charge of each company department."

Stella wasn't sure what Papa meant by going public, but she had read that Guinness, a major employer in Dublin, was selling more than a million barrels of beer a year now, and she had seen their fleet of custom-designed barges carrying cargo along the River Liffey.

19

"And," Papa continued, "the gift they have chosen is a custom-made watch for each of these twelve men of exceptional performance, and they have asked me to make these watches with special engravings on each."

"Oh, John, how wonderful," Mama cried as she rushed to his side to deliver a kiss to his cheek, as did Jo and Stella in turn. "But when must the watches be done?"

"Ah, that's the rub, my dear. They are to be given out at Christmas, just two months away."

The room became silent because each Manning woman knew how much time and meticulous effort was needed to make just one watch, and Papa was a perfectionist. Several seconds of silence stretched into a full minute.

Then Stella suddenly burst out with "Papa, you can do this! We'll all help by taking care of everything else in the household, doing all your usual errands for you, and we'll even, yes, bring your meals to you as you work."

"Yes, Papa, we'll all work together to help you," Jo echoed, "and I know Michael will help too, alongside apprentice Rob."

Mama and Papa exchanged fond glances as Mama nodded her head in active agreement.

"Oh, dear family," responded Papa, looking from one to another, "it will be a Herculean feat, but with your love and support, and working long hours, I believe I can do it, and the funds will mean so much to our family."

Stella did not miss the knowing look that Papa gave Mama, receiving her shy nod and hesitant smile in return.

The next few weeks flew by at the Manning home and shop. Papa acquired a couple of labor-savings tools he had long been considering for purchase, and each child did his or her part in sharing the tasks of daily living to free up Papa's time. Papa worked long hours in the ground floor shop, with Rob and young Michael carrying out watchmaking assembly steps that did not need Papa's fine hand.

Life carried on as usual upstairs, and even as the November and early December gray chill and rains settled on Dublin, family spirits ran high.

For her part, Stella was elated and utterly convinced that this new profitable business for such a well-known customer would increase Papa's reputation in the Dublin community and lead to new customers and orders. She was certain he would not consider leaving Ireland now for an unknown future across the ocean. Why, he might expand the shop, and even hire another master watchmaker or an additional apprentice.

And besides, she had begun to explore and consider a way for her to expand her personal situation right here in her beloved city. Last week, Miss D had taken her aside after the Poetry Society gathering—which Papa insisted she not give up for his sake—to tell her of an elocution contest.

"A contest?" Stella had said.

"Yes, Stella, and I'd like you to accompany me to learn about this spoken art in a larger setting than my parlor. The Sunday matinee next week at the Gaiety Theater will be a performance by Irish and English elocutionists of note, with honors going to the best. Someday, mayhap, I picture you on the stage in just such a role."

Speechless for a moment or two, which was not her normal response to anything, Stella gathered her wits about her and murmured, "Oh, Miss Dowling, I should very much like to go, but I shall have to ask Papa."

"Of course, and do tell him my parents will accompany us, and we shall take good care of you."

Stella nearly skipped home, thinking about such an event. If Papa agreed, she would wear her best dress, and Mama would help her with her hair. She had never been to a performance at the Gaiety. But she remembered that she and Rose and Mavis, while walking through Dublin from the South City Markets last summer, had passed the close-by Gaiety and spied a side door opened for a delivery. Never shy about adventures in the heart of Dublin, Stella had urged them to step inside.

Stella was filled with awe at the high-domed ceiling and its huge sparkling chandelier, the lush red velvet of the orchestra seats and curtains in the three rows of intimate balcony seating, all surrounded by intricate and ornate gold designs on the walls and ceiling. A three-tiered red velvet and gold curtain graced the back of the stage, which, on that particular day, portrayed an intimate drawing room set.

"Oh, how I would love to be on that stage," declared Rose, while Mavis ushered them out the door before they were caught inside, saying, "Dream on, dear Rose. Stella is more likely than either of us to walk upon that stage. She has the voice and the dramatic talent that you and I will never have."

Stella had laughed at the time, but now she remembered those words. And soon, if Papa allowed, she would perhaps be able to see a performance and judge for herself whether she might aspire to the stage as an elocutionist. But Papa would be shocked at such thoughts, she knew, so she dared not share Miss D's vision for her, nor did she actually know how she herself felt about it.

She certainly had no aspirations to be on the stage like the infamous and scandalous actress Lillie Langtry. But elocution was an art form for proper young ladies, becoming more and more popular as genteel entertainment, according to Miss D. There was at least a chance Papa would approve of her going to the elocution contest with proper Miss D and her parents.

Papa did approve, seeing no harm in Stella accompanying the Dowling family to a Sunday matinee to hear words of poetry and classic prose well-spoken in a genteel setting.

And so Stella, on a cold and blustery December day, found herself seated at the Gaiety in one of those plush red velvet seats she had so admired, escorted by the Dowlings and warmed by the cheerful and expectant chatter of her fellow Dubliners. She discovered she was eager to immerse herself into a world she could only imagine.

As the lush red velvet curtain parted with a whoosh of softness to reveal the stage, Stella observed a fine array of men and women in evening clothes, some seated and some standing within a beautiful stage set of Grecian motif, with white columns and draped fabric of gentle hues. Upon closer inspection, she saw that the women's garments were loose fitting but elegant, modest yet revealing enough to allow for arm and shoulder movement, while the men's garments were more attuned to the current fashions, yet not as stiff and formal. "Such beautiful people," she whispered as she touched Miss D's arm, receiving a nod and smile in return.

A moderator introduced the contestants, and then the judges, whom Stella thought looked rather stern, and announced the pieces that would be performed by each hopeful. Some selections were poetry by Milton, Byron, and Tennyson; others were declamations of a patriotic nature. Some performers were prepared to present Shakespearean verse, while others offered biblical narratives. Light and comic pieces were included in the program too, and Stella learned that each contestant was allowed two performances.

As the elocutions began, Stella was fascinated not only by the exquisitely spoken words but by the gestures and intonations, the postures and facial expressions, and the poise and movement of all. She was especially enthralled by the women, who showed no hesitation or shyness but, instead, spoke their recitations confidently, boldly, and fearlessly with such grace and composure.

At the intermission, Stella and the Dowlings mingled with other Gaiety guests, all adorned in stylish Sunday afternoon attire, pleasantly speaking and laughing in moderated tones with one another. Miss D introduced Stella to some of her friends, saying, "Please meet Miss Stella Manning, a student of the elocutionary arts," and Stella was immensely pleased with the smiles and gracious nods she received, and especially to be presented in such a way.

She enjoyed the other guests' easy, friendly conversation about the competition but felt too shy to comment herself. With her hair up and wearing a proper afternoon dress, though, Stella felt older and more mature. She sensed a comfortable affinity with this world of cultured, well-spoken, world-wise Dubliners.

As the competition wound down, along with Miss D and her family, Stella agreed with the judges that the prize for the male contestants should go to a Mr. Seamus MacDonald for his astounding recitation of Sir Walter Scott's "Highland War Song." But for the prize awarded to the female contestants, Stella's pick differed from the choice of the Dowlings, and she was pleased when her pick, Miss Bernadette Ryan, was selected as winner for her reading of George M. Vickers' "Aunt Polly Green."

The program ended all too soon for Stella. The Dowlings saw her home in their carriage, and she nearly floated up the front steps, lost in this new and amazing world she had just discovered, to join her family for Sunday supper.

Stella could not sleep. Earlier at supper, which Papa never missed, even in the midst of the Guinness watchmaking undertaking, she had described the Gaiety Theater and the elocutionary performance, bringing to life the excitement and drama of the matinee. Her family was mightily impressed, with questions such as "What did the costumes look like?" "How did they select the winner?" And, from young Michael, "Did anyone trip or forget their lines?"

Questions answered, and worn out from excitement, Stella chose to retire early, as Jo often did, only to discover a new surge of energy while in their bed and an urge to elaborate more details for Jo, who was quite exhausted from hearing the story and begged Stella to go to sleep and let her sleep.

Stella tried. But the details she could not share with the family played foremost in her mind. She knew, she absolutely knew, that she had seen her future. She knew she belonged on the stage as an elocutionist, and this knowing became her dream.

What to do next? She made a mental list: speak with Miss D to affirm her aspiration, find a tutor to advance and perfect her skills (because Miss D said all elocutionists had tutors or coaches), seek an entry point into a performance venue—no matter how small and insignificant—to get a start, and dedicate her best efforts to finding a way to true professional success on a large stage.

She reminded herself, though, that she was not yet seventeen, had no connections with the greater world at large, and would likely experience disapproval from her family, especially Papa. After all, was she not approaching "marriageable age" as Mama had stated? But surely Jo, as retiring as she was, would be the first daughter for whom Papa and Mama would seek a good husband because she was the eldest.

Likely a good husband for Jo, Stella mused, would be a quiet man, perhaps a librarian, to match Jo's quiet disposition. Or maybe the opposite would be better, a lively man to serve as counterpoint to Jo's placid nature. Yes, but whomever Papa approved to court Jo, she would be the first to marry. Jo would be settled first, and she, Stella, had time. But she had to move fast and plan her future because she didn't know exactly how much time.

Eventually, sleep came, but with it came dreams so vivid and real: the curtain lifting with a velvet swish, she in a beautiful flowing gown, poetic words streaming eloquently and effortlessly from her lips, an enthralled audience applauding, curtain calls, bouquets of roses placed in her arms, admirers crowding to meet her...

A light snow and fierce northwest wind descended on Dublin and the Manning home the next morning. It was now the middle of December, with barely a fortnight to go before delivery of the Guinness watches. All the family, except young Alfred, who slept late this early morning, gathered for an early breakfast and action plan for the day.

In spite of the weather, Michael and Alice would go to school, and Michael would help out in the shop after school, while Jo would pick up some supplies Papa needed from the local metalsmith. Stella would continue to delicately polish the finished watches and lay them out for inspection next to their small velvet pouches, ready to be tied with gold cord for packaging. Mama would take care of Alfred, assisted by Alice after school, and prepare hearty meals for all. And, of course, Papa would build the remaining watches, starting his day in the shop by gaslight.

Stella quickly lobbied Jo to switch tasks so that she could get out of the house, and Jo readily agreed. Donning an extra jumper and warm woolen cape with hood, Stella pulled on her most rugged high-top shoes and found a pair of mittens, before taking the stairs down, and scurrying through the shop with an "I'm away" to Papa as she closed the door. She trod carefully because the early morning light revealed a silvery film of slippery fragile snow on the sidewalks, and a fall would never do.

John O'Leary the metalsmith made fine gold chains for Papa's watches, and Stella had visited his shop many times with Papa, and on her own to retrieve a particular gold chain from time to time for Papa. His establishment was a few blocks away near the South City Markets, a neighborhood Stella knew well, and, as it happened, just three blocks from Miss D's home. Stella was sure she could pay a short visit to Miss D, retrieve the gold chains, and be home in a reasonable amount of time.

Calling on Miss D unannounced was not exactly the best of manners, but Stella knew Miss D was an early riser and felt she would understand the surprise visit, given their close friendship and fond companionship at the Gaiety last night. She would certainly understand Stella's urgency when they spoke.

Kitty, the Dowling maid, opened the door to Stella with a "Good morning, Miss Manning. I did not know you were expected," and then ushered Stella into the front parlor, taking her cape, while she sought out her young mistress. Stella stood nervously in this familiar room, and Miss D appeared shortly, still in her silk wrapper fresh from the morning room, to greet Stella warmly.

"Why, Stella, how lovely to see you. Such a grand surprise on this snowbound day. I had thought to ease into the day with a bit of Shelley, and now here you are instead to brighten a cheerless morning."

"Oh, Miss Dowling," replied Stella, "do forgive me for calling unannounced, and may I thank you again most heartily for taking me to the performance yesterday. I do hope you are well this morning and able to receive me for just a few minutes."

"Of course, dear," she answered, "but do tell me what brings you out so early on such an inclement day."

"A matter of most urgency, Miss Dowling. Well, at least to me," Stella confessed. "You see, after watching elocution performed on the stage, I know I have found my path in life, and I must speak with you to discover how to start walking that path."

Breathlessly Stella's words tumbled out, "And I know I need much training and practice, and of course, there is much to learn and acquire, and after all..." She stopped to catch her breath as Miss Dowling took both her hands and led her to a nearby settee and sat down next to her.

"Stella, Stella, do calm yourself and let me understand why you have come to me with this vision." For Miss Dowling remembered she was once a young, impressionable girl with many flights of fancy and ever-changing previews of her future. Not wishing to dampen Stella's enthusiasm, she nonetheless felt an obligation to engage in a rational conversation with her young mentee.

"You'll understand, Miss Dowling, I know you will, how I long to do something worthwhile with my seemingly boundless energy and abiding love of the spoken word." Stella paused a moment, gathering her thoughts, then continued, "You know how I love the poetry readings and recitations in our Poetry Society, and now I have found a proper and exciting outlet for my growing ability to dramatize the written word, bring it to life, and share it with others."

"Yes, dear, I know you have a gift for speaking well, but elocution is hard work, Stella," answered Miss D. "The people you so admired yesterday have spent untold hours rehearsing, training, practicing, and perfecting their art."

"I am very sure they have, Miss Dowling, and I am ready to do the same, no matter how much work it takes." Staring into the distance as if looking at a vision, Stella said, "Just to be on that stage, prepared to face my audience and be all I can be, is what I want to do with my life. Can you not see it?"

"I can, dear, I truly can, but there are practical considerations to bear in mind. You live in a family with certain expectations of you now, and in the future. You would need their approval and many hours of dedicated time each week to begin working toward this goal."

Looking thoughtful, Stella said, "This is a busy time with Papa's Guinness commission" — which Miss Dowling knew about — "and Christmas events are coming. But I might start my work between Christmas and the New Year."

"Yes, a fine time to begin new endeavors, Stella dear, but you must sit with your papa and mama and tell them of your ambitions to get their approval. If they are agreeable, I can begin your training, but you will need a more advanced tutor very soon if you are to progress."

"But you believe I have the talent and the spirit — the determination even — to succeed, don't you, Miss Dowling?" Stella waited impatiently while Miss Dowling paused and considered her question before speaking.

"I do believe you have the makings of the talent and spirit, Stella, but time alone will tell if you have the personal determination and commitment to succeed."

"But you'll help me?" asked Stella.

"With your parents' permission and your willingness to work hard, we can start. But, Stella, if you decide otherwise as you undertake this endeavor, please know that my regard for you will not be diminished, and we'll always be friends." Miss Dowling felt it was necessary to offer Stella a way out, a prespoken gentle letdown, if this goal was short-lived and proved too onerous for Stella to accomplish.

"Thank you, Miss Dowling," Stella exclaimed as she sprang to her feet. "Thank you for encouraging me and having faith that I can try to step onto this path, wherever it may lead."

"And, Stella," Miss Dowling warned as she too stood, "please pray about this vision. God has given us all gifts, which we are responsible to use for His glory and the betterment of our fellow man. Ask Him to confirm your gift and how He wants you to use it."

Knowing Miss Dowling was a Protestant, and not exactly sure what she was espousing or how such a conversation with God would go — and too embarrassed to inquire further on the subject—Stella assured her she would do exactly that. And with a quick hug, she retrieved her cape again and set out for Mr. O'Leary's and home.

The next few days seemed a blur, with all the Mannings working feverishly together to help Papa finish his commission for Guinness. In the early evening of December 23, Papa and Michael stood proudly in the reception area of the shop, dressed in their finest, as Mr. O'Malley appeared, as scheduled, to receive the velvet pouches of the twelve beautifully wrapped and packaged pocket watches, each inscribed with its recipient's name, the Guinness trademark, and words of thanks for services well delivered. He handed Papa a large cream envelope that bore the Guinness seal and thanked Papa heartily.

Mr. O'Malley had inspected each watch earlier in the day and had congratulated Papa on his fine work and ability to meet the short deadline. Stella and Jo had crept into the adjacent workshop to observe this inspection and were thrilled to hear Mr. O'Malley say to Papa, "Ah, Mr. Manning, finer watches I have never seen, and I am so pleased you were able to fulfill our order. I shall tell many others of your excellent workmanship and likely you shall prosper beyond imagining."

Papa had received the compliment humbly, Stella thought, and afterward she and Jo had charged into the shop to do some very unladylike whooping and hollering, followed by a grand hug with Papa. Stella rejoiced for herself too because she was absolutely certain now that Papa would not choose to leave Dublin for a new life in America. Her future and her ambitions seemed ever more secure. She felt so relieved.

Now, at supper, all sat serenely and happily around Mama's wonderful dinner of white coddle stew, savoring its flavorful pork sausages and streaky rashers of bacon, coddled in a creamy sauce made with milk and thickened with butter and flour. This delectable brew Mama had served over fluffy potatoes with a sizeable dollop of Irish butter on top—a celebration dinner she called it for the hard work of all.

The mood was quiet, with everyone—except Alfred—feeling tired and perhaps a bit let down, now that the excitement of the past few weeks was over. But then, young Michael broke the tranquil mood by declaring, "Now we can have Christmas!"

And Christmas they did indeed have, going to church on Christmas eve, visiting with friends and Mama's sister in Wicklow, sharing Christmas dinner and hastily bought gifts with one another, and also sleeping many restful hours in the chill and long December winter nights of the waning days of 1891.

CHAPTER 3

Dublin
Late December 1891 to May 1892

*T*he week between Christmas and New Year's Day had always seemed a peculiar week to Stella. The excitement of Christmas was over, activities for the New Year had not yet started, the winter solstice had just passed, but the time of darkness still exceeded sixteen hours each day, and the weather was predictably cold and dreary.

But this year, the peculiar week was a time of excitement for Stella as she spent the short daylight hours and many evening gaslight hours gaining new skills in elocution. Miss D had had the great good fortune to find at the Dublin City Library for Stella a training manual published in 1888 by a Scotsman, Alexander Melville Bell, called *Elocutionary Manual: The Principles of Elocution with Exercises and Notations, for Pronunciation, Intonation, Emphasis, Gesture, and Emotional Expression.*

This book was a treasure, and Stella had learned with great interest that the world-renowned Mr. Bell was not only the author of many works in the field of elocution, but also in physiological phonetics, which Stella learned dealt with articulation, and in orthoepy — another new word to her — which concerned the study of pronunciation. In addition, this Mr. Bell was also the father of the equally famous

Alexander Graham Bell, who had invented the amazing device called the telephone, and many other new and marvelous contrivances.

To have such a "tutor," in addition to Miss D's earlier coaching, was a major step forward in her training, Stella believed, and although the exercises were difficult and quite exhausting, she found great delight in her progress. Jo and Mama were busily engaged in teaching Alice how to sew, and Papa and Michael spent time in the shop on year-end inventory. With these various pursuits underway, Stella gleaned significant time alone in her bedroom to conduct her training, amid curious glances from Jo and occasional comments from all that Stella seemed quite consumed with her "reading," did she not?

Stella determined that soon she would speak with Papa and Mama about her goal to accelerate her work with Miss D and then receive more formal training to pursue her stage career. Thinking about how she would explain her plan, Stella decided to write a proper presentation of her ambitions, then present it in an elocutionary fashion to her parents, accomplishing the dual goal of relaying all the critical information while showcasing her growing elocution skills. "Yes, that will do nicely," she said as she began to write her script.

She was concerned about the timing of her presentation, however, because it seemed Papa and Mama were as busy as she was, aside from family endeavors and meals. She had noticed their hours spent talking in the shop in the evenings after the young ones were in bed and believed they were dedicated to planning the growth of Papa's business in the new year. Surely they had a lot to discuss with the earnings that would be available to them through Papa's newfound status in the community after the Guinness work.

"Yes," Stella said to herself, "1892 will be a wonderful, exciting year for our family with new business for Papa, the launch of my elocution career, and happy family times together."

She had no idea just how exciting the new year would prove to be.

On New Year's Day, Mama declared they would feast on an excellent meal to welcome the new year. She asked all three girls to help her prepare, which turned out to be a riotous time of cooking, talking, laughing, and keeping Alfred out of trouble in the kitchen, in turn, as the aromas of a variety of savory foods filled the cozy room.

Their hard work paid off in a much fancier meal than the Mannings usually enjoyed, starting with smoked salmon, a main course of roast goose and ham, accompanied by bread stuffing, roasted and mashed potatoes and gravy, and rounded out by Brussel sprouts, carrots, and peas. Mama's grand dessert was a plum and apple pie, which Papa declared was beyond superb.

As the girls cleaned up the dishes and platters and tidied the kitchen, with Michael drafted as a "drying man," Mama and Papa took Alfred to the parlor and bade all to join them as soon as the cleanup task was done.

Stella could hardly wait to rejoin the family in the parlor and darted upstairs briefly, as she finished her tasks, to gather her script. Although she had planned to present it to Mama and Papa only, with the family all together and in such a jubilant mood to welcome the new year, it seemed fitting to present it to all now. Surely they would be happily amazed, very excited about her plans and, of course, quite impressed with her elocutionary-style presentation.

Trembling a little with excitement and anticipation, Stella settled down next to Jo on the settee, with Michael lounging on the turkey carpet at their feet. Stella hid her script in the folds of her skirt and looked for the best opening, amid the gathering family's chatter, to speak.

As she timed her opening, she reflected on the joy she felt, being with her family in this comfortable home on Cook Street, in the welcoming and homey surroundings of the parlor, the scene of many genial and warm memories over the years. Like the time they had all seen young Alfred take his first tottering steps, collapsing into Mama's welcoming arms. Like the afternoon Alice declared she was "not a baby anymore" and would join her sisters in taking tea with the visiting ladies. And like the times Mama spent teaching her and Jo to sew and instructing them in ladylike manners ("Now, Jo, stand up straight and hold your head high as you walk, and, Stella, do look me in the face with a pleasant and demure visage as you speak...").

Yes, so many memories, and some of them sad too, like when they returned home from burying baby George and they all held each other and cried, or when Mama's dear friend Elizabeth had visited to receive comfort from Mama and the girls after losing her husband.

But most of the memories of this room were happy ones, Stella thought, and remembered the hopeful and poignant expression on Papa's face in this very place when they had told him, just a few short weeks ago, that they would all help him with the Guinness commission. They had all helped him. They were a family, and a knitted-together family, supporting each other, and ready to launch into a new year of growth for Papa's business and progress for all—and Stella's start to her future stage career as an elocutionist—a new year goal that only she knew right now. But soon all would know.

These memories and thoughts calmed Stella as she prepared to stand and speak, but Papa stood instead, cleared his throat, and began to address them all. "Dear family," he started, and Stella sat upright and gave him her full attention, "we have had a wonderful year and a peaceful holiday season celebrating our Savior's birth, and now a new time is upon us. A time that will see much change, but a hopeful and very exciting time, I am sure."

Alfred let out a little sigh and lolled his head on Mama's shoulder as he started to doze. Stella relaxed in anticipation of hearing Papa's plans for his business. Papa continued: "Your mother and I have prayerfully and fully considered the future for our family. We have made the difficult but very promising decision to emigrate to America, to settle in New York City. There we'll continue our lives and business in the new world, a place of much promise and opportunity for us all."

After a stunned silence from the Manning children, other words of assurance and details of the plans followed, with questions and answers flowing in abundance, but Stella did not hear any of it. She was sure her heart had stopped. She felt she was living in a dream state with slow-moving patterns of people and white noise surrounding her. Amid the clatter of conversation, she quietly excused herself and found her way to her room.

"It's over, my life is over," she cried into her pillow. "All my plans to gain a place in the world, in this world of Ireland that I know and love, are for naught. Now I will be a nobody, just one of thousands in a new and foreign place, with all dreams cast aside." Her sadness quickly turned to anger, though. "Why would Papa do this to our family?! Why would he uproot us from our beautiful Ireland and beloved Dublin, where my heart is, and shatter my dreams? He is so selfish!"

Having noticed Stella's absence, Mama had come upstairs and now tapped quietly on her door with, "Stella, are you quite all right? Are you well?"

Stella didn't reply, and Mama came in to sit on her bed and held her hand. "Dear Stella, it seems you are shocked and alarmed by our decision to go to America, but believe me, dear, it is well-thought-out and well-prayed-over."

Patting her hand, Mama continued, "There is much to consider, of course, and we have considered—"

At which Stella burst out, "No, Mama, there is nothing else to consider except the frightful news that my whole life is over. All my plans and goals for the future—my wonderful future here in Ireland—are ruined."

Mama, reaching out to hug her while Stella pulled away, asked gently, "What plans are these, Stella? Neither Papa nor I know of any plans you may have made."

"I was going to tell you—all of you—tonight, Mama, until Papa spoke and took away my words, and my life. I was so excited to share with you my dreams and to get your permission to take the next steps to fulfill them." And then a great sob broke out, "But now…"

"Stella, Stella," Mama responded, "Papa and I will hear your plans and dreams and see if they may be accomplished. We will listen and help you in any way we can. Come downstairs and let the three of us sit together in the kitchen and talk."

"Mama, it's too late. If Papa is making us leave Ireland, there is no time to pursue my dream. He is so selfish! Why is he doing this to us?"

Mama stiffened, wanting to comfort Stella but not willing to hear Papa declared selfish. Knowing Stella could be dramatic, and realizing it was actually one of her gifts when exercised coherently, Mama made the choice to end the conversation gracefully at the moment until Stella had some time to recover from the shock of the news and was able to speak rationally.

Instead, she squeezed Stella's hand, which she still held, and again invited her to speak privately with her and Papa at the earlier possible moment to share her heart—and her hurt. Stella responded by turning away.

Completely irritated by Jo's excited mood and after a nearly sleepless night, Stella arose early. Enfolding herself in her warmest woolen wrapper, she crept down two flights to the shop, knowing Papa would be up early and working there by gaslight, as was his habit. Not finding him there, she sat down to wait but soon found herself wandering around the shop, feeling the soft and lustrous wood of the clocks and savoring the soft scent of the linseed oil Papa used in his work.

"Stella," a soft voice called out from the doorway as Papa entered the shop. "You're up early today."

"Yes, Papa. I, I didn't sleep well, and I need to speak with you."

"Of course, dear, but I believe you really need to speak to both Mama and me together. She told me of your distress last night, and we are both concerned."

"Yes, yes, I know," Stella replied, "but first, I need to ask you if you will reconsider your decision to go to America, for my sake, but for all our sakes, really. There is no reason to leave our home."

Papa considered her question, then answered, "Stella, this decision has been long in the making, with many economic, practical, and, yes, even spiritual factors involved. Your mother and I are of one mind, and we believe it is for the good of all of us that we emigrate. The decision is final." He continued, "You are very young, not yet seventeen, and subject to your parents' decisions to know what is best for our family. I know you will miss your friends and life here, but cannot you try to trust us and begin to think about a new and promising future in a new land?"

Stella stammered, "No, Papa, my future is here, and I..." and with another sob, she sat down in Papa's work chair and sobbed into her hands.

Papa came over and placed his left hand on her shoulder as he lifted her chin with his right hand, and, looking into her tear-filled eyes, said, "Let's all talk tonight after supper, dear Stella. You can tell us about the dream you have for your future, the one you mentioned to Mama last night. We will listen and consider together."

Late that night, after the promised conversation had occurred, and Stella, now exhausted, was tucked under the warm covers with Jo, she reflected on the outcome. She had not used her script but had fearlessly explained to Mama and Papa about her passion for the spoken word, her love of elocution, and her desire to improve her skills so that she could become a professional elocutionist.

Mama and Papa had listened carefully and had affirmed her speaking talent, asking questions about her plan, but then expressed concern about so ambitious a goal at such a young age. They had finally agreed that she could pursue additional training while still in Dublin at a slow pace to test her enduring interest and commitment, but that performance, any "going on the stage," would have to wait until she was older.

Papa had said he respected her dream and loved her very much, and he had asked her to also respect his dream and to subordinate her wishes to his as his daughter. He told her, somewhat brashly, she thought, that if her vision for her future were meant to be, it would happen in God's timing, no matter where she lived. He had asked her to support his plan and the many activities that would be needed in the coming months before their migration in May.

Stella had grudgingly agreed. It was the best outcome she could expect for the present time, since they were definitely going to America. But in her heart, she held resentment against the importance of Papa's dream over hers. She vowed to herself that she would outwardly show tolerance and cooperation, perhaps even some zeal, for the coming move across the ocean in exchange for her continuing training in elocution.

But she also vowed she would retain and preserve her own identity and individuality — her own purpose and dreams — at all costs. She lived in a family, and she had loyalties to them all, but she would be loyal to herself first — and her own vision for her own future — above all. She would follow her dream.

It's amazing how fast four months can go, thought Stella as she closed the lid to her trunk. Tomorrow they would sail in second-class quarters from Dublin to New York aboard *Destiny*, a modern and fine steamship, according to Papa. Stella liked the name of the ship because it reminded her of her mission in life: to pursue her own destiny in the face of all circumstances. She and her family had celebrated her seventeenth birthday in March, although the festivities were brief, with so much going on. She felt, nevertheless, a step closer to the time when she would make her own decisions.

She had not faltered these past months in her elocution studies using Mr. Bell's book, several lessons with Miss D, and also a few short but robust lessons with a Mr. Brendan Boylan, an elocutionist of some note whom Miss D had located to tutor Stella. Miss D has insisted on paying the gentleman as a parting gift to Stella, a very kind and generous gesture, Stella knew, and she thanked her heartily. Mr. Boylan had worked with her intensively on her intonation and emphasis, but, more importantly, on her gestures and emotional expression. These latter skills came "most naturally" to Stella, according to Mr. Boylan.

All in all, Stella was pleased with her progress, but as her skills grew, so too did her resentment of Papa for removing her from her home, although she did not voice these feelings. Instead, she kept them to herself, allowing them to fester, while carefully guarding her heart and tongue, and cheerfully helping with all preparations for the move. And many preparations there were.

Papa's apprentice Rob helped Papa pack many of the watchmaking tools and supplies for shipment to Uncle Nicholas in New York, while Papa carefully packed the remainder of his most delicate instruments to accompany them. Rob, as it turned out, chose to finish his apprenticeship across Dublin with another watchmaker, with a letter of recommendation from Papa, and he moved into that new situation with ease and well-wishes from all the Mannings.

Many of the clocks in the shop were easily sold at good prices, and Stella was sad to see a couple of personal favorites go to new owners.

In an unexpected turn of events, a customer of Papa's was seeking a home for his son, a physician, and his family, who were moving into town from a rural location in County Kildare. Upon seeing the Manning home, this son found it ideal to locate his practice on the ground floor and his family on the upper two levels. They bought the house and much of its furniture and were eager to take up residence. Another and deeper sadness for Stella, although she pretended to be pleased for Mama and Papa with this very fortuitous and timely arrangement.

Mama had carefully packed all the family's clothing, except those garments needed for travel. She had also packed her precious linens and favored kitchen articles, plus family memorabilia and a few small pieces of porcelain and art. Her sister had arrived to take away some heirloom items from their family that she especially treasured.

Mama had encouraged each Manning child to carefully select personal and meaningful items from their lives in Ireland to pack in a trunk allotted for each to take along. Stella had chosen her poetry and literature books, a well-loved doll from her childhood, a favorite handmade quilt from her grandmother Manning, sweet letters from Rose and Mavis wishing her well, and of course, her Tara Brooch. She had decided to keep her own copy of Mr. Bell's book — another parting gift from Miss D — and other elocution training materials in her satchel for practice on the ship.

Documents were gathered: birth certificates for all the children, Mama and Papa's marriage certificate, medical certificates of smallpox vaccination they would need to board the ship, the family Bible, letters of reference from Papa's business friends, memorabilia, and personal correspondence.

So much planning, so many lists and activity. *And so unnecessary*, Stella thought.

A week of farewell visits from friends, a party given by all the girls of the Poetry Society, a tearful goodbye and promise to write from Miss D, packing of satchels for their use onboard the ship, and a blessing said over the entire family by the priest at church had filled the last week.

There was nothing left to do but say goodbye now, which Stella tearfully did as she strained to see through the early morning fog on the River Liffey to capture forever in her mind, for the last time, she knew, a view of Dublin: the old church spires, the peaked roof of St. Nicholas, the cupola atop the custom house, and Dublin Castle.

As she turned from the ship's railing, the fog nearly obscured the Poolbeg lighthouse, marking the end of the Great South Wall at the exit of the Port of Dublin. Secure with her family, but knowing her life was forever changed, Stella sighed as *Destiny* steamed into Dublin Bay and the Irish Sea toward the great and dark expanse of the North Atlantic — and her unknown future in a new land not of her choosing.

CHAPTER 4

New York City
May 1892

$\mathcal{T}$he steady clip-clop of the two Cleveland Bays pulling the open landau carriage seemed to provide a cadence missing in the chaotic and frenzied character of the city streets. The early morning fog had given way to a sunny day, although the sun had to work hard to find its way through the narrow streets and tunnel-like block after block of crowded tenement structures the Manning entourage passed after leaving the pleasant Battery.

The ship had docked at a pier on the Hudson River, and because they were second-class passengers, the family was allowed to enter the United States directly. Uncle Nicholas had met them as they had disembarked after their cursory inspection aboard the ship. Papa pocketed their birth and immunization certificates, which he had had ready to show if needed. He was prepared to tell the immigration officials that the Mannings had ample funds to settle in New York City and that Mr. Nicholas Manning would see his relatives settled in established accommodations and business arrangements. But these assurances were not needed.

It seemed to Stella, though, that the large masses of third-class and steerage passengers disembarking the *Destiny* onto ferries were not welcomed as easily and efficiently. They were literally herded onto the ferries amidst much clamor and confusion for transport to Ellis Island. She saw fathers strive mightily to keep all the family members together while both parents and older children alike struggled with baggage, trying at the same time to keep track of the smaller children. Most were poorly dressed and pitiful-looking, she thought, and she wondered how a city, with so many immigrants here already, could accommodate so many more of so little means.

But in contrast, because Uncle Nicholas owned a thriving carriage-making business, the Mannings were able to climb aboard and be seated comfortably in a handsome landau carriage for their trip into the city. With a sad look at other struggling families, likely from earlier ships, trudging the street under the weight of baggage and parcels, Stella gratefully took a seat in the landau. Facing forward and with the weather improving, she sighed and finally started to relax a little after a tense morning and to engage with her new surroundings.

She listened idly as her uncle gave a commentary on the neighborhoods they were passing through, with names such as Five Points, which aroused great pity in her, seeing the abject poverty; then the Bowery, which was crowded and noisy and little better; and then onto a broad boulevard called Broadway. As they proceeded "uptown," as Uncle Nicholas called it, the residences became larger and farther apart, with numerous fine homes and business establishments coming into view. They passed through a large square with many fine shops, which uncle named as Union Square, then another smaller one called Madison Square, this one more residential, with many elegant homes.

Stella craned her neck as they trotted around Columbus Circle to see the Merchants' Gate entrance to a huge greensward called Central Park, to which Uncle had drawn their attention. He proudly told them that in a few months, a grand and glorious statue of Christopher Columbus would be installed at this park entrance. Stella knew who Christopher Columbus was, of course, and could appreciate the remark.

As they traveled, Stella observed that horse-drawn carriages and carts of every size and description filled the streets, along with horse-drawn trolleys and omnibuses. According to uncle, an elevated railroad track, called the "El," also carried people over several routes throughout the city. It seemed to Stella that everyone was on the streets today: vendors of food products calling out their offerings, businessmen and tradesmen walking briskly, women strolling or shepherding children, and merchants opening doors and putting out signs for business. The noise was almost overwhelming, she thought, and she observed the streets were not kept as clean as Dublin's streets.

Seated between Jo and Michael, Stella turned from time to time to keep a watch on the wagon following with their trunks and marveled at the size and seemingly endless blocks of the city. *So much bigger than Dublin and teeming with people of every description*, she thought. How would she ever feel at home here?

Farther and farther uptown they travelled along Broadway, and Stella thought the city would never end. How would she ever find her way around this huge place?

The block after block of city streets finally led to a bridge over a river, the Harlem River, Stella learned, and eventually gave way to a more rural village environment. Uncle declared they were now in the Bronx borough of New York, the uptown area in the path of the city's rapid development. The carriage slowed as they eventually approached a residential neighborhood not unlike their Dublin one, and Uncle pronounced they had reached Woodlawn Heights, their new home in the Upper Bronx. All the Mannings looked up and down Katonah Avenue, the main thoroughfare, seeing homes and businesses and, again, people everywhere, but, Stella noted, not quite as many.

Papa and Mama listened intently as "Nicky," as Papa called him, extolled the virtues of Woodlawn Heights. "You'll find many Irish here, John, and a fair amount of Italians. Germans settled this area early in the century, but now it's so Irish that it's called 'Little Ireland' by many. More and more businesses are locating in the Bronx, along with fine craftsmen of all types, bringing shoppers north from downtown for their services and products." He continued with exuberance, "A boon to our growth happened last year when Manhattan's Third Avenue El extended to the Bronx, making it easier for customers to reach us." And then, "Oh and, Esther, don't be concerned about safety. Woodlawn Heights is home to 'lace curtain Irish,' not the other kind."

Mama raised her eyebrows at this comment, as Uncle Nicholas continued, "So I'm sure you'll meet many people with shared values and interests, and the children will meet good companions." Stella thought, *Of course, he's thinking of young men to meet marriageable daughters, no less,* but kept the thought to herself as she grimaced.

They all surveyed the pleasant village, wondering which place was their new home. The carriage soon slowed to provide an answer, with the baggage wagon close behind, as Uncle Nicholas told the driver to turn off Katonah Avenue and stop two houses down. They stopped in front of a modest but attractive three-story structure on East Two-thirty Seventh Street. With a shock, Stella realized that this place was really now her home and once more felt the sadness of leaving her birth home so faraway in Dublin, and yet somehow, at the same time, she began to feel a little excited about a new adventure.

The house was in a row with several others on the block, each similar but with varying shadings of brown stone clad over brick. A few steps down from the sidewalk level through a wrought-iron gate led to a lower level with two windows facing the street, and twelve steps up through the same gate led to the front door and an upper level with three windows. Above this floor was another floor, also with three windows. The house, Stella observed, had a pleasant air about it, almost a welcoming presence, she thought, and the midafternoon sun highlighted the warm brown tones of the façade.

Uncle had arranged for the Mannings to tour the house, which was nicely, but somewhat sparsely, furnished by its owner, who had moved his family to Chicago and wished to let the house for a number of years, or, as Uncle put it, "He would possibly consider a future sale." If the house met their approval, Papa would wire funds to the owner to consummate the lease.

Stella and her siblings climbed the front steps behind Mama and Papa as Uncle unlocked the door, all eager for the first peek inside. They walked from room to room on the main level, and the older Manning children clambered up the interior staircase to the top floor to see the bedrooms, while Mama inspected the kitchen, jiggling Alfred on her hip. Papa did a thorough walk-through of the rooms on the lower level, then he and Mama visited the top floor too.

They all reconvened in the large front parlor, and with Mama's nod of concurrence, Papa said, "Nicky, you have done a fine job locating a new home for us. It will do nicely. The lower level will make a welcoming walk-in shop, with an ample workroom in the back, and a rear exit."

Mama added, "And the kitchen will work well with our large family, while the small parlor is perfect for family meals and time together, and the larger front parlor is ideal for entertaining."

Papa looked at Jo, Stella, Michael, and Alice and asked, "Well, children, do you think this house, and especially your rooms upstairs, will do for us all?" Knowing his children, he figured that each child had already selected bedrooms. So true. Jo and Stella settled on a room at the end of the hallway across the back of the house behind the bathroom, which afforded a pleasant view of the mews and small garden. Alice was happy, she had decided, with the small, cozy bedroom tucked under the stairwell, and Michael had claimed the room across from the staircase, which he would now share with young Alfred.

They all looked at each other, smiling shyly, and Jo poked Stella to be the spokesperson for them, whereupon Stella said loudly, "Yes, Papa, we've all chosen bedrooms, and we are all content to live here."

And of course, Mama and Papa would have the largest bedroom in the front of the house, overlooking the street. All would share the roomy and commodious bathroom toward the end of the hall.

Mama, looking at Papa, asked if all might start to get settled, and Papa gave a resounding "Aye! Let's do it!"

The next few days were extraordinarily busy with set-tling in the kitchen, the linens, and the few household items that had crossed the ocean with the family. Mama and the girls did some shopping in the neighborhood to stock the pantry and also had time to make some delicate lace cur-tains for the large parlor windows, while each Manning child unpacked his or her trunk and put the new bedrooms to rights.

Stella assembled her elocution book and materials, plus her poetry and literature books on a bedside table she and Jo would share. Jo looked at the table and said, "Really, Stella, you have taken more than half the table with your books. You've hardly left room for my belongings."

To which, Stella answered, "Had you more books to inspire you with poetry and literature, we could fill the whole table. Perhaps you'd like to read some of my books." Jo sniffed and moved Stella's stack of books an inch or two toward the edge of the table and said, "There, that will do nicely."

Stella rolled her eyes, then they both laughed, remembering how different they were from each other and that Mama said they should emphasize instead their respect and love for each other. *Another sister truce*, Stella thought.

Michael helped Papa unpack all his watchmaking tools and supplies and set up his shop, and Mama and Papa bought a few additional furnishings for the house from a new neighbor who was selling various pieces. And everyone took turns keeping track of Alfred, who was elated to explore his new surroundings.

Eager to get to know the neighborhood and the Bronx itself, while the family settled in, Stella queried her uncle about the Bronx, ready to start finding her way around. Uncle told her that about a quarter of the Bronx was open space, deliberately reserved so by New Yorkers as the city pressed north and east from Manhattan.

These open spaces, Stella pushed to learn, consisted of a small park not far from their house, Edge Hill Park, and a grand park somewhat south and west of their location that Uncle called Van Cortlandt Park for the family who had owned the land for two centuries. The city had acquired this parkland of ridges and valleys in the northwest Bronx in 1888, he told Stella, and it offered more than a thousand acres of woodland and trails. Stella decided she would take a picnic lunch to this location with Jo as soon as possible.

"Ah, Stella," Uncle replied, "be sure you don't get lost. These open spaces are largely unimproved, although in future years, I'm quite certain they will be much developed."

Closer to Woodlawn Heights was the four-hundred-acre Woodlawn Cemetery, which Stella learned was opened before the American Civil War in 1852 but was annexed to New York City in 1874. And just established last year in April was the New York Botanical Garden, farther south but still in the Bronx. "So much to explore," Stella told her uncle.

Armed with such information, Stella was ready to visit these new and interesting places and begin to explore the larger world of the city itself, although she felt fairly intimidated by its size and huge population, and her ability to get around. But to pursue her dream of additional training in elocution and an opportunity to advance to the stage, she needed to start somewhere. But where? She had not forgotten her dream; it was ever before her. She told herself, "'Somewhere' is out there. I just need to find it."

With no big ambitions to roam far, Mama and Jo still wanted to explore their immediate neighborhood and meet some of their new neighbors, so Stella agreed their plan was a good place to start. Several walks around Woodlawn Heights with Jo and Mama, and with Alice and Alfred too, gave the Mannings an opportunity to meet neighbors and merchants and begin to form new friendships.

Mama met a couple of women from Ireland with whom she quickly bonded, and Jo met a sweet-faced Italian girl named Vittoria who seemed to share her interests. Stella made a few acquaintances, but she told Mama and Jo, "I know I'll never meet anyone as adorable and funny as Rose and Mavis," but she decided she would try to make some new friends, especially ones who might want to explore the city with her. How would she do that? Would Papa even let her?

She considered that reading a daily newspaper would give her an abundance of information about the city and about people and places she needed to discover. She was amazed to find out that the city supported nineteen English-language daily newspapers but finally settled on talking Papa into a subscription to the *New York Herald* because it claimed the best coverage of fashion, arts, and culture. She found its sensationalist tone, while somewhat shocking and brazen compared to Dublin's newspapers, refreshing and representative of the more audacious and bold character of this new country, and especially of New York.

With Papa busy getting his business set up and first orders coming in, and he and Mama exploring educational situations for Michael and Alice, Stella decided she and Jo needed an outing. She suggested a stroll the length of Katonah Avenue to visit shops and get to know more about the neighborhood. Jo readily agreed, and after chores were done, they both set out for their walk.

Strolling arm in arm, Stella and Jo enjoyed a sunny and warm late May day, with an early afternoon breeze. They smiled as the breeze encouraged the blossoms on flower carts they passed to wave delicately in greeting. They nodded and smiled to other ladies out walking, some of whom they had met, and exchanged greetings in response to "Good day, Misses Mannings" and "'Tis a fine day to be about, aye?"

Jo giggled as they passed a small group of young men who sent admiring glances their way and tipped their hats. Then she saw her new friend across the street and called out, "Vittoria, how are you today? Come join us for a walk."

Vittoria called back, "Ciao, Jo! Cross the street and walk with me here in the shade. It's much cooler." Stella said she would go with Jo, so Jo stepped out to cross the street.

The accident happened so fast that no one saw it coming. No sooner had Jo taken two steps into the street to join Vittoria on the other side than a runaway team of horses pulling a brewery wagon galloped into her path, pounding the street with eight wild hooves and kicking up a thick cloud of dirt and dust, with the driver yelling and pulling hard on the reins trying vainly to control the large animals.

Stella saw the team before Jo did and screamed, "Jo! Look out, stop!" and reached to pull Jo back but tripped in her eagerness to catch ahold of her sister. At that moment, seemingly out of nowhere, a young man flashed past Stella and literally threw himself in the path of the horses, pulling Jo out of danger within a hoofbeat of both being trampled and crushed.

Dusty and shaken, yet whole, he carried Jo back to Stella, who was crying and frenzied while trying to steady herself to help Jo, whose eyes were closed and who appeared pale and unconscious. "Oh, Jo, dear Jo, are you all right?" cried Stella as she followed the young man into a nearby merchant's building, whereupon two burly men helped him settle Jo on a nearby chair.

The young man brought water to Jo while Stella held her and rubbed her hands, while weeping and feeling pretty shaky herself. Others gathered around, and Stella was aware of Jo's friend, Vittoria, pushing through the crowd to get to them.

Stella hugged Jo and cried, "Oh, Jo, Jo darling, you will be all right. I know you will. You've been rescued and will be just fine." Jo, starting to come back to her senses, nodded, then gave Stella a weak smile and clung to her. Vittoria reached out and took Jo's hand too.

Jo said in a soft and weak voice, "Oh, Stella, I was so scared. I thought it was the end of me. But I think I'm not hurt," she said as she touched her head, arms, and legs, "but just frightened and shaken up. Who helped me? Where is he? And may we go home now?"

The young man, whom Stella noted had wavy dark hair and deep brown eyes, came forward and grasped Jo's hands, saying, "Miss, I'm so relieved you are all right. It looks like I reached you just in the nick of time, and I'm so glad I did."

Jo looked shyly into the eyes of her rescuer and smiled again, saying, "I am most grateful for your quick-acting help, sir. You have saved my life while risking your own."

He smiled back and replied, "It was my duty, miss, and a risk worth taking, to be sure." Vittoria nodded emphatically and smiled at the young man sweetly. Stella figured he was her sweetheart. But Stella noted his warm smile and genuine concern for Jo, however, and decided he was a very commendable young man. Gathering her manners, she introduced Jo and herself and asked him his name. He replied, "Luca, I'm Luca Rossi, and I'll be pleased to help you both home. Vittoria can help too." Stella thanked him heartily, and together they all helped Jo, who was still shaken, walk the few blocks back home.

Mama and Papa put Jo to bed immediately and called for a doctor, who examined Jo and pronounced her unharmed but likely to have sustained a concussion. He recommended rest for a few days, and Jo agreed. Stella said she would take good care of her.

Stella reflected on the vagaries of life that night. Anything bad could happen anywhere, she thought, even in a good neighborhood in broad daylight. But then, good things could happen too, and it seemed wise to not be fearful but reflect on hopeful thoughts. She wondered why God had let Jo be in the path of the runaway horses but then realized God was actually looking out for Jo by sending a rescuer. She didn't know how to talk to Him about any of this, though.

Then she remembered how Miss D told her she talked to God each day. Stella wasn't sure how that worked, even though she had learned all the questions and answers in her catechism, but she thought she would try, at least for Jo's sake.

She said simply, "Thank you, God, for saving Jo today," and fell fast asleep beside her sister.

Next day in the midafternoon, with Jo resting in a comfortable chair in the front parlor and Stella keeping her company, a visitor arrived: Jo's friend Vittoria, to see how Jo was feeling. As Stella ushered her in, Vittoria grasped Jo's hand and said, "I'm so relieved you were not hurt, Jo. Those runaway horses were very dangerous. I found out what happened, but first, may I invite my brother in to greet you? He too is concerned about you."

Jo had not met Vittoria's brother, but because she was fully dressed and Vittoria was such a nice new friend, she agreed to meet her brother. Vittoria went to the door and called him in from the sidewalk where he was waiting. As he entered the parlor, Jo was immediately elated and delighted to learn that Vittoria's brother was her hero from yesterday's unfortunate incident, Luca, Luca Rossi.

That explains the sweet smile Vittoria gave him yesterday, thought Stella. *Not a sweetheart but a brother. Hmmm. How interesting and serendipitous.*

Luca had come into the parlor with a tentative smile on his face, but as Jo's face lit up, her brown eyes generated a new sparkle in his as she greeted him. Luca was dressed in gray trousers, a white shirt rolled up at the sleeves, with a contrasting vest, and his wavy dark hair had been recently groomed. He wore a pair of black shoes shining neat and clean. In his hand was a small bouquet of flowers, which he shyly handed to Jo, and said, "Miss Manning, you are looking well today, so much better than yesterday."

Jo blushed as she accepted the flowers and as Stella offered Luca and Vittoria a seat, then replied, "Thanks to you, sir. In all the confusion yesterday, I did not hear your last name, nor know you were Vittoria's brother."

"Yes," said Vittoria, "my older brother by two years. My big brother has always looked out for me, so it was natural for him to look out for you too."

Luca blushed, which Stella noted that Jo found endearing.

Vittoria continued, "Luca was in the right place to help you, Jo. He had just walked a customer out of his shop when the runaways came down the street."

"How timely and excellent. And what kind of business do you have, Mr. Rossi?" asked Jo.

"A shoe emporium, Miss Manning, and it keeps me very busy with sales, and stock, and even repairs, but I needed to take some time off today to ensure you are well."

"How kind of you," said Jo, "and, please, you may call me Josephine, or Jo. Let's not be so formal."

Stella was struck by this request because Jo was ever the proper, formal young lady, always concerned about manners and etiquette. It was obvious she felt a close affinity to this young man so early in their friendship.

Luca replied happily, "And then please call me Luca, Miss Manning, oh, er, Josephine."

And then an awkward moment of silence occurred before Vittoria spoke up, "Tell them, Luca, what you found out about the runaway horses and wagon."

"Yes, yes, it's quite a story," Luca answered, gathering his composure. "It seems a small dog ran under the brewery wagon and began barking at the team. The horses took a fright and started on a brisk run, the driver being unable to govern them in their wild careening." He continued, "After your near miss, Josephine, they shied to the right and ran against a huge oak tree, taking a big patch of bark from it and damaging a nearby gate. The wagon then struck the tree with terrible force, breaking the neck yoke and pole at the same moment."

"How frightful!" exclaimed Jo, paling a little.

"But there's more," said Luca. "The crash with the tree then separated the horses, and they continued tearing down the street for several blocks until they were caught."

"Astounding, but what happened to the driver?" asked Stella, spellbound by this story.

"Well," Luca continued, "beside the broken wagon and brewery kegs strewn everywhere, the harness was badly damaged, and the driver's left arm was broken."

Vittoria then added, "So sad, but he will mend. It's fortunate no one was seriously injured or killed. Our father remarked last night that the runaway caused more excitement than a whole circus and menagerie turned loose in the streets."

All nodded and laughed, shaking their heads, but the excitement of the story was wearing on Jo, Stella could tell, and Luca noticed this fact too, so he rose and announced, "We are tiring out Josephine with the gruesome details of this dramatic story, so we'll be on our way now, knowing you are well," while bowing slightly at Jo.

"Thank you for your sensitivity, Mr. Rossi, oh, er, Luca, and I so appreciate your and Vittoria's kind visit."

"You are most welcome, and I am wondering if I may call on you again, Josephine?"

"Why yes, you may, Luca. I would enjoy getting to know you better and learn more about your shoe emporium."

Stella and Vittoria exchanged looks and nods, watching Jo and Luca smiling at each other as their guests departed. Stella, always quick to think through situations and draw conclusions, felt she knew now why God had let the horses run away.

CHAPTER 5

New York City
June 1892

Stella had found a friend. *A most excellent one,* she thought. Her friend did not come from the ranks of the several daughters of Irish and Italian families who made up Woodlawn Heights' population, although some good choices were possible there. Her friend surpassed all other alternatives, Stella knew, and was also delightful, outgoing, kind, and most of all, ambitious.

His name was Colin. He was her first cousin.

Uncle Nicky's youngest son had been ten when his family had moved from Ireland to New York ten years ago. Stella, three years younger, recalled vaguely playing with Colin at family picnics in Dublin's Phoenix Park, but she had little remembrance of him, or him of her. But now, at twenty and seventeen, respectively, they had reconnected on recent outings with Uncle Nicky's family, who also lived in Woodlawn Heights in a somewhat larger home than the Mannings'.

Colin was tall and handsome, well-built, with sandy hair and blue eyes, and, Stella thought, quite handsome. He dressed well and had good manners. He seemed to her a perfect example of an immigrant tradesman's son rising to the ranks of gentleman.

He had two older siblings, a brother and sister, who had left home, the sister to marry and move to New Jersey, and the brother to take a job in Chicago. A younger sister had arrived in their family long after her siblings had, and this sweet girl, Meghan, was now nine and a perfect playmate for Alice.

Stella felt she had found in Colin just the friend she needed. He was the big brother she never had. Colin was witty and creative and, like Stella, adventurous. Not in a dangerous way, Stella noted, but in a safe and fun way. And he was smart. He worked for Western Union, starting out training as a telegraph operator but was now rising through the ranks into management.

"And, Stella," he had told her at today's family gathering, "this whole industry is moving faster than lightning, with so many new technologies and inventions. Western Union may even ally itself with AT&T, the telephone company, which now has lines and metallic circuit connections in at least ten states, from New England to Virginia."

Intrigued, Stella asked about Western Union's reach, and Colin excitedly replied, "We are a nationwide company. Think of that! And now we have a transatlantic cable for overseas operations. The future is wide open for ambitious young men, and maybe for women someday too."

Colin's work took him from Woodlawn Heights to the fire-ravaged but recently rebuilt Western Union headquarters building on Broadway, which housed several hundred people, to all over New York City, as he trained new employees and oversaw several of Western Union's installations at the city's railroad stations.

As the family returned home that evening from Uncle Nicky's, Stella went to her room and gave some thought to her latest conversation with Colin, and to her situation. They had been in New York several weeks now, were settled into a family routine, and life was finally starting to feel reasonably good to her. Her resentment of Papa still simmered, however, and it was time to begin pursuing her dream again. She had never given it up, even in all the excitement of the transatlantic journey and move into her new home.

Colin's mobility was Stella's ticket to get to know New York City and find the connections she needed to renew her elocution training and get to the stage. But how? She thought it all through: Papa liked his nephew Colin and had a lot of respect for him. He admired Colin's hard work and energy. Stella remembered Papa's words to Mama last year when she had first overheard their discussion about coming to America, recalling Papa saying that "our sons will have many doors open to them." That exact thing had happened in Colin's life, so his example, she knew, spoke to Papa's belief in opportunity in America and his ambitions for his sons. But what about her? Her ambitions? Was she allowed to have opportunities too? Instead of just resentment?

Although Papa, and Mama too, had honored her aspirations in elocution, and even encouraged her, they had asked her to proceed slowly, and she had. She had been willing to put her vision for her future in second place to honor Papa's dream of a new life in America. She was a good daughter. But she had her dreams too and was not ready to delay them any longer. She didn't want to continue to resent Papa for the delay, but she did.

She reminded herself of her vow to retain and preserve her own identity and individuality — her own purpose and dreams — at all costs. She was ready to move forward, but what was the next step? Maybe Colin could help her. And then she remembered Miss D's advice to pray about her vision of her future, but she wasn't sure how to ask God for advice, so she decided she would just sleep on this question.

Sleep, however, was elusive. So after a while, Stella slipped out of bed, careful not to wake Jo, and went to the window. She looked out on the night sky, so full of stars. She thought she might try to pray like she did after Jo's accident. She wasn't sure how to begin, so she simply said,

"God, please help me find a way to pursue my dream if you are willing." Crawling back into bed, she soon fell asleep.

Picking up the *Herald* the next morning, Stella was astounded to see an announcement in the Arts section that rocked her world. It read:

> The First National Convention of Public
> Readers and Teachers of Elocution will
> meet at Columbia College on June 28.

Stella read the article following the announcement and was so excited she could hardly breathe:

> For many years there has been a rap-
> idly growing interest in this country in the
> subject of elocution, so that today the need
> of the incalculable benefits arising from
> the exchange of ideas and from fellowship
> with those interested in our work is keenly
> felt...

The article gave details for the coming event and further explained that the convention had been called by the public readers and teachers of elocution in New York City and Brooklyn. These people had to be the local elocution community, Stella figured.

"What an opportunity to meet the people I want to connect with," exclaimed Stella, but then she sadly realized that the conferees would be those already performing elocution or teaching it. She was not qualified to attend. "But perhaps I could find my way into the convention as a listener and make some contacts, seek some direction, and find a teacher willing to work with me," she said aloud. She figured that

among everyone at the convention, there would be someone who could help her take the next steps.

And she remembered her conversation with herself a
few days ago when she concluded that a start on her dream
was "somewhere" out there, and she needed to find it. This
convention seemed to be her "somewhere," and she was
determined to go.

But what would Papa say? She imagined the conversation: "Stella, you do not know your way around the city.
You've never been to Columbia College, and you certainly
cannot go alone." All that was true.

She needed Colin. Yes, that was the answer. She would
ask Colin to take her into the city, and if he couldn't accompany her to the convention, he could escort her to the site and
then return to escort her home. It had to work. She would
seek out Colin and ask, beg if she had to, for a yes, and then
present her plan to Papa. Papa trusted Colin, didn't he?

June 28 was less than a fortnight away. She needed to
get her plan into action. As it happened, Colin and his family were coming for Sunday dinner, so she would find a private opportunity to explain her dream to him, her passion
to get started in elocution in America, tell him about the
convention, and see if he would help her.

It had to work. It just had to.

"A fine supper, Mrs. Manning and Mrs. Manning,"
Papa said as he smiled at Mama and Aunt Beatrice, Uncle
Nicholas' wife, after supper with the family. "And we have
you to thank for the delicious dessert from your parents'
Italian bakery, Mr. Rossi. Tell me again what it is called."

"Zuppa Inglese, sir," replied Luca Rossi. "It's one of
my mother's specialties. Even though the words translate
as English soup, it is a traditional Italian dessert made for
the first time in the sixteenth century. My mother can tell

you the whole story! I'm so glad you liked it, Mr. Manning." There were nods of agreement all around the table, and young Michael asked if he might have the last piece.

Stella had been surprised to see Luca arrive for supper, but was not surprised to see Jo's glowing and happy face throughout the meal. She knew that Luca and his father had paid a visit to Papa in his shop two days ago so that the fathers could meet. After a friendly exchange, Mr. Rossi the elder had asked Papa about customs and expectations of proper courting behavior in Ireland, and then Luca had humbly asked Papa if he might be permitted to begin to court Jo.

Papa had agreed, but, *typical conservative Papa*, Stella thought, had asked for a slow courtship until the families became better acquainted and the young people had ample opportunity to get to know each other. Both fathers agreed, and Papa had announced the news to Jo, who was elated and ran to tell Stella.

But Stella had not known Luca was invited to supper, which Jo admitted later, when quizzed, was a momentary invitation on her part as Luca was leaving after a short "proper" visit yesterday. But Stella had little time to think about Luca joining their family for a meal because she was so busy rehearsing her imminent conversation with Colin and looking for an opportunity to get him aside.

That opportunity arose when Jo said, "Mama, it's such a cool summer evening. May Stella and I, and Colin and Luca, take a walk before helping with dishes?"

"What a lovely idea," chimed in Stella. "Colin and Luca, sound good to you?"

"Absolutely," both replied almost in unison.

Aunt Beatrice said, "Let's let the older girls have an evening off, Esther, and I will help with the dishes, along with the younger girls." Both Alice and Meghan groaned but agreed to help.

So perfect, thought Stella, *and I will have to do a nice turn for Jo for such a timely and serendipitous suggestion, even it was for the purpose of spending some time alone with Luca.*

And so Luca and Jo, and Stella and Colin headed down the front steps and set out into the fresh early evening air, enjoying a light breeze from the east.

Stella said to Jo and Luca, "You two walk ahead, and we'll walk behind, serving as your chaperones, which is only proper." Jo and Luca laughed and walked ahead of Stella and Colin. Stella walked slowly, letting Jo and Luca get ahead of them about ten feet, then said to Colin, "Dear cousin, I've a favor to ask of you, an important one, but first I'll tell you about something very dear to me, my dream, in fact."

"Why Stella," replied Colin, a little surprised at Stella's intensity, "I'll help you in any way I can. It's so wonderful to have my cousins nearby, and I feel such a big brother to you. Do tell me."

Stella smiled and told him of the Poetry Society, her brief training in elocution in Ireland, and her passion to become a professional elocutionist and perform on the stage. Colin was quite amazed and asked some questions about the elocution art, but they were running out of time, so Stella had to get to the point.

"On June 28, there is a convention of elocution teachers at Columbia College, and I must be there to pursue this dream in New York, Colin. I believe Papa will let me go if you will escort me to and from Columbia College and perhaps stay with me there."

"Ah, Stella, I can certainly ensure your safe travel to and from the college on that day, but I cannot stay there with you. My boss would be very unhappy if I took a Tuesday off from work. Hmm, let me think a minute."

Stella felt very tense as Colin thought, but then he spoke. "I've got it. Clarence! Clarence Curtis. He is a friend of our family and a close friend of mine, and he attends Columbia

College. I'll ask him to attend the conference with you or at least look in on you several times during the day between classes."

Relieved, Stella cried, "Oh, Colin, such a wonderful idea. I knew you would help me."

"But do you think your papa will approve this plan?" asked Colin.

Stella hoped with all her heart he would.

Papa was hesitant and asked for some time to think about Stella's proposal to attend the conference. He asked Uncle Nicholas and Colin about travel safety issues and about the character of young Clarence. He quizzed Stella on her purpose in going and instructed her on her deportment at such an event, if he should decide she could go.

Stella was hesitant to tell Papa very much about her intention to meet teachers of elocution and others who might instruct her and help her gain entry onto the stage, thinking he would deny her the trip because she was too bold. So, instead, she explained her desire to attend so that she could learn how elocution was done in America and take a good look at the profession she was considering for the future. "That is all true too, right?" she told herself.

Papa finally agreed after speaking with Mama.

Stella hugged him and declared, "Oh, Papa, thank you, thank you. I am so excited, and I am grateful you've agreed to let me go. I shall be mindful of all your admonitions."

But in her own heart, she wished she hadn't had to plead so hard to go. She resented being treated like a child. It was her right to be her own person now that she was, for all practical purposes, a young adult.

CHAPTER 6

New York City
June 1892

$\mathcal{T}$uesday, June 28, dawned clear and slightly cool. The entire Manning clan gathered on the front steps to see Stella off early in the morning as Colin drove up in a curricle to take her to the city.

"We'll trot to the El in the lower Bronx," Colin announced, helping her to her seat, "and take it to Forty-Seventh Street and then walk a few blocks to the college. It's at Forty-Ninth and Madison, between Fourth and Fifth Avenues."

"But where do we leave the horse and carriage after we get to the El?" Stella asked.

"Ah, a simple solution. They'll stay at a trusted livery until we repeat our journey in the opposite direction and pick them up later this afternoon." Colin continued, "Most Mondays, I drive the cart into the city and stay over with Clarence or with another friend, then drive back to Woodlawn Heights on Friday after the week's work."

Stella remarked, "So here I am, disturbing your weekly pattern."

To which Colin replied, "No, no, cousin. I am on the go all the time anyway, and I'm delighted to help you. Having a father in the carriage-making business has proven beneficial. He has contacts everywhere and knows the best livery businesses. Besides, I may borrow his best carriages, like for today's trip."

"You know the city so well, Colin," Stella replied, "and I am so grateful for your escort today."

Stella settled down in the curricle, a reasonably comfortable two-person small carriage. She smoothed her soft gray skirt and admired Colin's handsome profile as they began their journey. Along with the skirt, she wore a white cotton blouse connected to the skirt by a black suede belt. Atop her carefully upswept and tucked hair was a perky straw hat adorned with soft pastel silk flowers, a treasure Mama had brought from Ireland.

She wore her own treasure today too at the neck of her blouse, her beloved Tara Brooch. Her gloved hands clutched a black reticule that contained a biscuit, some writing paper for notetaking, and two pencils.

The horse's iron shoes tapped a rhythm on the early morning's unpaved streets as the curricle swayed slightly, creating a relaxed mood for casual conversation. Colin talked some about his work and then asked Stella if she was excited about attending the conference.

"I'm beyond excited, Colin, and can hardly wait to get there."

"It's a fairly long ride, Stella, but soon the scenery will change, and you'll see a lot of the city."

As the surroundings changed from villages to more densely settled streets and paved roads, Stella remembered this route from the day she had arrived, which seemed a long time ago now, even though it was only a few weeks. She thought about the fact that she was beginning to be entranced by this new land. Sure, she missed Ireland, and especially Dublin, but New York was exciting. Woodlawn Heights had turned out to be a pleasant place to live, and she had met some nice — and delightfully different — people, like the Rossi family.

And then there was Colin, her big brother. It would all start to be ideal if she could find a way in this vibrant, growing place to pursue her dreams. *Yes,* she thought, *today is an important day in my life.*

The scenery changed to busier and busier streets as they entered the lower Bronx, found the livery, and then the El. Colin paid their five cents fare each and then secured seats as faraway as possible from the soot and ash the coal-fired, steam-driven cars produced. "Maybe someday, electric trains will replace these steam-driven ones," said Colin with a sigh.

Stella agreed but found the El very efficient for travel in the city. Yet, as they left the El and began to walk the remaining short distance, she felt that the overhead tracks plunged the sidewalks into perpetual shadows, even on a sunny day.

A few short blocks' walk brought them to the downtown buildings of Columbia College, and Colin soon saw his friend Clarence waiting for them at their usual meeting spot.

"Colin, there you are, and this young lady must be your cousin," called out Clarence enthusiastically.

"Yes, Clarence, please meet Miss Stella Manning."

At which, Clarence swept off his hat, made a courtly bow, and greeted Stella. He was tall and lanky, a bit underfed, Stella thought, but charming and friendly. "I've found the hall for the conference," Clarence said, "and I'll take Miss Manning directly to it."

"Excellent," said Colin, and turning to Stella, he said, "I'll meet you in this exact spot at 5:00 p.m., and Clarence will look in on you during the day."

Thanking him profusely, Stella walked amiably with Clarence as he escorted her to the building for the conference.

"It is a great pleasure to meet you, Miss Manning," chatted Clarence. "And although I do have classes today, I will stop by at the noon hour and then in the midafternoon to ensure you are well, then meet you shortly before five to deliver you back to Colin."

"You are so kind, Mr. Curtis," said Stella as he deposited her at the entrance.

No one except Stella knew that she was not invited to the conference, was not a guest of a conferee, and might have to talk her way in.

As she entered the building, she immediately saw a sign: "Welcome to the First National Convention of Public Readers and Teachers of Elocution." And Stella could hardly believe she was here. Her first impression upon stepping inside was a sea of white. Many dozens of ladies in white dresses filled the lobby, dotted here and there with men in black suits. The women's dresses were of fine fabric, and each wore a fashionable hat. And they were all speaking with each other, it seemed.

Stella realized she was perhaps not as well or as properly dressed, and she didn't know a single soul. Not wishing to feel overwhelmed, however, she nonetheless determined to put on a confident air and held her head high. She decided immediately to mingle within a large group of ladies, who were all chatting excitedly with one another, and pushing their way into the auditorium, which she did along with them and gained entrance easily. She breathed a sigh of relief since no one seemed to be collecting tickets at the door. Taking a seat toward the back in a quiet corner, Stella looked around and noted the women sitting straight and tall in their corseted white dresses, so she assumed the same posture. She removed her gloves sedately and began to look at the program she had been offered as she entered.

The program was for the entire five-day conference, and she learned that yesterday was the day for the officers to conduct business, form committees, and hear opening remarks by Mr. F. F. Mackay, the chairman of the event, and welcoming remarks by Dr. John L. N. Hunt, president of the college. So today was the first actual day of the conference, although she had missed some elocution performances that were presented last evening to inspire and entertain the attendees.

No matter that I missed that performance, thought Stella. *I'm here today, and this will be a wonderful day in my life.* She noted that four plenary sessions were scheduled, two this morning and two in the afternoon, with discussions after each one.

She was quite amazed by the wide range of topics the program listed. Some she was familiar with; others were rather mysterious. From her previous training in Ireland, she could relate to "Passion and Emotions" and "Psychology and Expression," but the topics "Steps to the Artistic" and "Voice Culture" sounded intriguing and new territory for her. Territory she would have to conquer, she decided.

Prominent in the program, it seemed to Stella, were listings featuring presentations and discussions of the "Delsarte Philosophy and System of Expression," and Stella was very curious about this system. It seemed to be a system of elocution, and she had never heard of it.

"I have so much to learn," she lamented quietly as she scanned the program.

But her attention was soon drawn to the platform at the front of the hall, decorated with lavish ferns, with a carved wooden podium in the center, elaborately draped in bunting. A very young and small woman stepped forward at that time, and her youth and size startled Stella. *Why, she can't be much older than me,* she thought to herself.

The young woman had just been introduced as Miss Lily Hollingshead from Cincinnati, Ohio, and although

Stella wasn't sure where that was, she listened intently as Miss Hollingshead began to speak. She began by explaining to the audience that her grandfather, the well-known elocutionist James Murdoch, has been asked to speak but had been too ill to attend. Indeed, Miss Hollingshead continued, he had been too ill even to write the requested address, so she had penned it on her own.

Stella noted bemused expressions on the faces of some of the attendees as they briefly glanced at each other. Miss Hollingshead continued by saying that as a teacher of elocution herself, she felt deeply the honor and responsibility of addressing the assembled educators and performers. With these opening remarks, she then began to speak boldly, and with much confidence and authority declaring, "This is the day of schools of oratory—schools of expression—schools founded on the methods of Delsarte."

There was that word again, thought Stella. *I must find out its meaning.*

As Miss Hollingshead continued to speak, Stella knew she was seeing an elocution performance, not just a speech. She noted the attendees' bemused expressions had turned into admirable ones as they became riveted by Miss Hollingshead's passion, eloquence, and body posture.

Stella admired this young lady so much. She decided that she could be intimidated or inspired by her, and she chose to be inspired.

The morning flew by for Stella with a discussion of Miss Hollingshead's quite long presentation, and then a presentation by another elocution teacher and discussion of that subject. Stella discovered that "discussion" in the program following a presentation was the time for the audience to ask questions, and she could hardly keep up with the notes she was taking.

At the noon break, Stella hustled out of the auditorium to avoid speaking with anyone who might challenge her attendance, and she found Clarence outside the front door with a small lunch neatly wrapped for her.

"Hullo, Miss Manning. I hope your morning was excellent. Do sit over here with me for some refreshment," Clarence urged as he settled himself on a nearby low stone wall.

"How very thoughtful of you, Mr. Curtis," Stella replied. "I did not bring any food, save a small biscuit that would fit in my reticule, so I am delighted with your offering."

"'Tis not much, Miss Manning, merely a small cheese to go with your biscuit and a hearty apple."

With a grateful smile, Stella proceeded to spend half a pleasant hour with Clarence before joining the throng filing back inside the hall and finding her earlier seat. Another presentation and another discussion began, this one on "Psychology and Expression," which Stella was very keen on. Her notes filled the remaining space on her paper, and she had time for only a brief wave when Clarence looked in on her from the door, as promised.

As the afternoon was wrapping up with another plenary session, this one on business aspects of the conference, Stella was surprised to see a well-dressed couple approach her and sit down next to her.

"Good day, miss," said the woman, a stylish but somewhat portly person about Papa's age, Stella guessed.

"Good day, madam, and sir," replied Stella, somewhat nervous about being approached by a stranger, and in this case, by two of them.

"I do hope you are enjoying the conference, and I see you have been taking many notes on the presentations and discussions," the woman said, looking at the pages in Stella's lap. "May I introduce myself, please? I am Mrs. Sophie Delacourte, and this gentleman," she said, motioning to the man beside her, "is my husband, Mr. Bernard Delacourte."

"How do you do, Mrs. Delacourte, and Mr. Delacourte," Stella said as she nodded pleasantly. "I am Miss Stella Manning," thankful that Mama had taught her good manners when meeting someone new.

"It's a pleasure to meet you, Miss Manning," declared Mr. Delacourte, a handsome, older man, also stylishly dressed, but not so portly. "You have seemed highly engaged with the presentations and discussions. We have watched your studious note taking."

Slightly embarrassed and surprised that she had been watched, Stella was not quite sure of a response, or if these two older people might scold her for attending uninvited, so she decided to tell the truth. Didn't Papa always say something about the truth setting you free? And although she didn't know exactly what that meant, it seemed a good rule. "I am a student of elocution, here today as a listener, and I found the conference speakers most interesting. My notes will help me remember many details that should prove useful."

"Indeed," confirmed Mrs. Delacourte, "and do tell us about yourself and your training. It seems you have a lovely Irish accent and a very well-modulated voice."

Surprised at this question and compliment, Stella's mind went into high gear. Perhaps these people were the contacts she was seeking to make by attending the conference. Perhaps they could help her take the next steps toward more training and performance. At the same time, she knew caution was always good when not knowing to whom one spoke.

"I have recently come to New York from Dublin, where I had begun my training in elocution and would like to continue my training and advancement in the field here," was her simple answer.

The couple smiled in a friendly and supportive way, Stella thought, and Mr. Delacourte asked her more about her training. So she told them about the Poetry Society and her readings there, about attending an elocution competition and Miss Dowling's tutoring, and about her training with Mr. Boylan in Dublin. She also told them about her study of Mr. Bell's book and her practice of the exercises therein.

"So I have much to learn, but I am passionate about elocution being my life's work," Stella decided to confess.

The Delacourtes looked at one another and then at Stella, and Mrs. Delacourte spoke first. "Miss Manning, my husband and I are opening a school in September here in the city for aspiring elocutionists, young ladies who have what we call 'native talent and presence.' We have a sizeable home and have converted part of it to classrooms and living quarters for students, in which the young ladies will live and study the art and science of elocution intensively.

"We are seeking to qualify eight young ladies of good moral standing, solid family background, and excellent manners to be our first students. The course will consist of six weeks of intensive training and initial performances in the Delsarte method of elocution, of which my husband and I are practitioners and teachers."

Stella's eyes grew wide, and she could barely contain her excitement about such a school. She didn't know what to say, unusual for her.

But Mr. Delacourte continued, "Would you be interested in auditioning to be selected as one of the initial eight students, Miss Manning?"

Stella was not sure what an audition was, but it sounded like a performance of some kind, and she had a lot of confidence in her growing elocution skills, so she asked a few questions. She learned that the Delacourtes were holding auditions in two weeks for candidates for the eight openings in the class. She would be required to select a reading, practice it on her own, and recite it, and then be handed a reading to study briefly and then recite, all of which would be judged for entrance into the program.

She also asked about the cost for such a program, and Mrs. Delacourte told her the fee would be very modest because, quite frankly, of their wealth and desire to advance the art and science of elocution as a contribution to society.

By way of explanation, Mrs. Delacourte revealed, "We believe we are obligated to do so to be good citizens in these times when so much vulgarity and coarseness seem to be arising in New York's many forms of mass entertainment. Elocution is the antidote, we are convinced, and training new practitioners is a positive step we can take."

Gathering her wits, Stella thanked them for the opportunity to be considered and said she would discuss it with her family and write to them within one week if she might be allowed to attend the audition and try for a place in the class.

"Very well, Miss Manning," said Mr. Delacourte, giving her his card. "I do hope you will consider joining in the audition. Your speaking ability is quite pleasing and engaging, and you do seem ambitious. With training in the Delsarte method, you may well make a fine elocutionist."

As they parted, Stella stood still for a few moments as if in a trance. She remembered her prayer the night before she had found the news article about the conference and wondered if her prayer had made a difference to God. Did He do things like this — point the way forward so clearly?

She collected her notes and reticule and met Clarence outside the door, who handed her off to Colin at the agreed-upon location. During the long trip back to Woodlawn Heights with Colin, who thankfully brought along some food for the journey, she couldn't stop thinking about the world she had seen today, and the opportunity presented to her.

She told Colin all about the Delacourtes and the school and enlisted him in the plan she was beginning to form in her mind to convince Papa to let her audition for placement in the class. Colin agreed to help all he could.

"But, Stella," he cautioned, "your Papa is very protective, and you are very young. I wouldn't get your hopes up too high."

CHAPTER 7

New York City
Late June 1892

Stella's safe return home was welcomed by all, and Papa thanked Colin for taking such good care of her. Stella was exhausted, she told everyone, and said she needed some soup and then her bed.

"But tell us about your day, Stella," Jo begged.

"It was wonderful, but I'll tell more tomorrow, I promise." And Stella was off to bed after Mama served her some nutritious soup.

As she lay down, before sleep could claim her, Stella knew she had to finish her plan to present to Papa for permission to audition for the Delacourte class. Picturing Papa's face and his tendency to question and analyze all information (is that where she got this trait?), she sat straight up in bed as she came to one startling decision. She would not beg or plead or cajole. She was nearly grown, and she would not ask for permission as a child might ask for a special outing. No, she would approach Papa and Mama as a young adult, more or less like presenting a business arrangement. She would be respectful and deferential, and she would explain the opportunity clearly and courageously, not seeming bold or brash but in a factual and unemotional way.

If necessary, she would remind them of their promise back in Dublin to support her dream, to let her pursue her goal. And, if further necessary, she would remind them of Papa's statement that night that if her vision for her future were meant to be, it would happen in God's timing. Those were his exact words, as she remembered, and although she had secretly scorned his attitude at the time, she now would be able to present humbly, she thought, some evidence of God's timing.

This mature, reasoned approach seemed right to her, almost a fresh awareness that a serene, more peaceful and thoughtful attitude was much better than holding resentment inside. Had God somehow calmed and refreshed her heart? Did He do that?

Very early in the morning, Stella made her way down to Papa's shop, where she knew she would find him working, as was his habit.

"Stella, good morning," Papa said as he rose from his worktable to greet her with a kiss.

"Papa, the same to you. It looks like a beautiful day out there," mused Stella.

"Yes, and, Stella, I have some excellent news. So many new orders. My business is starting to blossom here in America."

"I'm so happy for you, Papa. Tell me more."

"Your uncle Nicholas has a lot of wealthy customers, and he has told them of my skills in watchmaking, and they have told others. Several new customers have come to me through his introductions. And also, I've been welcomed into the New York watchmaker's guild in downtown, and they have sent me referrals. 'Tis a wonderful start for us, Stella."

"Indeed, Papa, and your business will grow. The well-crafted sign you have placed out front will bring new customers too, as the Bronx continues to rapidly expand our way. I love to see the words 'J. Manning, Master Craftsman, Watches and Clocks' when I go out. So very nice!"

"And, Stella," Papa continued, "I'll be making weekly trips into the heart of the city for guild meetings and to expand my associations with businessmen of all types."

This bit of information was very good news to Stella. She could use Papa's mobility and visits to the city in her presentation if needed.

"I'm so pleased, Papa, and I'd like to ask you and Mama to meet with me in the parlor tonight, after the young ones are in bed, to tell you my news. Would you do that?"

"Why, of course, Stella," answered Papa, giving her a curious look. "Must it wait until tonight?"

"Yes," said Stella and gave him a peck on the cheek as she waved her hand and went back upstairs.

As requested, Mama and Papa convened in the front parlor late in the evening. The young ones were indeed in bed, as was Jo, who always retired early. Stella walked confidently into the parlor and took a seat facing her parents, a relaxed but studious look on her face.

"Well, Stella, what is this news you have to tell us?" asked Mama. "How very curious we are!"

Stella began slowly and methodically, reaching for the peace she had felt earlier. Everything counted on this performance. "The conference was quite exciting, Mama and Papa. I was able to observe professional elocutionists and teachers of elocution present valuable and stirring information about the elocution movement in America. I took some excellent notes. I was completely engrossed in the subject matter and learned a lot. But the most beneficial part of the conference was my introduction to a Mr. and Mrs. Delacourte of New York City, practitioners and teachers of elocution."

Stella explained the genteel way in which she had met the Delacourtes and how they had conversed about her elocution training and their work in the field. She explained factually about the new school, the audition process, and that she had been invited to try out for one of the eight available student positions for the September program. If she were selected, she told Mama and Papa the facts she knew about the six-week residential training. She was forthright in her explanation, gave Papa Mr. Delacourte's card, and asked if Mama and Papa had any questions. Of course, they did.

Mama's concerns centered around her housing and the characteristics of the potential students, and Papa's about her transportation, safety, and, primarily, the reputation of the Delacourtes.

Stella laughed, "Mama and Papa, you're both assuming I will be selected as one of the eight students after the auditions. I may not be, but thank you for the compliment. Could we do this: take it a step at a time, please? Perhaps you could inquire about the Delacourtes, Papa, to assure yourself they are good people. And if so, then you could accompany me to the auditions to meet them."

She continued, "This plan would seem like the reasonable next steps in looking at this opportunity for me, and we can see what the potential is. It seems like a genuine offering to move forward in work I feel I am called to do."

Mama and Papa seemed to relax a little with Stella's proposed approach, and Papa said, "As it happens, I am going to the city tomorrow to a meeting of the watchmaker's guild. I will make discreet inquiries and also ask Uncle Nicholas to do the same."

Mama added, "Stella, we want to help you find your way in the world, but we need to be sure this situation is a good one, a respectable one, and that these Delacourtes are trustworthy."

"I do understand, Mama, and I appreciate your support and concern," Stella replied. "Then we have a plan, and we'll work together on it just like we all worked together on the Guinness watch project."

Mama and Papa smiled and agreed, and Stella felt she had won a victory by being mature and logical and setting the stage for family teamwork. She actually enjoyed her newly found peace; it seemed to dispel the bitter taste of resentment. And, after all, Papa did have a point: she did not know the Delacourtes, even though they seemed very much on the level, and it would be wise to find out more about them. Her goals were important, but she didn't want to take any missteps.

Stella busied herself with sewing projects, helping Mama with Alfred, serving as chaperone in the parlor when Luca came to call on Jo, and rereading Mr. Bell's entire book on elocution training. She wrote a long newsy letter to Miss D about the conference and her potential opportunity, and also loving letters to Mavis and Rose, asking about their lives and the meetings of the Poetry Society.

By the week's end, she was beginning to feel anxious about Papa's investigation of and findings about the Delacourtes because she had told them she would confirm her attendance at the auditions within a week. What if it was too late?

But that evening, Papa requested another meeting with her and Mama in the parlor, and she eagerly attended. Again, she vowed to be rational and sensible, and above all, peaceful.

Papa started, "Well, Stella, it's been an interesting week, and it seems you have found some admirable people to consider as teachers. It appears, from all reports, that the Delacourtes are upstanding citizens. They are known as wealthy philanthropists by many, but not haughty and self-aggrandizing as some wealthy New Yorkers are. They are indeed elocutionists and teachers of note, and their money comes from longstanding family resources, not business. They seem to have a high social conscience, supporting the arts in an effort to offer a higher level of culture to New Yorkers in the face of so much growth in the lesser and more coarser forms of entertainment that are growing rapidly throughout the city."

"Yes, Papa, they told me they see elocution as an antidote to so much vulgarity," Stella mentioned.

"And," Papa continued, "they are known as kind and gracious people, who have done much good to improve the social and moral tenor of the city. Alas, many think they fight a losing battle though."

"Always trying to do the right thing is good, though, isn't it, Papa?" Stella asked.

"Yes, absolutely," he answered. "So your mother and I have agreed you may write to the Delacourtes your acceptance of their offer to audition. I will take you into the city for the audition, meet them and talk to them about the program, and then we'll see what happens."

"Thank you, Papa, and Mama too," said Stella in a grown-up manner, but then she reached over and gave each a kiss.

Again, Stella found it necessary to keep herself busy while waiting for a reply from the Delacourtes. It arrived within three days, in a cream envelope addressed to her in an elegant hand. It read "Miss Stella Manning is cordially invited to attend an audition for the inaugural class of the Delacourte School of Elocution" and gave details about preparation for the audition and the date, time, and location.

Stella was elated, and Jo took time out from her daydreaming about Luca to share some of Stella's joy.

"Really, Stella," she said (*there was that "really" again,* Stella thought), "you are stepping out in the world, as I knew you'd always do. I'm happy for you." By this comment, Stella felt less the little sister and more an adult peer to Jo, a good feeling.

"Thank you, sister," Stella replied, "and I'm happy for you that you seem to have found a wonderful man with whom to consider a future." At which, Jo blushed as Stella gave her a hug.

Mama and Papa were pleased at the reply from the Delacourtes too, and Stella sensed some parental pride as Papa began to make plans for their journey to the city for the audition.

Stella knew she had a lot of preparation to do, foremost of which was to select the reading she would present and then to practice, practice, and practice it until she felt she could do it well. She began by searching her poetry books to find a poem that lent itself to dramatic and emotional expression. Her two finalists were both from Shelley, although one of her favorite Keats poems placed third.

She finally selected Shelley's "Hymn of Apollo," one of her much-loved poems because of its beautiful description of nature and the stirring flow of the words. She thought she could perform it well. She studied it verse by verse to try to understand the emotion Shelley felt as he wrote the words and how best to express those emotions. She wished she had Miss D to discuss the poem with, but using the kind gift of Mr. Bell's book from Miss D, she felt she had a good tutor.

After a few intense practice sessions, Stella asked Jo and Luca if she might perform for them, and they readily agreed. The pair were settled in the parlor with Stella, who stood, assumed a somnolent posture, and began to recite:

> *The sleepless Hours who watch me as I lie,*
> *Curtained with star-inwoven tapestries,*
> *From the broad moonlight of the sky,*

Fanning the busy dreams from my dim eyes —
Waken me when their Mother, the gray Dawn,
Tells them that dreams and that the moon is gone.

Jo and Luca looked at each other with startled expressions and then fixed their gazes on Stella, seemingly fascinated by this side of her neither had seen before. Even though Jo had observed Stella practicing some nonsensical, it seemed to her, articulation exercises from time to time, this presentation was quite different and astonishing.

They were amazed not only at Stella's dramatic presentation of the words but by her changing body postures and gestures, quite different from everyday motions, they thought.

Stella seemed in a different world as she recited the poem and finished the last three lines with an acclamation, bold and ringing.

All prophecy, all medicine, is mine,
All light of art or nature — to my song
Victory and praise in its own right belong.

Then she returned slowly and methodically to the self they knew and took a bow. After a stunned silence, Jo and Luca applauded, and Luca said, "I had no idea what elocution is, Stella, and I am amazed. Your presentation was astounding."

"Thank you," said Stella, "and I hope to improve it over the next few days. There are still a few rough places. I'm trying various gestures for some of the lines that may be interpreted differently. I'm so new at this and have much to learn."

"But, Stella, really," said Jo, "I think you're off to a fine start."

Stella filled many hours practicing and trying out variants of her interpretation of the poem, and finally she asked if she might perform it for Mama and Papa, and they agreed, as she knew they would. Their reactions were similar to those of Jo and Luca, and Papa said, "It is amazing how you seem to go into a different world, Stella, as you perform. It's as if you are here, but not here. You make eye contact with us, and then you don't. I had no idea this art form was so different from, say, a sermon or speech. It's truly quite amazing."

Stella thanked them and felt she had stepped closer to helping them understand she was quite serious and committed to this path, that it was not a flight of fancy. That it truly was her dream.

As the audition day drew nearer, she and Mama and Jo planned her wardrobe, deciding on a flowing soft cotton skirt of pale green with a small train. A creamy white blouse with pin tucks and small ruffles on the bodice and full sleeves would pair with the skirt, and she would wear her favorite bright green cloth belt, and of course, the Tara Brooch. Papa approved the green choices and said again how well green went with Stella's eyes. He said she looked the perfect Irish young lady, as she modeled her outfit for him.

As to her hair, Mama and Jo suggested a style they had seen in *Peterson's* back in Dublin, which they had both admired. It consisted of a loose swept-up look with a large bun piled on top of Stella's head and secured there, with the occasional ringlet allowed to fall down at the nape of the neck. As they tried out this look, her thick curly brown hair adapted well to it, and she felt quite grown-up and very stylish.

Alice, who was having a happy day after her chores were done, was spending time with her cousin and new best friend Meghan. Observing Stella's hairstyle, she said she would like to wear her hair in this same way, and Jo advised her to ask again in a few years.

Papa saw to the carriage, arranging for another pleasant curricle and horse through Uncle Nicholas, and Colin advised the best route through the city to the Delacourtes' address.

All was in readiness as the audition day approached. Stella admitted to herself that she really did not know if the preparation and anticipation were in vain or not. She might not be good enough to qualify for a place in the school, after all. She didn't know who the competition was. But it seemed to her that she had at least a decent chance, and she would do her best and be hopeful for a good outcome.

And although the outcome was not sure, and even if she were accepted, there were still hurdles to overcome. After all, Papa had not given his full permission for her schooling in elocution with the Delacourtes; he had granted her a chance to take a step, a chance to explore this audition opportunity, as she had suggested. He might decide otherwise, after all, if he felt it was not right for her.

She had recently felt much of her earlier resentment toward Papa lessening, about his dream being more important that hers. He had seemed willing, and Mama had too, to help her in her pursuit of her dream. But yet, he could still disallow the next steps if he so decided. What would she do then? Was she prepared to defy him, if necessary?

Stella wanted to get a good night's sleep before the audition day, but again, sleep eluded her. Perhaps, she thought, my sleeplessness is God's way of letting me know I should pray to Him. So she asked Him, quite simply, to help her if He wanted her to attend the school. As she drifted off to sleep, she thought of the Lord's Prayer, the part where it said, "thy will be done," and realized for the first time she was actually asking Him to help her, not just because she wanted help, but if it was His will.

CHAPTER 8

New York City
July 1892

Papa reached up to ring the very elaborate door chime at the top of the stone steps that led them to the tall and elegant townhouse on Fifth Avenue, between Fifty-Seventh and Fifty-Eighth Streets, just as a young lady came out the door, nodded, and walked down the steps.

"Ready, Stella?" he inquired, smiling down at her.

"Yes, Papa, I am more than ready," Stella replied, wondering how the young lady who was leaving had fared in her audition.

A maid in a crisp white-and-black uniform received Papa's calling card and led them to a small front parlor, ushering them to seats on a lush velvet-covered settee. The brocade wallpaper, silken drapes, and thick carpet celebrated the color of the sun in clear yet muted gold tones. Only a minute or two passed before Mrs. Delacourte appeared with a hearty greeting.

"Miss Manning, how delightful to see you again, and we are so pleased you have chosen to audition today."

Stella and Papa stood, and Stella said, "Good afternoon, Mrs. Delacourte. May I present my father, Mr. John Manning."

Papa did a short and gracious bow, and Mrs. Delacourte nodded in return, welcoming Papa and turning to Stella. "Mr. Delacourte and I are looking forward to your recitation, Miss Manning, and he will be available shortly. He is just finishing with another audition. It's been quite a busy day, with nine auditions so far, and more to come later this afternoon."

Stella's heart sank a little because she knew there were only eight places in the class, and she was likely the tenth one to audition, with others still to appear. How skilled and prepared were these other candidates? she wondered. Were they more qualified than her?

Mrs. Delacourte chatted amiably with Papa about the hot July weather, and Stella tried to relax. Shortly, she saw Mr. Delacourte in the entry hallway saying goodbye to someone, and then he joined them in the small parlor.

"Miss Manning! And this gentleman—"

"Is my father, Mr. Delacourte. Please meet Mr. John Manning, who has been kind enough to accompany me into the city today."

"Excellent, and welcome, Mr. Manning. Several of the fathers and mothers of our candidates have accompanied their young ladies today, and we are pleased to meet family members. Perhaps you would enjoy some refreshment while Mrs. Delacourte and I hear your daughter's recitation."

"Indeed, that would be pleasant, Mr. Delacourte," said Papa. "And I do have some questions about your school if you might have a few minutes to speak with me between auditions."

"Yes, yes, Mr. Manning, we will make that time available. Please sit comfortably, and our maid will attend you shortly. Miss Manning, please come with us."

Stella smiled back at Papa as she followed the Delacourtes into a larger parlor across the entry hallway from the small parlor, and they closed the door.

Mrs. Delacourte spoke first: "Miss Manning, do not be at all nervous. This is a friendly and welcoming room, and we are at ease. We will all just take a seat and let you gather yourself, then you may speak when you are ready."

Stella was only slightly nervous because she had prepared so extensively. The room was large and elegant, done in the same golden hues, which Stella found very pleasing. Serene artwork highlighted the soft lemon color of the walls, and a spacious bay window let in long rays of the afternoon sun through the high, lightly draped windows. A glorious grand piano highlighted the beauty of a nearby marble and gilded fireplace. The room was indeed inviting and set a tranquil mood for elocution.

Stella relaxed amid the serenity of the room and the Delacourtes' peaceful and expectant faces. She knew she could do this. She stood and said, "Today I will recite Percy Bysshe Shelley's 'Hymn of Apollo.'"

She assumed her starting posture, paused, and began.

As she finished the last two lines and took a bow, the Delacourtes came to their feet, extended their hands to touch hers, and said, almost together, "Well done, Miss Manning!"

Mr. Delacourte remarked, "Your presentation showed much preparation. It seems that your prior training and study have been of great benefit."

"Thank you," replied Stella.

"And now you may remember, Miss Manning, we will give you a short recitation to study for a few minutes and then will ask you to recite it as best you can, with a minimum of preparation. This part of the audition tests your ability to assess a new piece, think through a possible interpretation, and demonstrate spontaneity of articulation and pronunciation, all qualities we look for in potential students."

"We will let you prepare for a few minutes while we speak with your father," said Mrs. Delacourte.

"Very well," replied Stella. "I love a challenge."

She then received a sheet of paper with a short selection from Cervantes, the noted Spanish poet, wit, and playwright. The piece was just a few lines and read:

Blessings on him who invented sleep, the
mantle that covers all human thoughts,
the food that appeases hunger, the drink that quenches thirst,
the fire that warms cold, the cold that moderates heat,
and, lastly, the general coin that purchases all things,
the balance and weight that equals the shepherd with the king,
and the simple with the wise.

What a delightful piece this is, mused Stella and began by reading it slowly two times, then thinking through the pauses, the words that needed emphasis, the voice modulation that would work with each phrase, and the body posture that would best interpret the piece. She recited it to herself twice to test her interpretation, making a few adjustments as she proceeded through the piece.

She was ready to present her first rendering of the reading when the Delacourtes returned in just a few minutes. Standing, she began, "I will now recite a poem from Cervantes" and delivered her elocution, followed by a bow.

"Bravo, Miss Manning," said Mr. Delacourte and reached out to shake her hand. "Thank you very much."

Stella wasn't sure what the next step would be, so she waited for the Delacourtes, who opened the door and returned her to the small parlor where Papa was waiting. Standing, he greeted Stella and the Delacourtes, preparing to speak further or take their leave.

Mr. Delacourte spoke then, saying, "Mr. Manning and Miss Manning, we are so pleased to welcome you today, and you have done well, Miss Manning. Very well indeed.

We shall make our selections for the class and be in touch with you within three days."

Stella knew they had to be noncommittal until they had completed all the auditions, so she graciously thanked them, as did Papa. Mr. Delacourte asked Papa if he had all his questions answered, and Papa replied he did. Also noncommittal, noted Stella. But it was done, and she had done her best, and Papa seemed calm.

This time, the wait was more tense but shorter. Stella concentrated on household duties and tutoring Alice in her handwriting skills, as Papa had requested, but waited eagerly for the post. She rehearsed the negative scenario in her head, what she would do and say if not accepted. She also rehearsed the positive outcome, but when the cream envelope arrived, she opened it with great trepidation. Surely it was God's will for her to be in the class.

But maybe it wasn't.

The elegant script read "Miss Stella Manning is cordially invited to become a student of the inaugural class of the Delacourte School of Elocution" and included an information page with all the details she needed about the opening day in mid-September, the six-week schedule, what to wear, what to bring, and so forth. Also included was an RSVP card with a three-day receipt date.

Stella held the letter, enclosure, and card in her hands and whispered, "Thank you, God," before running to tell Mama and Jo, who exclaimed over the news but were kneading bread in the kitchen and couldn't give her a hug with flour on their hands. So she rushed downstairs to the shop to tell Papa. At his workbench, Papa looked up and smiled as she entered the workroom, almost breathless.

"You have good news, I suppose," he said with a smile on his face.

"Yes, Papa, the best news ever. I have been accepted. May you and Mama and I meet tonight to review the details and discuss the way forward?"

"Indeed, we may, Stella," replied Papa, "and I have given much thought to such a conversation should you be accepted."

Stella wasn't sure if his response augured good or bad news, but again, she decided to stay peaceful and positive and continue to approach this opportunity like a young adult reasoning with her parents, not a child asking permission. Yes, she needed their permission, but she wanted all of them to reason together and mutually agree on the next chapter in her life.

The evening couldn't come fast enough. Papa opened the conversation by saying, "You have worked hard to get to this day, Stella. Ever since your readings with the Poetry Society, your brief training in Dublin, and your study and practicing here, you have shown a keen and enduring interest in elocution. It was the same as I was learning watchmaking. I was drawn to every way to acquire knowledge and skill. I can see the same determination and resolve in you.

"But tell your mama and me, Stella," Papa continued, "what you would like to do with this skill, this gift, and how it may fit into your life in the immediate and coming years. As you know, most young women marry and have families and homes. Do you see those goals in your future too, in addition to pursuing elocution?"

Stella wasn't sure at all about her future. She had never met a man she was vaguely interested in enough to consider marriage, and the idea of children and a home seemed far off. Still, these things were worthy goals too, and she might embrace them someday.

She wanted to answer honestly, so she just began to share her heart. "Papa and Mama, someday it would likely be wonderful to have a husband and family, but I would like to do something that is uniquely mine first. I'd like to explore my potential and find my own place in the world, and although that may be unusual for a young woman in these times, it is the path I'd like to walk now."

"What would be your goal after you complete the six-week class, Stella?" asked Papa.

"I should like to perform elocution in genteel settings, such as salons and lycea, perhaps churches, or in other settings where art and culture are appreciated. New York offers many stages for performers, and elocution is growing as an art form. Indeed, the Delacourtes see it as an antidote, to use their words, for the coarse and common entertainment that abounds in New York."

"You do not intend to use your skill in the new entertainment called vaudeville, then, like the variety shows performed at New York's Fourteenth Street Theater?" asked Papa, "because such places would not be fitting for a properly raised young lady."

"I do not anticipate performing in such places, Papa, which I haven't even heard of. And, Papa, we might be getting ahead of ourselves. Let's take my elocution work a step at a time. If performance possibilities arise, the Delacourtes may be able to advise, and they know the good and not-so-good side of New York entertainment."

Papa seemed satisfied with this answer, and Stella waited for the next round of questions.

"Stella, we want you to receive this training and also be safe in the city," Mama said. "Papa has questioned the Delacourtes quite closely about your regimen, and it seems you will have a highly structured schedule with strict guidelines. You will be kept safe but given reasonable freedoms and responsibilities for your free time."

"And, Stella," Papa added, "the Delacourtes have asked me to give them names of any friends, specifically young gentlemen, you may associate with under supervision. I will give them your cousin Colin's name, and when accompanied by Colin, his friend Clarence's name. I will visit you from time to time as I go into the city for the watchmaker's guild meetings, and I will task Colin and your Uncle Nicholas to pay visits occasionally to ensure you are well."

"And perhaps your sisters and I can visit also," said Mama.

But Papa continued, "There is one other matter, Stella, and it concerns expenses for the class. Although they are minimal, the Delacourtes believe each student should invest in her training, either financially or in kind, which I think is wise. We will pay the fee, but in the several weeks before classes start in September, I'd like you to help me in the shop, and I'd also like you to work with Mama to sew the clothes you will need for the city."

"Investing in my future sounds right, Papa, and I will surely take on those two assignments. I've helped in your Dublin shop, as you know, and Mama has taught me to sew a fine seam."

"Then we have a plan, Stella," announced Papa. "Mama and I agree that you are becoming a mature and sensible young lady, which we've seen in how you have approached this situation. We trust you to proceed mindfully as you study elocution with the Delacourtes under the conditions we've discussed."

Stella replied, "I am so pleased we have agreed and that I may accept the invitation! Thank you, Papa and Mama."

Stella's mind whirled in at least a dozen directions as she climbed the stairs to her room. Her dream was beginning to be realized. It seemed God had a plan for her life in America after all, and He was showing it to her bit by bit. He had given her a peace she didn't understand too, and she was grateful.

CHAPTER 9

New York City
July and August 1892

*T*he Manning household was amazed how hot it was in America in the heart of the summer. Sure, Dublin could have warm summer days, but New York's location thirteen degrees of latitude below Dublin's offered a climate that took some adjusting to, they all admitted. The family settled into the "inferno," as young Michael called it, adjusting their lives with less heavy cooking and slower activities.

Papa had related an article he had read just this morning in the *New York Times* about the July heat wave: "On the East Side many families moved into the streets which were lined with baby carriages and cribs while the grown-up persons lounged about in doorways or took cat naps lying on trucks or stretched out on the pavement. While some city residents headed outdoors to sleep on the street, others headed to Central Park or out to Coney Island." All were amazed at this report.

Everyone agreed the lower floors were cooler than the upper floors, of course, and Stella found her work assignments in Papa's shop on the lowest level to be the coolest location in their home. She enjoyed her work for other reasons too. She liked to help Papa receive, catalog, and organize the delicate parts for his watchmaking and keep the clocks dusted and oiled, but her favorite task was greeting customers and showing off Papa's fine watches and clocks.

Her outgoing personality and ability to engage in polite conversation with strangers were assets she felt she offered Papa in his business.

Papa was always available to meet with customers to advise and answer questions, but his time was best spent crafting new products and filling orders while Stella greeted the increasing steam of potential customers who came up from Manhattan and the lower Bronx.

One warm Tuesday afternoon, with thundershowers threatening, a kindly older man came into the shop saying he had heard downtown of Mr. Manning's fine skills in watchmaking and had traveled to Woodlawn Heights to see if he could order a special watch. He introduced himself as Thomas Kane.

"So pleased to meet, you, Mr. Kane," said Stella. "I am Miss Manning, the watchmaker's daughter. How may I help you today?"

As he began to speak, Stella noted how handsome Mr. Kane was. She observed he was tall and well built, with gray streaking his handsome beard, and touches of gray at his temples. He had a friendly and open face, and she could tell he smiled a lot because of the smile lines at the edges of his eyes.

He began his business by saying, "My son, also Thomas Kane, has recently received a promotion on the Pennsylvania Railroad. He started at the bottom rung on the railroad as an engine cleaner, then rose to fireman and, being ambitious and a quick learner, is progressing up the engineer ladder on his way to become an engineer of passenger trains. He has just been promoted to engineer on local freights, an important step in his responsibility."

"Congratulations, Mr. Kane. It sounds like you have a fine son," said Stella.

"Indeed, he has been a great blessing to me, especially the last few years since I have been widowed. For his hard work and his promotion, I should like to gift him a new and better watch, custom-made, not store-bought, with an engraving. Watches are important tools for trainmen, as you might imagine, Miss Manning, because they always have schedules to meet, and I have a list of all the standards the railroads require in chronometers."

"Indeed," answered Stella, taking the list, "and I'm sure your son will appreciate a new watch as a gift in honor of his new responsibilities."

Stella thought it was admirable how proud this gentleman was of his son, and she hoped Papa would be as proud of her someday when she had reached a new level of accomplishment in her elocution work.

She showed him several specialty watches that Papa had made, opening each one's handsome case and explaining its features. She spoke of the different styles of engraving that could be done and the selection of watch chains. Mr. Kane seemed pleased and eager to make a selection.

She called Papa out to meet him, and the two spent quite a lot of time considering various styles and engravings. Finally, Mr. Kane made a selection, and Papa made notes on all details of the order, telling Mr. Kane he might return to receive his watch on Monday next week. They sat and spoke pleasantly for several minutes after the sale was concluded.

"Excellent, Mr. Manning," said Mr. Kane as he rose to leave, "and might I bring my son to receive his watch here and meet the creator of his very special new timepiece?"

"Certainly, Mr. Kane, but would you not wish to present it to him in a more illustrious or intimate setting?" replied Papa.

"I think he will be pleased to receive it in the craftsman's own workshop," Mr. Kane said, thanking Papa and Stella for their careful attention to his request.

As he left, the smile that Stella predicted crinkled his face, and he said, "Thank you, Miss Manning, for your help, and, Mr. Manning, I am so delighted you can work with me, and I look forward to receiving a fine watch for young Thomas."

"Such a kind and thoughtful father, Papa," remarked Stella as he left. "Do you know, Papa, he is a widower, and thus, I imagine his son is very important to him. I'm glad we can help him." And she thought, *I wonder what his son might be like? The father is so kind and caring.*

Stella divided her time between working in the shop and fulfilling her other task, sewing her wardrobe for the classes, set to start in a few weeks. She and Mama and Jo decided she needed comfortable and everyday blouses and skirts and, perhaps, a dress or two for outings. Coordinating colors would allow her to mix and match to expand her wardrobe. New nightdresses and a wrapper would be useful too. They assessed her current holdings and planned the new garments to fill in as needed.

Their sewing times were animated with stories from new friends Mama had made and Jo's description of Luca's boisterous Italian family and her times spent with them. Alice joined in sewing now too, and Alfred kept them all entertained with his small-boy conversations and endless energy. Young Michael continued to work with Papa, bit by bit learning watchmaking, and also took Alfred out to play just about every day in nearby Edge Hill Park. Family summer routines settled in amid the steaming days of August.

Friday of the week found Stella helping Papa in the shop, when Mr. Kane paid a surprise visit, it seemed, for his watch was not to be ready until Monday. "Good day, Miss Manning. I hope you are tolerating the heat well," said Mr. Kane in greeting.

"Hello, Mr. Kane, so nice to see you," replied Stella. "And, yes, we are hoping for cooler weather come September. We were expecting to see you and your son on Monday..."

"Yes, yes, I know, Miss Manning, and I'm terribly sorry to startle you by an early arrival. Might I speak with you and Mr. Manning about an important favor?"

"Certainly. I'll tell my father you are here," replied Stella, very curious about what the favor might be. Papa had the Kane watch well underway, but it was not ready to be presented today. As Papa came out to the reception area to greet Mr. Kane, Stella stayed close by too.

"Mr. Manning, please forgive the interruption. As you know, I was planning to arrive on Monday with my son Thomas to receive the watch, but his schedule has just been published for next week — his first run in his new position — and he will be leaving Monday morning for several long-day shifts. He is coming off duty Saturday and has just one day off, so I would be ever so much grateful if you would consider letting us come by on Sunday afternoon to receive the watch.

"And, of course, I realize that Sunday is the Lord's day, and I would be interrupting your family time, so I totally understand if the imposition is too great," Mr. Kane continued.

Papa smiled his most engaging Irish smile, and said, "Mr. Kane, it would be my pleasure to have the watch available for you to present to him Sunday. And, in view of the timing, might you join me and my family for Sunday supper? We should like to meet your son and hear of the railroad."

Stella noted Mr. Kane seemed quite surprised and even somewhat overcome with a degree of emotion, which was given away by the light mist that formed in his eyes. He spoke softly, "An extraordinary and most kind offer, Mr. Manning. We shall humbly and gratefully accept and look forward to the occasion."

In all her years, Stella had never seen Papa so drawn to a customer and invite him for a meal, but she agreed Mr. Kane was a singular sort of man, and, after all, he was a widower, and he and his son could probably do with some company and a good Sunday supper.

Sunday was usually a relaxing day for the Mannings. In Dublin, they always went to church, but because there was yet no church anywhere in the area, Papa usually gathered the family in the front parlor, read some devotions, and then said some prayers from his prayer book. From time to time, an itinerant priest gathered the Catholics in one of the nearby barns for a Mass, but not today.

Because the weather was so hot, Mama had planned a cool summer supper of cold sliced ham with a potato salad that included hard-boiled eggs, pickled beetroot, onions, tomatoes, cucumber, and radishes with lettuce. She added Irish soda bread and fruit for dessert. Luca had again been invited for supper, and Mama had included extra helpings in the meal for him and their expected guests, the two Thomas Kanes.

Stella went down to the shop with Papa, at the time the Kanes were expected, to greet the gentlemen and satisfy her growing curiosity about the younger Mr. Kane. She did not have long to wait as the two gentlemen entered the shop at the agreed-upon time.

The first things she noticed were his eyes: the deepest brown with flecks of amber. Tall and well built like his father, Thomas the younger had the same handsome face but without the beard. Light brown, neatly trimmed hair framed his face, and he had an earnest, forthright look, but with a relaxed and friendly air.

Introductions were done all around. Stella gave him her most gracious smile, and he returned it. No smile lines yet around his eyes, she observed, but such lines took time to grow.

Stella had done her usual beautiful job wrapping the watch, adopting the wrapping style she had used with the Guinness watches, including the velvet pouch, and she handed it to Papa to present to Mr. Kane, who in turn proudly presented it to his son, with heartfelt words of congratulation and love.

"It is truly a treasure, Father," said the son as he examined the beautiful watch. "And I am most grateful. Thank you, sir, for your generosity and loving kindness."

Stella felt it was almost a private moment, and she and Papa were intruding, but then the younger man said, "And thank you, Mr. Manning, for your fine craftsmanship and the kindness and friendship you have shown my father." Turning to Stella, he said, "And Miss Manning, I understand you have been instrumental in helping my father make his selection and have also shown him much kindness."

"It has been a pleasure to meet him, Mr. Kane," Stella replied. "And we are looking forward to your joining us for supper and hearing about your work on the Pennsylvania Railroad. I believe we can join the others upstairs now."

"Yes, yes," confirmed Papa, "and you may bring your watch to show it off!"

Stella's first few hours with young Thomas Kane were memorable. Amid the clatter and chatter of her family and the serving and enjoying of the food, she found him to be a most gracious and authentic man. He smiled and laughed, he asked the younger children questions about their interests, and he spoke in a friendly and relaxed manner with the adults, but did not seek to draw attention to himself. He seemed truly interested in the lives of everyone at the table.

His father was equally amiable, and the meal was enjoyed, in spite of the hot weather.

Alfred, who loved to use his newly developing conversational skills, took a special liking, it seemed, to young Thomas. Upon learning he was a train engineer, Alfred asked questions about trains and announced that he too would like to drive a train someday. Young Thomas was gentle and thoughtful with Alfred and happily answered his questions and encouraged him.

A breeze came up as supper finished, and Jo, always eager to spend time with Luca, suggested a walk to enjoy the freshening air. She said, "Papa, I think you and Mama would enjoy speaking more with Mr. Kane, while Stella and I might ask Luca and the other Mr. Kane" — nodding toward young Thomas — "to walk a bit to enjoy the breeze."

To which Papa replied jovially, "Jo, I'm thinking you are not thinking so much of us, but rather thinking of some time away from the older folks. Am I right?"

"Well, actually, yes, Papa," answered Jo a little sheepishly.

"Then take Alfred with you and stop by Edge Hill Park to let him play for a while to burn off some energy," said Papa. Turning to the Kanes, he said, "Because we could not bring his rocking horse and wooden trains and blocks and other larger toys on the ship, he is lacking in some of his play activities, and the park is a treat for him."

Alfred whooped with joy, and Papa asked Alice and Michael to clear the dishes. "While Mama and I visit in the parlor with Mr. Kane," said Papa.

Feeling a need to issue the invitation herself, Stella said, "Mr. Kane, would you enjoy a walk around the neighborhood with me, my sister, and Mr. Rossi?"

"That would be delightful, Miss Manning, for a short while. My father and I must be on our way soon because I need to be at work very early in the morning to start a long week."

And so Stella and the younger Mr. Kane, Jo and Luca, and an eager Alfred set out for a short stroll around

Woodlawn Heights and a stop at the park. Alfred led the group, running and jumping a few paces of Jo and Luca, who agreed to keep track of him. Stella and Mr. Kane followed, and he offered Stella his arm.

Stella had not walked with a gentleman who was not her father or her cousin, so she was not sure if she should take his arm, but his offer was kind and gentlemanly, and it seemed polite to accept, so she did. She looked up at his very brown eyes and saw the late-afternoon sun reflected in his amber flecks in a most appealing way, and she felt flustered, not sure what to say to start a conversation.

Mr. Kane solved the problem by asking, "Miss Manning, do you work in your father's shop each day, or do you have other work or interests?"

"I'm quite busy these days, Mr. Kane, helping Papa, but also preparing to start a new school program in September in the city. I will be studying elocution in the new Delacourte School of Elocution, a unique and wonderful opportunity for me."

"*Elocution* is a term I've heard, Miss Manning, but I'm not sure exactly what it is," Mr. Kane replied. "Tell me about it and about your new program."

This was a query Stella could easily answer, so she told him of her enduring interest in poetry and literature, about the Poetry Society and her elocution training in Dublin and how she had met the Delacourtes. Mr. Kane was highly engaged with her story and asked her a couple of questions.

As their walk continued and they reached the park and sat down on a grassy hillock, Stella felt she should allow him to tell her more about his life, so she asked him how he had gotten into railroad work. "It's always been in my blood, Miss Manning. You see, my father was a railroad man, and I grew up around the railroad all my life. His work was in the nonoperating part of the railroad, first as a dispatcher, and then as an assistant station master for the New York Central and Hudson River Railroad. When I was small, my mother would take me to the Grand Central Depot to meet my father as he finished work so that I could watch the arriving trains." Speaking with great enthusiasm, Mr. Kane continued, "As these mighty machines, billowing great clouds of steam and shaking the ground, pulled into the station, I knew someday I'd be an engineer to bring the trains in. It takes a lot of experience to serve as an engineer on passenger trains, but that is my ultimate goal."

Stella loved this story, as she watched Alfred chase a butterfly in the park, and she pictured a small boy's fascination with the steam engines and his dream to drive one. It seemed Mr. Kane had the same passion for trains and railroad work as she had for elocution. He was a man on a journey to follow his dream, just as she was following hers. This thought was exciting to Stella.

As they strolled home, Stella asked him more about his work and then said, "I can appreciate your keen interest in your chosen line of work, Mr. Kane. It is a thing we share, this seeking to fulfill a closely held dream. I wish you the best of success in pursuing your goals."

"And I wish you the same, Miss Manning," said Mr. Kane as they reached her front steps again, finding Jo and Luca, ahead of their pace and waiting on the steps with an exhausted Alfred.

As Stella released her hold on Mr. Kane's arm, he looked down into her eyes and said most earnestly, "How extraordinary it has been to meet you and have a chance to talk with a fellow soul on a chosen path in life. I admire your tenacity and energy, Miss Manning. I'm hoping we can speak again, and I shall think of you and your fine family each time I look at my new watch."

"I would enjoy the opportunity to speak with you again," replied Stella. "But I know we must send you on your way because of your early-morning departure."

The Kane men thanked Mama heartily for the fine meal and Papa again for his craftsmanship and new friendship.

As they bid goodbye to everyone before climbing into their carriage and setting out, Stella felt a loss. She barely knew the young Mr. Kane, but they had connected in a special way, she felt, sharing their closely held dreams, being so candid with one another in such a relaxed and natural way on such short acquaintance.

She wondered if their amiable connection was a normal experience because she had known so few young men. Whatever it was, she found it, like he had said, to be extraordinary.

CHAPTER 10

New York City
Late August 1892

*T*homas Kane was up before dawn, walking the short distance from his home at Ninth Avenue and West Twenty-Ninth Street to the El, which took him downtown to the ferry terminal at Pier Eighteen. The so-called Cortland Street Ferry was his ride to Jersey City. Someday, he mused, "Pennsy" trains will come into New York City through a tunnel beneath the Hudson River. Wasn't there already talk about this feat? But for now, his locomotive awaited him in Jersey City at the roundhouse, from where he would drive it to the freight yard to pick up his train.

Today was a signal day in his railroad career. Being promoted to local freights after his years as a fireman, and after much training and mentoring by senior engineers, was a huge step up for him toward his goal of becoming an engineer on passenger trains. Thomas knew the most precious cargo the railroad carried were people, and aspiring engineers had to prove their skills and gain much experience with freights before training and qualifying for the lofty goal of passenger train engineer.

His grand aspiration was to someday drive the famous Pennsylvania Limited, an extra-fare all Pullman train that served New York through the Jersey City to Chicago route.

This flagship train was the fastest on the Pennsylvania Railroad line, with a runtime to Chicago of twenty-six hours and forty minutes. Inaugurated in 1881, it had the distinction of being Pennsylvania's first named train, and it joined the railroad's timetable as Train 1 Westbound and Train 2 Eastbound.

Thomas had seen this sleek and beautiful train during his five-year tenure with the railroad and was fascinated with its vestibule cars, which allowed passengers to move freely from car to car through enclosures located at each end. He figured that someday this feature would be standard on all trains, but his railroad had done it first. The Pennsy's forward-thinking and innovative business model, and extraordinary growth, were primary reasons he had chosen to work on the Pennsy, even though he had had opportunities to sign on with his father's railroad company, the New York Central and Hudson River Railroad.

He told himself to stop dreaming of the Pennsylvania Limited and concentrate on doing excellent work on the freights and gaining new skills. For now, he would be content. Yes, not merely content, but absolutely delighted that he was moving into local freight service. Local freights operated throughout the Pennsy system, he knew, and he would gain valuable experience.

Just about everything was shipped by rail these days to move manufactured goods across the huge country, he mused. Newark, New Jersey, as just one example, was booming with factories producing all kinds of products that shipped hundreds of miles on the Pennsy. Even newly improved refrigerated train cars moved meats and fruits and delivered these in-demand products to warehouses for distribution. Thomas believed firmly that he was in the business of the future, and he was grateful.

Yes, he thought, on his newly assigned local freight service, he would serve industries on the Pennsy's New Jersey main line and branch lines, gaining knowledge throughout the area system. He was indeed blessed, and being a man of faith, he thanked God for each new day's opportunities to pursue his dream.

As he stepped aboard the ferry, he stood at a rail and looked back at the cluttered waterfront, already coming to life with shouts and the clatter of horses and carts. A glance eastward toward the city gave him a striking view of the rising sun, its bright early morning rays glinting off the ever-taller buildings that were arising in lower Manhattan. His thoughts turned to the crowded and crime-ridden city, and he wondered how safe Miss Stella Manning would be once she came to the city for her elocution schooling.

Stella Manning. A most extraordinary young lady, reflected Thomas. He wasn't sure of her age, but she had the maturity and ambition not usually possessed by young women under twenty, which he was sure she was. And he had been mightily impressed by her natural beauty: those startling green eyes, lush and curly brown hair with just a touch of gold, her heart-shaped face that radiated so much zest for life as she spoke, and her delicate, ladylike ways. The warmth of her nearness as they walked together tugged at his memory and lent an extra warmness to the rising sun.

Yes, she was one of a kind, Thomas mused. She had an abundance of natural charm, and her forthrightness in sharing her dream with him on such short acquaintance was remarkable. Her dedication to training in elocution was inspiring—much like his dedication to his goals—and he had no doubt she'd be a diligent student and do well.

He had to admit he was smitten, not a common emotion for him. But he had never met anyone like Stella Manning. Most young ladies were wrapped up in social activities, shopping trips, and the like, based on his limited experience. She was a girl with a purpose in life, with whom he could share his heart and feel relaxed yet energized in her presence.

He would like to become better acquainted with her. But how? His schedule changed from week to week, she would be busy getting ready for school and then highly engaged with her studies, so it seemed fairly hopeless. And besides, what interest might she have in him when she was ensconced in the literary circle of the city, surrounded by people whose world she sought to enter? No, it was likely unpromising. Yet, a glimmer of hope stirred him to consider a way.

As he offered a silent prayer for the opportunity to see Miss Manning again, young Alfred's face came to mind, and he remembered Mr. Manning saying that many of Alfred's toys had to be left behind for their passage from Dublin to New York.

He had an idea.

Saturday morning found the Manning clan preparing for a picnic in Edge Hill Park. Mama and Jo were wrapping sandwiches in napkins wrung out of cold water to keep the bread moist and packing small meat pies and cheese in paraffin paper along with several other items. Stella was in charge of packing the square grape basket solidly, using every corner to best avail. A smaller basket was packed with tissue paper napkins, a sharp knife, a fork, a few spoons, and a tin drinking cup for each person, along with salt-and-pepper boxes.

Papa and Michael were finishing up a few chores in the shop below before setting out, and Alice was getting Alfred dressed for their outing. The door chime announced the arrival of Luca and Vittoria, with more wrapped picnic food in another sturdy basket and jugs of water to make lemonade. Frivolity was in the air. Everyone had had a busy week, and today's sunshine augured well for a fun and relaxing time.

Another door chime was heard, and Stella stepped into the hall to open the door and find the young Thomas Kane standing at the top of their steps with a large crate in his hands. Her heart skipped a beat at his ready smile.

"Mr. Kane! What a pleasant surprise," announced Stella as she recovered from her happy discovery. "Do come in."

"Miss Manning, good morning. I apologize for visiting unannounced, and I won't interrupt if you are busy, but I have a small thank you for your family's hospitality of last Sunday, something that might be welcome."

Stella was delighted to see Mr. Kane again. She had thought often during the busy week about how she might spend some time with him, but it had seemed hopeless, with his travel schedule and her near-imminent departure for school in the city. How serendipitous that he was here. *How very pleasant*, she thought.

As she ushered him into the parlor, the Manning women came out to greet him, and Alfred rushed to him, grabbing him by the legs and nearly toppling him over with joy. "Mr. Kane, Mr. Kane," he called, "you have left your train to come see us again!"

Thomas Kane stooped down to Alfred's size and said, "Ah, so I have, young Alfred, but instead, I have brought a train to you." Having said that, he invited Alfred to sit with him as he opened the large crate and removed six finely crafted wooden train cars, each with pegs to attach to one another.

Alfred was beside himself. He jumped up and down, exclaiming, "Trains for me?!" Then he sat down to examine each car, discovering an engine, two freight cars, two passenger cars, and a caboose. Thomas Kane then produced from his pocket, next to his watch, a wooden train whistle and explained to Alfred some of the various whistle signals, demonstrating that three short whistles meant the train will be backing up, and one short and three long whistles meant the flagman should protect the rear of the train.

"There are twelve different whistle signals, Alfred,"
Mr. Kane said, "and you can learn them all as you move
your train around."

"This train, it's mine to keep, Mr. Kane?" asked Alfred.

"Yes, indeed, it is," was the answer. "This set was mine
when I was a small boy, and I loved playing with it. But now
I have big trains to run, so this one is just for you to enjoy."

Alfred threw himself on Mr. Kane, gave him a huge
hug, and said, "Thank you, thank you, sir. Just wait until I
show Papa!"

At that point, Papa and Michael arrived, and Mr. Kane
quickly got to his feet to greet them. "Papa, Papa," cried
Alfred, "look what Mr. Kane has brought me. Now I have
my very own new train set, even better than the one we left
in Dublin." Michael sat down to play with him, and they
soon had the train in motion all over the parlor.

"Mr. Kane, how wonderful," exclaimed Papa, shaking
his head and smiling broadly, even more so than Mama, Jo,
Stella, and Alice.

But Stella's smile was misty because she was so touched
by the thoughtfulness and kindness Mr. Kane had shown.
She imagined what this train set had meant to him as a
small boy and how hard it must have been to give it up. But
he had done so and gladly, it seemed, as she observed the
complete delight on his face while he watched Alfred blow
the whistle and move the trains.

"Mr. Kane," Mama began, "such a superb and astonishing gift. I don't know what to say about such a considerate
present for our small son. Alfred will spend many happy
hours running his trains."

And Papa added, "We are most grateful for your generosity, Mr. Kane. I am sad, though, that someday you might
have your own boy who would wish the set."

"In that far-away case, Mr. Manning," Mr. Kane said,
smiling pensively, "perhaps Alfred will be grown-up and
have tired of it, and will share it with such a boy! But it is

indeed his to keep. It's a small thank you for your family's kindness and hospitality to me and my father."

"Mr. Kane," spoke Mama again, "we are all preparing for a picnic in Edge Hill Park, and we'd be most pleased if you'd join us. We have plenty of food for all."

"Yes, yes," chimed in everyone. Stella looked directly at him and saw pure joy on his handsome face.

He returned her gaze with an expectant smile and said, "Why, I'd be delighted. Thank you so much."

The picnic proved to be a great idea, with everyone carrying picnic food and supplies to the park. Even though Alfred was loathe to leave his trains behind in the house, he and Michael, Luca, and Thomas Kane soon found themselves engaging in a lively game of baseball with a bat and ball Luca had brought. Luca was a big baseball fan and had told them all that the game of baseball was growing rapidly in America. He reported that Brooklyn already had several leagues, along with the New York Knickerbockers, although organized baseball was still chaotic with competing leagues and unsettled rules. But he didn't care; he just loved to play.

The ladies spread old sheets on a grassy knoll in a shady area of the park, and soon the men and boys came over to share the picnic food. Mama and Jo and Vittoria spread out the feast: sandwiches made of both white and brown bread that contained thinly sliced roast beef seasoned with Worcestershire sauce; lamb, also thinly sliced combined with tomato catsup; and chicken, seasoned with celery salt. Fruit sandwiches appeared too, and everyone's favorite was the sliced banana with lemon juice and a small amount of sugar between slices of bread and butter. An array of cheeses, chopped nuts, Mama's meat pies, and cucumbers and tomatoes rounded out the meal.

Vittoria and Luca shared juicy pies, turnovers, and cakes with cream filling from their parents' bakery and had brought tea brewed at quadruple strength to be diluted with the water and served cold, along with the lemonade.

Conversation centered on, of course, the weather, and everyone's workweek, with lively chattering all around. As the afternoon wound down, Jo and Luca, with Vittoria as chaperone, and Michael tagging along, decided to walk to the other side of the park. Alice dozed, enjoying the sunshine on her face, and Alfred tugged at Thomas Kane's sleeve to see if he would play with him. Stella said, "Let's go for a walk with Mr. Kane, Alfred, to give Mama and Papa some time together to relax." Alfred readily agreed, and so did Mr. Kane, and the three set off to explore.

Alfred ran on ahead and asked for help in climbing a tree. "It's a pretty tall one, Alfred," cautioned Mr. Kane, "but I'll boost you up and stand guard here in case you tumble. Do be careful, or I shall get in trouble with your mama."

Stella laughed, remembering how she used to love to climb trees in Dublin's parks. "And I shall be here to catch you too, Alfred," she said.

As Alfred climbed the tree and Stella and Mr. Kane stood watch, she turned to him and said, "Mr. Kane, I don't know how you could part with such a precious toy as the train set, but you have made a small boy very happy. And your generosity and kindness have made me very happy too."

"It's quite all right, Miss Manning," replied Mr. Kane. "The set gave me such pleasure as a young boy, and I felt Alfred would love it too."

"You see," Stella continued, "Alfred is a very special little boy to Mama, who is always seeking his happiness. Of course, she loves us all, but before Alfred was born, she had another little son named George who died, and we were all very sad until Alfred came along. Mama calls him her 'last little baby,' and she dotes on him."

"Ah, Miss Manning, how very sad to lose a family member. I too have felt this sadness when first my younger sister died of pneumonia, and then this dreaded disease took my mother too shortly afterward. It's been most difficult for Father and me, but we have each other for consolation and company, and we know our dear ladies are safe in heaven." Mr. Kane's eyes misted over for a few seconds, and then he said, "And we shall see them again someday, we know too."

"Oh, Mr. Kane, I am so sorry," said Stella. "When did you lose these dear ones?"

"It's been four years now, Miss Manning, and it's been especially hard on Father because he sees himself as the protector of our family, and he was helpless to save them, even though we had good doctors."

"Such experiences leave such an empty place, Mr. Kane, and I've noticed how you seem to appreciate being with our large family."

"Yes, indeed," he replied. "Father and I do well keeping each other company, but we both miss the warmth and love of my mother and the gaiety of my sister. She was only fourteen when she died, just turning into a lovely young lady."

Stella placed her hand on Mr. Kane's arm, looked into his eyes, and said, "I am truly sorry and wish it were otherwise. I can only imagine how lonely you and your father must be from time to time as you remember earlier times."

"We try to reflect on the good times, Miss Manning, and stay thankful for our blessings. And we have relatives in New Jersey whom we see occasionally, Father's brother and his wife and family."

Alfred squealed from a high perch in the tree and said, "Look how high I am!" Both Stella and Mr. Kane warned him not to go any higher. "But I want to touch the sky," he shouted.

They laughed to break the solemn mood, and Stella turned and said, "Mr. Kane, I am wondering if I might address you by your Christian name since we are becoming friends. It seems only right to drop our formality after we have shared our dreams for the future and our sadness of the past."

"I would be delighted and honored, Miss Manning, I mean, Stella. It's such a beautiful name, you know, reminding one of the stars."

"Ah yes, Thomas..." began Stella.

"Call me Tom, Stella. That's how I'm usually called."

"All right, Tom. Pleased to meet you," Stella said as she held out her hand for a handshake, and they both laughed.

"As I was saying, Tom, my family has always called me Stella because Papa said when I was a baby, my little eyes twinkled like stars when he tickled me and I laughed. My baptismal name is Mary Esther Manning, but I've always been called Stella. What is your full name?"

"It's Thomas Herbert Kane, Stella, and my mother was named Sarah, which was also the name of my sister, but she was called Sallie all her life."

With a shriek, Alfred went hand over hand out onto one of the sturdy tree branches and called, "Catch me!" as he let go. As they did, they all ended up on the ground laughing.

"Let me help you up, Stella, and you, Mr. Alfred, should not live so dangerously," said Tom sternly but with a smile.

Walking on together with Alfred bounding ahead, Stella asked Tom about his first week in his new position driving the freights, and he asked her about her preparations for school. They enjoyed a relaxed and easy conversation and soon found themselves linking up with the others, returning from their walk. All reconvened at the picnic site, and then Luca announced, "Tonight, we're having a bonfire to mark the near end of the summer season. Everyone is invited."

Tom Kane looked perplexed, but Luca said to him, "Mr. Kane—Thomas—you can help build the fire, enjoy it, and then spend the night at our house." Winking at Jo, he continued, "Please say you'll stay. Mama has planned some special late-night food for us."

Tom looked at Stella, who grinned and nodded, and Tom replied, "Sounds like a delightful evening, Luca. I don't have to work until Monday."

The bonfire lit the night sky in an area of cleared ground safe for fires right outside of Woodlawn Heights beside a grassy knoll. The evening cooled down to a pleasant degree, and stars came out brightly. Young and old gathered, and Luca's father brought his fiddle. Others from town came too, including Stella's cousin Colin and his family, and Stella introduced them to Tom. One Irishman brought his mandolin, creating a sweet and haunting sound.

As promised, Mrs. Rossi provided wonderful food: doughnuts with cheese and cakes with cream filling, and others brought food too. Traditional folk songs from Ireland and Italy filled the air.

Luca pulled Jo into a lively Italian tarantella, and young Michael did his version of the Irish jig, which caused everyone to laugh, including Michael.

Sitting together, Stella admired Tom's strong profile in the shadows cast by the fire and the night sky. When he smiled down at her and took her hand to gently tug her to her feet and lead her to dance to a slow Irish folk tune, she thought she had never been happier in her life as she swayed loosely in his arms. She wanted to be held closer, though, and this feeling was new and overwhelming to her, but propriety prevailed, and she smiled up into his eyes while keeping a proper distance apart.

Papa and Mama danced to the slow tune too, and she watched how closely Papa held Mama and wondered if she would ever be held that close by someone who loved her.

She saw Luca whisper something into Jo's ear and saw Jo blush and smile.

As the dance ended, Tom bowed and thanked her, releasing her hand slowly, and she returned the bow. The magic of the evening ended as the bonfire grew dim and the musicians finished the last tunes. She bid farewell to Tom as he joined Luca and she walked home with her family, Papa carrying a sound-asleep Alfred.

Lying in bed next to Jo, Stella reflected on all she had learned about Tom Kane today. He had been through some hard times and sad losses but was striving to be a companion to his father and diligently pursuing his railroad career. He loved being a part of a family and had a friendly, outgoing nature. He was a caring and generous man. And his arms were strong. She loved being held, however loosely, by them. It seemed when his luminous dark brown eyes looked down at her that he was seeing into her very soul. He was a perfect gentleman, but she could imagine him pulling her close in a loving hug, like Papa did, but she thought the feeling would be much different.

She liked him very much and would like to see him again and again, but finding time to see each other would prove difficult in the coming weeks. She would be so busy with school, and he was on the rails many days each month with his work. Stella decided to talk to God about this situation. She asked Him to bless Tom for all his kindness and to show her how their friendship might continue as she drifted off to sleep.

Early Sunday morning afforded a quick visit with Tom as he stopped by early to accept Mama's invitation to enjoy her special porridge breakfast before he had to return to the city to spend time with his father.

"Have a wonderful week, Stella," he said softly at her front door, as he handed her his card with his address. "And write me a note to let me know how your plans are coming along for starting classes next week. With your Papa's permission and the Delacourtes' address, perhaps I can pay you a visit when you are settled in the city, if you have time."

"Please ask him, Tom, because visitors must be on an approved list Papa will give to the Delacourtes."

"Then I shall work up my nerve to write to him to see if he will give permission," answered Tom lightly, seeing that only Mama and Stella were up and about so early.

"Excellent, Tom," said Stella, masking her sadness at his leaving, "and please greet your father for all of us and have a good week. I promise to write." She wanted to touch his arm but, instead, just said, "Godspeed into the city, Tom Kane, my exceptional new friend."

Tom's long trip back into the city gave him time to think through and savor the highlights of the past twenty-four hours in Woodlawn Heights. He was truly pleased that young Alfred was delighted with his train set. Remembering all the many happy hours he had spent as a boy playing trains, and now seeing another young boy just as entranced as he was, did his heart good.

Time with the Manning family was to be cherished. They were good people whose love bonded them together, much as his family had been before it was shattered by loss. Yes, he and his father were close and loved each other, in addition to having much in common with their railroad lives, but they were so alone. Nonetheless, he was as happy as he could be right now, with a secure and decent home with his father and a good job. His prospects were excellent, and he knew many others who were not so fortunate. And yet, he yearned for more, for a fuller life, one with a wife and children. A family. *Someday,* he thought, *I might find that, but how many years in the future?*

For now, he reminded himself, he needed to trust that God was leading him day by day and would show him the next steps. Was Stella Manning part of his future? She was so young and ambitious and just beginning to follow her dream of becoming an accomplished elocutionist. What then? He should ask her and support her in any way he could. But was there any room in her life for him?

She was so lovely, and holding her in his arms, even loosely, as they danced under the stars last night, was an enduring memory. They had begun a good friendship, and he valued that highly, but could he hope for anything more, a future with her? Could they even work out their schedules to spend any significant time together?

He would leave it in God's capable hands.

CHAPTER 11

New York City
September 1892

With a promise of cooler weather to come, the Mannings prepared for a new season of their life in America. Papa's business was growing fast, with referrals from the watchmaker's guild and the steady stream of wealthy people who made their way to Woodlawn Heights as the upper Bronx became more heavily populated and accessible. Although watches were now mass produced by companies such as the American Waltham Watch Company, many gentlemen preferred the personalized service and high-quality work Papa offered.

Alice and Michael were preparing to start school through a special situation that had developed in the absence of any public schools being stood up in Woodlawn Heights. As it happened, a young Irish immigrant, a Mr. Patrick Brady, had come to make his home in the neighborhood with members of his family already settled there, and fortunately he was a schoolmaster.

The village's Irish and Italian families seeking nearby educational opportunities for their children, and Mr. Brady seeking work as a schoolmaster, were a perfect match. He had readily agreed to take on the task of operating a local school supported by funds pooled by all the families. With materials from the 50-year-old New York City School Board, he would teach the children in borrowed warehouse space on the edge of town, with parents contributing chairs and tables and school supplies. Papa was adamant that Michael and Alice should finish their schooling, so this situation proved ideal.

Jo and Mama had the household running smoothly and were helping Stella finish preparations for her school wardrobe, and Stella herself was in a whirl helping Papa in the shop and preparing to leave for the city. Jo would take over some of her work in the shop, although she was not as eager to meet and greet customers as Stella had always been. She told Stella she was hoping her responsibilities upstairs and downstairs would not keep her too busy to spend time with Luca with whom she was getting along famously.

Everyone was enjoying watching Alfred play with his train set and blowing his train whistle to signal the movement of the trains, although Papa had requested that the whistle signals be issued less frequently in the evening when all were relaxing at the end of the day. Each time Stella watched Alfred's happy face, she remembered the warm and tender feelings she had for Tom because of his most gracious and unselfish gift.

Stella had spent the last week reviewing her elocution exercises, tuning in again to her studies and literary books in anticipation of her coming training. She had purposely pushed aside thoughts of Tom, and the fun and frivolity of the end of summer, to focus her mind on her schooling. She had written to him to let him know of her progress in all the preparations and to give him the Delacourtes' address. She had signed her letter "Affectionately, Stella" and hoped that this closing was not too bold.

She had eagerly examined the post each day to see if there had been a letter from him to Papa asking permission to visit her in the city, but none had arrived. She was disappointed but hopeful it would still come. Tom had seemed keen to visit her, hadn't he? And she knew him to be a sincere person, but maybe he wasn't that interested in seeing her after all, with work priorities and needing to spend time with his father. She would be patient and not worry too much about their friendship now with all her new activities coming up. Yet, she still did.

She had also written a long, newsy letter to Miss D and shorter missives to Mavis and Rose, all of whom had written to her recently. She thought she would have little time for correspondence once her classes started.

The night before leaving home, as Stella climbed into bed, she reminisced on the almost four months she had spent in America so far and what it meant to her. She remembered her feelings as *Destiny* had reached shore, how she felt her dream was shattered forever, how resentful she was of Papa, but those feelings had not proved true. And a peace she didn't understand had happened. Yes, she had given up a whole way of life that was satisfying and meaningful to her, but this new life was showing promise. New friends and new opportunities had appeared. As Jo had advised her the night before they docked, she would make the most of it. She would follow her dream in this new land wherever it led.

"Good night, God," she whispered. "Let me be all that You want me to be, and let Tom be in my life too. It seems He knows you, God, and that must please you. Amen."

Papa took the day off to take Stella and her trunk to the city at the beginning of the second week in September, on a breezy mild day, to move into the Delacourtes' Fifth Avenue residence and school. The whole family wished her well and stood on the doorstep to wave goodbye as Papa urged Uncle Nicholas' horse and curricle to move forward, with Stella's trunk firmly strapped on. Soon Papa would be buying his own rig, he told Stella.

Stella felt a stab of sorrow to leave everyone; she had never left home and family before except for the occasional overnight at Rose or Mavis' homes. What would it be like to be away for several weeks? Would she be homesick? She hoped not, as she waved goodbye and then turned her face toward the city and her future.

She and Papa drove all the way into town, not wanting to take the El in the lower Bronx because of her trunk. As they left Broadway and went around Columbus Circle and alongside Central Park, Stella looked for the new statue of Christopher Columbus Uncle Nicholas had mentioned on their drive past this location the day they arrived. It was there, but covered-up, and Papa told her the statue would be dedicated in October for the four hundredth anniversary of Columbus' arrival in America in 1492.

Papa turned onto Fifth and soon they arrived at the Delacourtes' impressive Victorian mansion. Waiting on the steps was a young man who asked Papa if he was delivering a student for the class, and receiving an affirmative nod, he said he would take the rig around back to the mews and bring in the trunk.

"I'll have it upstairs for you right quickly, miss, so you and the gentleman may go directly into the house. The Delacourtes are in the large parlor greeting the arriving students."

Stella could hardly contain her excitement. Was this day really happening? As Papa helped her down from the carriage and up the steps, she breathed a grateful prayer to God and gave Papa a quick kiss on the cheek with a "thank you, dear Papa."

His dream had become a reality, and now it was her turn.

Mr. and Mrs. Delacourte greeted Stella and Papa heartily and invited them into the main floor's large parlor, which was abuzz with the excitement of several young ladies and parents. Tea and small, delicate sandwiches were being served, and Stella noticed a gentleman playing the grand piano in the corner, creating beautiful classical background music to match the ambiance of the elegant room.

Stella looked at the young ladies first and counted six others, seemingly about her age, all looking eager and somewhat overwhelmed, much like she felt she looked. The various parents, like the girls, seemed well-dressed but not so much as the people in the pictures Stella often saw in the *Herald* of The Four Hundred, the ultra-elite socialites who dominated the city's social scene. Everyone looked friendly and typical of their friends in Dublin and in Woodlawn Heights.

One girl seemed missing as Stella smiled and counted students. And at that moment, another young lady arrived to bring the student count to eight.

"She must be Irish," Stella said to herself, seeing the red hair, shining blue eyes, and tilt of the head of the last arrival. This girl looked right at Stella and smiled, then came over to her and said, "You must be Irish," and Stella was amazed at the concurrent conclusions each had of the other.

"Yes, I am," said Stella as she held out her hand. "Stella Manning, originally from Dublin."

"I knew it," said the red-haired beauty. "And I am Jessie Byrnes, New Yorker, but my family is originally from Dublin."

"But how did you know I was Irish?" asked Stella.

"Ah, the green eyes, the tilt of the head, and your Irish way of composing yourself," said Jessie.

Stella laughed, and so did Jessie. Their fathers began speaking to each other, and Stella noticed many in the room seemed fairly in awe of Mr. Byrnes. The conversation in the room accelerated until Mr. Delacourte called for order and announced in a firm by friendly manner that the parent tea-time was over, and the young ladies needed to unpack, get acquainted, and prepare for supper.

Fond goodbyes were said by all, even a few tears fell, and Papa gave Stella a hug, with assurances the whole family would pray for her and he would pay her a visit next week when he came to the city for his guild meeting. Then he and the other parents drifted toward the front door and waiting carriages brought around by the young man who had ushered them in earlier.

And that was it. She was here, Papa was on his way home, and her new life had begun.

The Delacourtes asked the students to sit down in the velvet chairs spaced around the parlor and gave them a hearty welcome speech.

"We're so pleased to see all of you," Mr. Delacourte said. "Each of you has been selected from a larger group of applicants to attend the inaugural session of our new Delacourte School of Elocution. We see much talent in elocution in each of you, and we are highly enthused about developing that talent to enrich your lives and the lives of many in this city."

Seeing the smiles and eager faces all around the room, Mrs. Delacourte continued, "Classes will begin at eight in the morning tomorrow, Monday, in the second-floor parlor, and your schedules and all details about your training will be provided. For now, it might be good for each of you to stand, introduce yourself, and tell us in one or two short sentences about yourself and your family. Let's start with our two sisters," she said, indicating two blonde and pert young ladies sitting side by side.

"Thank you, Mrs. Delacourte," one of the sisters said as she stood, and nodding to Mr. Delacourte, she began, "I am

Emily Billingham, here with my sister Charlotte Billingham. Our father is a professor of English literature at Columbia College, as you might have guessed from our names. My parents are great enthusiasts of the Brontë family, and had we another sister, she surely would have been named Anne."

Laughter ensued as the other Billingham girl stood up daintily and disclosed, "And we do not have a brother named Branwell, but I am Charlotte, younger of the two, but only by fourteen months, and we have always been each other's best friend."

A petite raven-haired girl arose next and introduced herself an Anne-Marie Cariveau, born in New York of parents who emigrated from Paris, France in 1872, and who owned a very busy bakery in midtown Manhattan. She told the others she was blessed to speak both English and French to their customers, although she preferred English for elocution.

Curly-headed and vivacious, Gianna Ricci introduced herself as a third-generation American of Italian background whose parents were involved in textile manufacturing, and she told the others she was the only girl in a family of five brothers, at which all the girls who had brothers groaned.

Jessie Byrnes, sitting beside Stella, stood to tell of her father's emigration from Dublin, Ireland, as a child, how he had served in the American Civil War, and was now superintendent of the New York City Police Department. She stated she had four sisters, and she was the youngest. Her father, she reported, had a dramatic flair, which she greatly admired, and she had thus gained an interest in pursuing elocution.

Another dark-haired and vivacious girl arose to introduce herself as Rachel Polonsky, of Jewish heritage, from a close-knit family of five, she said, and that her father was a buyer at the A. T. Stewart Department Store.

Two introductions remained, and Stella smiled at the other young lady and encouraged her to go ahead, so Anna Bentley stood and told the others her family had been in America since before the Revolution in the last century and that her papa was a physician.

Going last, Stella announced herself "as the other Irish girl, recently arrived," and that she had missed Ireland and her brief elocution work there after her family emigrated this past spring. She reported they were now happily settled in Woodlawn Heights, and she, her family of two sisters and two brothers, were the children of a fine watchmaker.

Mrs. Delacourte thanked everyone for their introductions and said she would take them to their third-floor rooms, where their trunks and belongings already resided in the hallway. With four bedroom and two bathrooms, each girl would have a roommate, and four would share each bathroom. She announced the Billingham sisters would room together, she had paired the two Irish girls in one room, and the other four could choose a roommate as they saw fit.

As Stella climbed the stairs with the others, she marveled at the large and commodious house, elegantly furnished with high ceilings and tall windows on each floor. A lavishly carved central staircase led to each level, and she guessed a back staircase was in the house to accommodate servants. She loved her room. It looked out on Fifth Avenue at the constant parade of finely dressed people. Repeating the gold tones of the entrance level, which she found cheerful and bright, soft silk drapes and linen window shades with tassel pulls framed the room. The soft turkey carpet of muted gold-and-brown tones felt luxurious underfoot and stretched between two finely crafted beds. She would have her own bed! Never before had she had this luxury.

A tall and ample wardrobe, plus a dressing table for her to share with Jessie, and even a closet for additional storage, completed the room. She and her new roommate happily unpacked and settled their clothing, and looking to be of the same size — although Jessie was about an inch taller — they giggled how they might share clothes from time to time to enlarge their wardrobes.

A fine dinner in the first-floor dining room, aglow with candles for atmosphere — although the new electric lights were prominent through the house — found everyone chatting amiably after Mr. Delacourte said a blessing, and using their very best manners, as expected in such a setting. Again, Stella could hardly believe she was here.

Later that night, Jessie told her, "I know you will be able to tell me wonderful stories of Ireland, Stella, and we'll have fun sharing our lives in great detail over the coming weeks, but for now, we need to rest up. Tomorrow will be a big day."

Stella couldn't agree more.

CHAPTER 12

New York City
September 1892

"*He*'s resting now, and he will recover," said the doctor to Thomas Kane.

"Thank the Lord, and thank you for your excellent help, Dr. Brooks. You have been so attentive to him with my absence this week on my routes."

"You are quite welcome, Mr. Kane, but do see that he rests and receives fluids and good nutritious meals as he recovers."

Stella's final exciting week of preparation for school had been a week of sheer worry and difficulty for Tom. His father had fallen ill shortly after he left for work the Monday after the Woodlawn Heights picnic. Upon returning that night, he had found his father febrile and weak, while insisting "it was nothing." Tom took his symptoms seriously and promptly called for a doctor.

Fearing a bad influenza might do substantial harm to the older man, the doctor had put him to bed with medications and instructions for his care. Tom was in a panic because of his work schedule, but two small miracles, as he called them, had happened. Their neighbor, a robust and capable German widow, whom they had befriended, offered to look in on him, ensure doctor's orders were carried out, and bring him food. The Pennsylvania Railroad was able to change Tom's schedule, giving him a day off every other day to see to his father's care, and the doctor had stopped by too. The fever had broken late Saturday, and Tom spent extra time at church on Sunday being thankful.

Now he knew he needed to have a talk with his father about his work at the University Settlement Society on Forsyth Street, where the elder Mr. Kane taught English to the immigrants that swelled the Lower East Side and were beset with problems of poverty, hunger, disease, crime, and housing. His father believed that his small part in helping them find a livable wage and improving their lives was needed, so each week he spent time there and was subsequently exposed to various diseases.

Tom respected the work the Society had been doing since 1886 and was proud that his father supported the first such settlement house established in the United States, and the second in the world. Like the elder Thomas, his fellow workers were men and women from mainstream middle-class Anglo-Saxon backgrounds who aimed to perform a bold new social experiment by creating oases of hope in the squalid immigrant neighborhoods. Although his father did not live among the recipients of the settlement house services (Tom had insisted he not do so because of his age) as many did, traveling to and from, and exhausting himself with long hours, left him vulnerable, Tom believed, to illness. A noble concept and wonderful work, but perhaps it was time for it to end. Yes, he would have to have that talk after his father was feeling better and stronger.

And now that life was settling down again, he needed to write to Mr. Manning to see if he would allow him to call on Stella at the Delacourte home, and he needed to write a short note to Stella. He had received a pleasant letter from her during the week's trials and had admired her neat, orderly handwriting and then had smiled broadly at the way she'd closed the letter. He'd hardly had time to think of her with this week's challenges and exhaustion, though, but each time he did, the image that came to mind was the feel of her in his arms as they danced under the stars. Stella, the stars, he thought, a perfect combination of images.

"Are you as tired as I am?" asked Jessie as she and Stella climbed into their respective beds.

"I'm sure I am, and perhaps even more tired," replied Stella. "But it's a good tired, isn't it, Jessie?"

"Oh, to be sure," was the reply.

"Let's say it together, Jessie, before we sleep," said Stella, and the two launched into their memorized objective together: "We are training our bodies to make them willing, graceful, and obedient servants to our wills and emotions. We are training our minds to abandon themselves to the spirit of the selection in hand, forgetful of self and surroundings, becoming for the time the real character or the soul of the lines rendered."

This was the purpose of the Delsarte Method of Elocution, as the Delacourtes explained the first morning of class. Each girl would memorize this intention and keep it foremost in her head as the training commenced and grew more intense. Stella and Jessie took this directive quite literally and had memorized it the first day.

Now it was the end of the third day, and the girls were finding many challenges in their training so far. The first challenge had been the imposing syllabus, a new word to Stella, which Mr. Delacourte declared was a standard instructional tool in university classes. This document listed the order of the training and all its component parts and seemed not only comprehensive but completely exhaustive. The Delacourtes had reviewed this master plan with the entire class and had cautioned all not to be intimidated.

"Yes, it is very thorough and all-embracing," said Mrs. Delacourte, "but we will work through it a subject at a time, with demonstrations, class exercises, and ample time for questions, and as you master one skill, we'll move on to the next."

The syllabus started out reasonably nonthreatening, listing *The Correct Position for Reciting* and *Walking* as the first two topics. But immediately thereafter and highly prominent in the syllabus, the class discovered, was a long series of exercises that needed to be understood, practiced, and mastered to train the body for elocution. Among these exercises were:

>*Exercises for poise and to properly place the weight*
>
>*Exercises to acquire a narrow base and avoid bending the front knee*
>
>*Pivoting exercises and exercises for bowing*
>
>*Exercises to give lightness to the body and to add dignity to the stage walk*
>
>*Exercises in walking backwards*
>
>*How to pick up anything, how to sit, how to rise, and how to go up and down stairs*

And there were many more.

The syllabus' training path then moved into the art of gestures, including *Delsarte's Laws of Gesture* and exercises (again) for the "Harmonic Poise of Arms and Hands," and this section was followed closely by breathing exercises.

The heart of the syllabus seemed to focus on tone and voice training, and the students in reviewing it the first morning saw more exercises for focusing tone, and then training in loudness, distinctness, difficult sentences, flexibility of the voice, and speed of speaking. Most interesting looked the sections titled "Words in which Long U is often

Mispronounced" and "Words in which Short Italian A is often Mispronounced." This last section generated raised eyebrows by Gianna Ricci, their Italian-descent classmate.

The syllabus' listing of "Different Styles of Reading" looked to be the most interesting and included two sections. The first was "Styles of Reading in the Natural Voice" and included "Pathos; Solemnity; Serenity, Beauty, and Love; Common Reading; Gayety; and Humor." The second, which seemed mysterious and intimidating to all was "Styles of Reading in the Orotund Voice" and included "Effusive Orotund, Expulsive Orotund, and Explosive Orotund." Not to be impolite, but quite overcome, Emily Billingham had said she was not sure she ever wanted to be "explosive."

But to the surprise of all, ahead of all the topics in the syllabus was an entire section on "Physical Development," which included numerous exercises for relaxing one-by-one all the parts of the body, and then exercises for strengthening all parts of the body. These initial exercises started each day with the students stretched out modestly in the second-floor parlor, the primary training site, learning to both relax and strengthen their muscles.

In addition to the imposing syllabus, Stella and the others conceded they had had no idea of the physical training required in elocution. Although young and fit, Stella had to push herself to do each relaxation and strength-training activity with the exactness required before each day's training in the subjects. Then, as each lesson progressed, more challenges arose in mastering the concepts and performing the elocution exercises.

But she was here, following her dream of becoming a professional elocutionist, no matter how much work it took. That was what mattered. And she remembered Miss D telling her that elocution is "hard work," so she was not surprised at the level of effort she had to expend each day.

Besides, she had received a note from Tom that day telling of his father's illness and ongoing recovery and his very hectic week. He included news from his work, inquired about her training, and said he hoped to receive permission to see her soon. Stella said a prayer for the elder Mr. Kane and decided life was good.

The daily schedule and rhythm of training fell into place quite quickly with breakfast at 8:00 a.m., class from 9:00 a.m. to noon with a short break at 10:30 a.m., then lunch in the dining room, with selections of food presented on the long mahogany sideboard, and class again from 1:00 to 4:00 p.m., with another short break at 2:30 p.m.

"Free time" was from 4:00 p.m. to dinner time at 6:00 p.m., which was a sit-down meal shared with the Delacourtes and served by their maids. Short walks outside on the avenue or in the close reaches of Central Park before dark in groups of three or four were fine, but speaking to strangers was not. Time was available in the evening for personal pursuits such as letter writing, visiting with one another, music for those interested in listening to the Delacourtes' graphophone, browsing the home's extensive library, and any other personal interests. The cooler September evenings often found a small group of girls sitting and conversing on the front steps enjoying the early evening air and the sights and sounds of Fifth Avenue.

The students had firm rules about their conduct, which, Mrs. Delacourte advised, included being respectful and considerate of each other; kind and patient with all, including any student who was struggling with a concept or an exercise; and excelling in good manners at all times. Jealousy and teasing were not permitted, and all were expected to be prompt for class and meals. These rules suited Stella just fine because she disliked discord and liked structure.

The eight who shared the two bathrooms worked out schedules that were compatible, and evenings often found them visiting in each other's rooms, talking about events of the day, sharing stories from their lives, and commiserating about sore muscles before the mandated lights-out at 10:00 p.m. Friendships formed, and rapport grew steadily.

Weekends offered opportunities for the girls to visit family as long as a parent came to escort them home and returned them by Sunday evening after the dinner hour. Friends on the approved list might visit, with gentlemen allowed in the parlor only with a chaperone, but list girl-friends could go upstairs and have an informal visit. The students might go for a stroll or carriage ride in the park with a list gentleman friend, again with a chaperone, or with a couple of list girlfriends, and with stated departure and return times for both situations.

Colin surprised Stella on the first Friday evening as others were departing and she was beginning to feel home-sick for family. He appeared out front with a fine carriage and Clarence onboard, offering Stella a ride in Central Park and guaranteeing a fine time if she would bring a girlfriend along to keep Clarence company.

"'Tis a new carriage my father is bringing along, Stella, and we need to give it a try and let him know if we like it," teased Colin.

Jessie was staying over, and she was Stella's first choice. Mrs. Delacourte approved the arrangement because Colin was on the list, was also Stella's relative, and Clarence was a student at the college and on the list. Jessie was delighted at the prospect of an outing after a very busy week.

And Colin was absolutely delighted to meet a striking red-haired Irish girl, who was also Stella's new friend, as he took no time at all in stating. Noticing his immediate inter-est in Jessie, Stella volunteered to sit with Clarence so that Colin could become acquainted with Jessie.

Amid laughter and good cheer, the four trotted away toward the park, promising Mrs. Delacourte the hour of their return. No one noticed the two men hidden in the shadows of the nearby alley as the carriage departed.

"There she goes, the Irisher girl, his girl, the one I tole ye about, aye?" said one.

"Eh, and bonny she is, mate. The flamin' red hair makes her an easy mark to spot, and the brown-heided one is a beauty too," answered the second.

"We'll follow a ways back and keep our eyes on 'em, ye hear?"

CHAPTER 13

New York City
October 1892

*F*all leaves began to swirl in colorful flight, and wind gusts lifted the outlandish hats of pedestrians in their stylish fall outfits along Fifth Avenue, but Stella barely had time to admire the new fashions from her bedroom window as she rushed downstairs to morning exercises. The end of the second week of instruction was just about here, and the Delacourtes had arranged for an afternoon salon event right after lunch. This morning would be spent preparing for it.

Each of the students had progressed well, and they were deep in the syllabus by now, so the Delacourtes had announced yesterday that a few of their friends, patrons of the arts, would be coming for afternoon tea and to hear recitations by the students. This announcement had set everyone to exclaiming "but we're not ready to perform, we don't know everything yet, we've just begun," and other disclaimers. But the Delacourtes, admitting that much training still needed to be done, nonetheless insisted that standing up in front of strangers, even with two weeks' training, was an essential step in gaining poise and presence.

"And such an event," Mrs. Delacourte explained, "will begin to expose you to various important people in the arts community, ones whom you should start getting to know for your future careers in elocution." Great sighs issued all around, but great expectations also began to build among the students.

Mr. Delacourte had chosen patriotic readings as the theme for the event and presented compilations of readings to review, so each student had selected a reading and put her nascent elocution skills to work in practicing for the salon event.

Stella had selected "Washington to His Soldiers," an address delivered by George Washington to his soldiers before they began the Battle of Long Island in 1776. She had found this piece inspiring and uplifting when reviewing the compendium of selections, and she loved the lines:

Liberty, prosperity, life and honor, are all at stake...
heaven will crown with success so just a cause.

Her early stirrings of American patriotism had been fueled by many stories in evening bedroom sessions with the other girls whose families had prospered in America, and she had learned more of her new country's history, especially about colonial times, through browsing the Delacourtes' huge library. And recent instruction and exercises on voice tone and gestures were good preparation for this particular recitation, she thought. She was excited to have the chance to perform the address for even a small audience.

Jessie was just as excited and was hard at work preparing her chosen piece, "Napoleon's Farewell to His Army at Fontainebleau in 1814," and the two had critiqued each other well into the evening upstairs in their room last night.

And just as exciting, even more so, was the good news that Tom Kane had received permission from her father to call on her this evening. Even with all the immersion in her training, she had thought of him each day and was eager for news from his life. But most of all, she wanted to, well, just gaze on him.

The salon event proved to be memorable. Everyone had done well, some more noticeably nervous than others. Stella's recitation was well-received, and in the social time after the presentations, several of the six invitees had complimented her personally. Although Jessie had done exceedingly well too, with the Napoleon piece, Stella noticed that a few of the people seemed to purposely keep their distance from her, and she wondered why. Jessie was charming and friendly and outgoing, so the slight shunning Stella saw didn't make sense. She determined to find a way to discuss it with Jessie later, delicate though the subject might be.

But now with dismissal from the salon, she hastened to her room to freshen up for dinner, and then Tom's visit. Dinner would not be a sit-down event this evening because of the late afternoon social activity and refreshments, and the girls were asked to select food that cook had prepared for a light supper and placed on the sideboard. Stella liked this plan because it meant she would have more time with Tom, and she had asked Jessie to meet him and spend some time together as their chaperone. Jessie promised to do so but said she would fulfill her chaperone duties in such a way that Stella might have some proper one-on-one time with Tom too. Stella especially liked this plan!

Waiting for Tom to arrive in the small parlor, Jessie asked Stella about Tom, and Stella told the story of how they had met and how much she respected and admired him.

"So are you in love with him?" Jessie asked.

"I'm not sure what it's like to be in love, Jessie," Stella answered. "I love the kind things he does, his gentlemanly ways, his love for his father and family, his dedication to his goals, and the way he makes me feel."

"And how does he make you feel, Stella?" Jessie asked.

"I feel treasured and respected and able to share my heart with him. And I feel so comfortable around him, and I want to get closer to him, to have him hold me in his arms. Scandalous thought!" Stella blushed a little.

"Not scandalous, just normal," laughed Jessie. "He sounds like a wonderful man to have for a friend and even for a husband someday. You are fortunate to have met such a good man."

"My family likes him, too, and he fits right in with all of us, it seems," Stella continued. "My little brother especially adores him."

"Stella, hold onto this man," said Jessie. "There are so many scoundrels out there, and it seems you have found an exceptional man."

"Yes, but it's difficult with his work schedule and my school schedule, and I don't know how I'll be able to spend enough time with him anytime soon."

Just then, the doorbell chimed, and both girls flew to the door before the maid could answer it.

"Colin!" called out Stella. "I didn't expect you, but how wonderful to see you."

"Well, I was in the neighborhood, so I decided to stop by and say hello, and..." Spotting Jessie beside Stella, he immediately grinned even wider and laughed. "Good evening, Miss Byrnes. What a pleasant surprise to see you again."

"And you as well, Mr. Manning," answered Jessie somewhat shyly.

"Do come in," said Stella. "We were actually waiting for Tom Kane to arrive."

"Perfect," said Colin, "because I have that same carriage again that we are still testing, so perhaps we can all..."

At that moment, Tom came bounding up the front steps, surprised to see Colin but beaming at seeing Stella. She returned the smile, reached out and took both of his hands, and said simply, "Tom."

Their eyes met, and Stella remembered her scandalous thought and blushed but instantly then remembered her manners and introduced Jessie to Tom.

"Miss Byrnes," said Tom, nodding graciously.

An awkward moment occurred before Stella said, "Come in, come in, Colin and Tom."

But Colin cleared his throat and mentioned the carriage again, so after Stella had introduced Tom to Mrs. Delacourte, who was in the large parlor and gave permission for the carriage ride—having received Tom's name from Stella's father to add to the list—all set out for Central Park.

The evening was cool and crisp, and Stella was glad she had run upstairs to grab her warm woolen cape. The four-passenger Park Phaeton was a comfortable carriage, and she and Tom climbed in the back, tucking a light robe around their laps, while Colin helped Jessie into the front seat. The ride wasn't far to the park entrance at Fifth and Fifty-Ninth Streets, and many others had chosen to enjoy the park on foot, horseback, and in carriages on such a fine fall evening.

The winding drive took them around the green and the pond, and finally Colin turned into the mall, its long and elegant path leading into the heart of the park. It was a moon-filled night to enjoy the park's natural beauty, but the carriage occupants seemed more interested in each other than the lush surroundings. Colin seemed to be telling Jessie a story or two about his work adventures, and she was laughing. Stella and Tom, sitting close together but not so close as to be improper, thought Stella, were more serious.

"Tell me first about your father, Tom," inquired Stella.

"He is recuperating well, and I'm thankful, after a few difficult days trying to ensure he was cared for and keeping up with my work schedule. My dilemma is speaking to him about his settlement house work, which I know he won't want to give up but which seems a threat to his health."

"Tell me about it," said Stella.

And Tom did, and Stella commented, "It's difficult to give up a work that is meaningful and important, so I can understand his determination to serve there, but at the same time, I can share your concern about his health. Perhaps there's some compromise that would work. Could his students meet him in a park?"

"Stella, you are always looking for good outcomes and ways to solve problems," said Tom. "It's an admirable quality. Maybe there is a compromise situation I can help him with. Now tell me all about your classes and new friends."

And Stella did, with Tom asking questions, especially about the lengthy syllabus. And then they talked about his last two weeks on the railroad and all the assignments he had had and new things he had learned.

"But I have a question about being an engineer, Tom," Stella said. "And you may think it silly."

"No, Stella. There are no silly questions. Just ask!"

"Well then, here it is," said Stella. "I've been wondering, since it seems many people can run an engine, what other skills and experience do you need to run a train? I guess, I mean a locomotive with other cars attached. How complicated is it?"

"Ah, that's a good question, Stella, and one I had many years ago. The heart of the matter is managing not only the power of the locomotive but also the coupler slack between the cars, the momentum, and the braking of all the cars. I have to plan ahead so that when I apply the brakes, the pressure wave, as it's called, needs time to reach the rear of the train, to all the cars attached. I have to factor in grades, curves, and speed, and this task requires careful judgment.

"At the same time, I have to observe the timetable, signals, and track conditions, while watching the track ahead and the train cars behind, and also be sure the engine is running safely and efficiently. I have to blow the whistle for grade crossings and plan ahead for meets with other trains."

"Oh my goodness, Tom," said Stella. "I had no idea how many things you have to do at once!"

"And my answer was pretty technical, Stella, so I'm sorry to overwhelm you with information, but that's what I have learned to do over the years of my training, and I'm still perfecting it all. Each day presents new conditions and challenges."

"Not too technical at all, Tom. I am fascinated and quite amazed. Thank you for telling me the whole story. In a sense, learning elocution has similarities. I have to keep in mind posture, balance, gestures, breathing patterns, voice tone, and so much more all at once. Of course, no lives or valuable freight are at risk," laughed Stella.

"You are quite welcome, and once again, our lives have parallels, Stella," replied Tom easily. "And here's a question for you: I've told you my path forward, to move from freight to passenger trains, which will require much training and experience. But now tell me what you expect to do with your training and experience in elocution."

Stella paused a little because she hadn't really thought through a path for the future other than to become a professional elocutionist and fulfill her dream to be on the stage. What did it really mean to be "on the stage" anyway? Which stage and for how long, and what kind of career path might that involve?

As usual, she decided to share her heart with Tom. "Last year in Dublin, my friend and mentor, Miss Dowling, asked me that question, Tom, and I told her how much I love reading and reciting poetry and literature—bringing it alive—and that elocution seems a proper and exciting outlet for my energy and love of the spoken word. And then Papa and Mama asked me the same question after the Delacourtes selected me to be a student, and I gave them two answers: I'd like to do something uniquely mine—find my own place in the world. And I'd like to perform elocution in genteel settings where art and culture are appreciated."

Tom was quiet for a few seconds then said, "Those are noble and thoughtful goals, Stella. How do you see your career flourishing here in New York?"

"Ah, Tom, I just do not know. Perhaps it will be revealed to me as I progress. The Delacourtes have a lot of contacts in the city. But honestly, I'm not sure of the next steps after my training is finished, or what I will actually do with my new skills." Then she thought about her possible future as they both grew silent for a few moments, and she decided to share one more piece of her heart. "Tom, one more thing Miss Dowling asked of me, and that was to pray about my vision. She told me God has given us all gifts, which we are responsible to use for His glory and for the betterment of our fellow man. I've never forgotten these words. And she advised me to ask God to confirm my gift and tell me how He wants me to use it."

"A remarkable woman is Miss Dowling," Tom observed. "She is quite right."

"But, Tom," Stella continued, "even though I've started talking to God and I'm starting to see how He directs our lives and answers prayer, I'm still not sure how to ask Him to confirm my gift and tell me how He wants me to use it."

Tom took Stella's hand softly in his, looked so intently at her she thought she would melt, and said, "Just keep talking to Him, Stella, and you will receive His confirmation and direction, but maybe just bit by bit, so be patient. Each new day is a gift from Him, and He will show you the way."

Upstairs later in their room, Stella and Jessie talked into the night. They had parted with their young men after returning from the park and after taking coffee with them in the small parlor, which the maid, still making rounds before retiring for the night, had offered to bring. Colin had agreed to give Tom a ride home, and Tom had, in turn, invited Colin to join him and his father at their home for the night and a big breakfast in the morning. Colin, ever the friendly vagabond on his trips throughout the city, had agreed.

"It's good that the gentlemen can be together tonight," said Jessie. "Seems they are forming a nice friendship."

"Yes," replied Stella, "and I'm glad Tom has some time with a man friend near his age. He works so many long hours and spends most of his nonworking time, it seems, keeping his father company."

"I wonder if they are talking about us?" giggled Jessie.

"Probably not, I'm thinking. Men usually talk about men things, not girls, from what I've heard. Girls, on the other hand, love to talk about men," answered Stella laughingly.

"Very true! So what are your thoughts about Tom, Stella? I noticed how you two held each other's hands sweetly, and you seemed sad to part as he was leaving."

"He is as wonderful as ever, Jessie, and he shared more of his heart with me tonight, and I with him. We talk so easily with one another. When I am with him, I quite forget about elocution and all the things we need to focus on here. It's amazing to me because before I met Tom, elocution was my whole world, well, in addition to my family," said Stella.

Hmmm, mused Jessie.

"And what about you and Colin? How did you enjoy your time with him again?" asked Stella.

"He is such a fine fella, Stella, and I had a wonderful time listening to his adventures in the city and stories of his family. I believe I could become very fond of him, but I'll need to ask my father to investigate him first before I see him again."

"Investigate him? Is that what you said?" asked Stella.

"Oh, to be sure, Stella. You may remember my father is superintendent of the police department in the city, and he has methods of finding out about just everybody. Whenever my sisters and I have met a new gentleman whom we'd like to get to know, my father must be sure he has no criminal record or connections. That's just a regular thing in our family."

"Gracious, Jessie!" exclaimed Stella. "Colin is just a young man from good Irish stock working for Western Union. He would never commit a crime or spend time with any criminals. Why, I know his whole family, and his father is my father's brother."

"Oh, I know, Stella, and I'm sure it will be just fine, so I'll ask my father to get this step out of the way this week. Really, it's nothing. Just something we do."

"All right, I guess I understand. Please tell me more about your father, though. I had noticed some people at the opening tea session seemed to avoid him, and I thought that was rude. And Jessie, I saw a little of the same thing at the salon event today concerning you, which I thought was most unkind."

"Ah, Stella, we Byrnes are used to certain degrees of shunning because of my father's work and reputation in the city. We take it in our stride. I will tell you the backstory, and you'll understand." Jessie started: "Remember I told you at our opening day that my father had come to America from Dublin as a child, grew up here in the city, and then fought in the Civil War?"

"Yes, I remember that part," said Stella. "And then you said he was head of the New York City Police Department."

"Yes, he is, and before that, he was head of the city's detective bureau for twelve years. He rose rapidly in the police force, and a fine detective he is, Stella. He solved a very famous murder case way back in 1872, the Fisk case, and then a big robbery case at the Manhattan Savings Bank in 1878. Many others too, and he became known not only in New York City but across the nation as a legendary crime fighter."

"Oh my, how amazing, Jessie. I had no idea," said Stella. "Tell me more."

"There's much more to tell, Stella!" Jessie continued. "My father invented an intense form of interrogation called 'the third degree,' which helped to break many criminal cases, and a police tool called 'mugshots,' which are pictures of criminals that help identify and catch them. He also acquired the literary name of 'Inspector Byrnes' and starred in a series of novels by Julian Hawthorne called *From the Diary of Inspector Byrnes*.

"And he published a book in 1886 called *Professional Criminals of America* to educate other police on fighting crime. This book is pretty well known, Stella, and recounts the careers of notable thieves and provides detailed descriptions of notorious crimes. Then, just last year, he solved a terrible bombing crime against a Mr. Russell Sage."

"So your father is pretty famous as a leading detective in the city and known across the nation? He's a national hero, it seems," suggested Stella. "You must be very proud of him. That's quite a story, Jessie! But why the shunning I observed? Shouldn't people admire and respect him?"

"Oh, many do, Stella, but there are rumors of corruption flying around the city. Because father has connections with many men of wealth, like Mr. Jay Gould, and has invested his earnings wisely over the years with their advice, many think he has broken the law. He is considered controversial, sad to say. He may even face questions about our family's personal finances one of these days. Nothing has been proven, Stella, and I know him to be an honest man, but some people will still shun us."

"I find that shocking, Jessie, and I'm sorry it also comes down on you."

"'Tis just something I've learned to live with, Stella," replied Jessie. My father is very dear to all of us, and, as I've said, he has a wonderful dramatic flair, which I may have inherited from him."

"Indeed, Jessie. And thank you for sharing your story. Getting to know you has been one of the chief delights of our training," Stella said, as she grew weary from the long and exciting day. As she drifted off to sleep, she whispered a prayer thanking God for Tom and also asking Him to protect Jessie's father from slander, and to keep his family safe, especially Jessie.

CHAPTER 14

New York City
October 1892

Far south and east of Stella and Jessie's peaceful slumber stood a sleazy and rat-infested tenement, plunked down in the Lower East Side in the unsavory neighborhood of Mulberry Bend, part of the crime-ridden Five Points area. This slum, plagued by disease, prostitution, and every kind of crime, boasted the highest murder rate in the city. Efforts had been underway since the 1830s, mostly by Christian and charitable organizations, to clean it up and help its suffering poor, but vice still thrived throughout the neighborhood.

Into one of the squalid apartments came two men up to the second floor, laughing loudly and smoking foul cigarettes, kicking aside the debris of rancid garbage just outside the door. Tapping solidly on the door, the two were welcomed by a third man, who rose from a broken-down chair as they entered, and greeted them with, "Ye've come. Good. The big man will be 'ere soon, and we've much to plan."

One of the newcomers spat in the corner and laughed as he sat on another dilapidated chair, announcing, "We've got a bead on the girlie. His girlie. She's uptown in un of them fancy gret t'onhouses wit a passel of oth'r lasses, bein' all prim and proper, she is, sportin' that flamin' red har. Goin' out for rides in the park, they are, of a night."

"Who is 'they'?" the house occupant asked.

"Another girlie, this un wit great brun curls. And two bruisin' chaps keepin' an eye on 'em. They's both beauties, even if I do say."

"Have you seen them out alone?"

"Nay, nae yet," the second visitor reported.

At that moment, a walking stick clicked on the stairs outside the door, and the scent of cigar and fine cologne drifted in to combat the rancid odor of the flat.

"He's come. Go find him a decent chair."

Uptown a considerable way and a world apart from Five Points, two other men climbed the stairs to a second-floor apartment also, this one in a modest but well-appointed building on West Twenty-Ninth Street and Ninth Avenue, the horse and carriage well secure in a nearby trusted livery.

"I know Father will be pleased to meet you, Colin," said Tom as he unlocked the door. "We've little company these days while Father is recuperating from his illness, and it will do him good to have a new acquaintance to talk to."

"Tom!" said the elder Kane, rising from a chair. "I am hoping your visit with Miss Manning was pleasant, and, oh, who is this fine gentleman?"

"Father, please meet Colin Manning, Miss Manning, er, Stella's, first cousin, son of her father's brother."

"How delightful, Mr. Manning, that you've come along with Tom. I was just preparing a late-night bite for him."

"I've invited Colin to spend the night, Father, torment-ing him with reports of your famous Saturday morning breakfast."

"Excellent," said the elder Manning. And the three sat to talk and exchange news of the day, enjoying the late-night biscuits and cheese and a light libation. As the elder Manning retired, Tom gathered linens for Colin's bedding, and the two chatted as the evening was winding down.

"Tom," said Colin, "you and Stella seem quite fond of each other. She is an amazing, talented young lady, and I've grown quite fond of my cousin and her family since their arrival here in New York."

"Indeed," said Tom. "She is remarkable, and we have shared so many things close to our hearts in the short time we've been acquainted. We get along so very well. I am blessed to know her."

"I'm hoping your relationship will continue and bloom into something special in the future," said Colin. "You are a steadying influence on her, and she responds well to your kind ways."

"Thank you, Colin. She is very special to me, and I'm hoping I can spend enough time with her in the coming weeks with her school demands and my work schedule to allow our relationship to grow."

"I know that would make her happy," Colin said.

"And, Colin," said Tom, "it seems you are getting along well with Miss Byrnes."

"Yes, remarkably so, Tom," answered Colin. "She has allowed me to call her Jessie, and she is a really delightful girl. And if I pass muster with her father, the very well-known Superintendent Byrnes of the New York City Police Department, I hope to spend more time with her."

"*That* Mr. Byrnes? Oh my goodness, Colin. I should have guessed with the name *Byrnes*, but I was so focused on seeing Stella again that Jessie's last name just flew by me. I'm sure you'll pass muster."

"I certainly hope so," said Colin.

And so Stella and Jessie were wrong; sometimes men do talk about girls when they are together.

155

The next week of elocution training, though intense, flew by, as Stella, Jessie, and the other six studied, practiced, exercised, presented to each other and the Delacourtes, received feedback, and overcame difficulties with the multitude of concurrent skills required to deliver an elocution presentation. Their training was now half over but with much more to learn and master.

Free time found the small group of girls bonding closely, helping each other, and getting to know each other's life stories. Parents visited, friends came to call, some group outings to enjoy the crisp fall air transpired, and it was altogether a busy but satisfying time for all. Stella enjoyed a brief visit from Papa, who exclaimed she looked a little tired but exuberant.

She received a hasty note from Tom telling her that he was booked for heavy hours this week, some days at much as sixteen hours. He asked if he might come to call on Sunday and inquired if he might take her to church. She considered going to church with Tom would be highly worthwhile and wondered what his church might be like.

In thinking about Tom's work, Stella considered that it might be a lonely and exhausting job, even though he had train-mates, these long hours with little sleep and no relaxation. He had told her he needed to work hard to progress, and he was willing to do so, but it seemed to her his work could be quite fatiguing. She dropped his father a note to say hello and to let him know she was thinking of him during Tom's long hours.

The Delacourtes took all the girls to A. T. Stewart's Department Store to consider the type of clothing they would need for future elocution performances. Stella remembered the garments from the performance she had seen in Dublin: modest but looser fitting, flowing dresses and gowns to allow freer movement of the body, and especially the arms. She decided she and Mama and Jo could sew any garments she might need, and she wrote a letter to Mama describing the style and fabrics.

On Sunday morning nine days after she had last seen Tom, he came to call to take her to church, with Mrs. Delacourte's permission, of course. Stella was happy to see that he looked rested, and also very handsome in his more formal churchgoing attire. But she was mostly happy just to see him again. She had been busy, but nine days was a long time.

She greatly admired his gray herringbone frock coat with black trousers and the double-breasted vest in a subtle gray-and-black floral scroll fabric. His white shirt with the high collar and silk puff tie completed the outfit, and in his hand was a John Bull top hat.

"Tom!" she exclaimed. "How wonderful you look!"

"Thank you, Stella," he said as he drew her closer to him and kissed her gloved hand, then said, laughingly, "Father said I must have one good outfit to be a proper gentleman for proper outings, and this is it."

Stella had borrowed a light blue wool outfit from Jessie, a soft skirt with a long duster of the same color, to which Stella had added her best high-collar embroidered white blouse accented by the Tara Brooch at her neckline. A darker blue felt hat with a sloping brim and adorned with small silk flowers in varying shades of lavender completed her outfit. When she and Jessie had planned her Sunday clothes on Friday before Jessie went home for the weekend, Jessie had remarked how beautiful Stella looked in this ever-so-fashionable outfit her father had bought for her.

And seemingly, Tom agreed. "Stella, you look absolutely lovely," said Tom as he admired her borrowed outfit and led her down the front steps into the sunshine-filled cool air.

"Thank you, Tom, and I am pleased to be going to church with you, but where are we going? You did not tell me the name of your church."

"Its formal name is the Church of the Transfiguration, Stella, but everyone calls it 'The Little Church Around the Corner,' and therein lies a tale. It's an Anglo-Catholic church that my family has attended for many years, and it's at One East Twenty-Ninth Street, between Madison and Fifth.

"As we travel, I'll tell you the story of its name, Stella. It's such a fine day, I thought we'd walk a block to the Sixth Avenue El, take it to Twenty-Ninth Street and then walk the last two blocks. Is that all right?"

"Absolutely," replied Stella as she took his arm and remembered how strange that felt at first, but now it was natural and easy and felt so right.

As they set off toward Sixth Avenue, Tom said, "The story goes like this, Stella. A few days before Christmas in 1870, Joseph Jefferson, a well-known actor, approached the rector of a church called the Church of the Atonement to request a funeral for his friend and fellow actor, George Holland. When the rector learned that the deceased was an actor, he refused to hold a funeral for the man in his church.

"Joseph Jefferson persisted," he continued, "and asked if there was a church in the area that would hold the service. The rector said, 'I believe there is a little church around the corner where it might be done.'" Jefferson replied, 'Then I say to you, sir, God bless the little church around the corner.' And so it has been called such all these years since, Stella, and will likely be so in the future," Tom said as he finished the story.

"It's quite amazing that the rector considered the actor to be so unworthy, Tom," said Stella. "Judging someone because of his profession seems so wrong."

"Indeed, Stella, but it has always been such, this judging thing, even though our Lord told us not to do it in the gospel He inspired Matthew to write."

"There is so much I need to learn about the Lord, Tom, and I just don't know where to begin," said Stella. "It seems you are a man of faith, so you must have started somewhere."

"I did, many years ago, but a step at a time works best, Stella, and maybe today you'll learn a few things," said Tom lightly.

As they stepped off the El and walked the last block to the church, Stella was amazed at the beauty of the church at her first glimpse. Built of deep red brick in English neo-Gothic style, she soon discovered that the sanctuary was set back from the street, allowing them to enter through a peaceful garden. Amidst the city landscape surrounding them, this garden reminded Stella of the Irish countryside, and she was entranced.

Inside the church were a guildhall, transepts, and beautiful stained glass in the graceful arcs of the gothic windows. Tom pointed out the tall tower, which he said was added in 1852, two years after the church was dedicated.

The service was very much like the Catholic masses she had attended in Dublin, and Tom told her Anglo-Catholics emphasized their Catholic heritage and also honored the identity of the Anglican Church in England. Because his father's English family had been Anglicans before immigrating to America, they had been drawn to this church since its early years, he explained.

Tom introduced Stella to the rector, the Reverend Doctor George Henric Houghton, who was the founder and first rector and had served the church since 1850. This particular congregation, Tom related to Stella, had always stressed service to the poor and oppressed since its earliest days, serving as a stop on the Underground Railroad during the era of the Civil War, which Tom then quietly described to Stella just before the service started.

Stella found the service moving and beautiful, the rector's words reassuring and comforting, and she felt very peaceful and yet energized, as the bells tolled them homeward. She had noticed Tom quietly praying, with his eyes closed, at the communion, and had felt so close to him as they received communion together.

Back in the Delacourtes' neighborhood, they strolled a short way into Central Park, laughing at some of the games the children were playing nearby, and then Stella remembered that cook had invited all the girls going to church with friends and beaux to return for a casual lunch to be laid out on the sideboard.

She invited Tom, and they returned to a house full of several of the students and their friends. Tom was able to meet more of her classmates and unwind from his long week with friendly and easygoing conversations and joking with all. The gentlemen removed their frock coats, and the girls their dusters and suit jackets, and they all laughed and relaxed and joined in a lively game of charades for a while, after which one of the young men declared, "Best to not play charades with elocutionists; you will never win!"

They sat for a while in the small parlor, and Tom admired the brooch Stella was wearing. "The design is so unusual, Stella. What does it mean?" asked Tom.

"Its meaning is lost in history, but the design is Celtic, Tom, and the original was made by early medieval Irish metalworkers in the eighth century. It was found in Ireland in 1850 and named after the famous Hill of Tara, the seat of the ancient kings of Ireland. Before we left Dublin, Papa took me to the new Museum of Science and Art, and I saw it displayed there. I thought it was strikingly beautiful, and Papa gifted this replica to me for my birthday. It's my most treasured piece of jewelry."

"It's truly unique and singular, Stella, much like you," said Tom, smiling and taking her hand.

Their parting at the front door was sweet, as Tom held both her hands in his, looked deep into her eyes, and said, "Thank you for coming to church with me, Stella. I am so blessed to know you and to have shared this day with you."

"And I with you, Tom," answered Stella softly, wanting so much to be held in his arms. "The Little Church Around the Corner is a special place to me now, and I'd like to go again with you."

"We will do that, Stella dear, and I hope to see you again very soon."

"May that time come quickly, dear Tom," said Stella, squeezing his hands, and not wanting to ever let go.

CHAPTER 15

New York City
Late October 1892

All the members of the Manning household were enjoying their first fall in Woodlawn Heights and were surprised how nice the weather had been, with cool days, cooler nights, but abundant sunshine with only a little rain now and then. But Papa knew from his neighbors who had lived through last winter that colder air, blustery winds, and even snow and sleet were on their way, so he arranged for delivery of coal for the steam heating system that would keep them warm all winter. Mama and Jo began sewing some warmer garments for all and, using their canning and preserving skills, put away the last of the late summer and fall fruits and vegetables for winter enjoyment.

The household was running smoothly, and Jo's relationship with Luca was running exceptionally smoothly, as was her friendship with his sister Vittoria. Papa and Mama had made some Irish friends within the community and enjoyed social times now and then with neighbors, Uncle Nicholas' family, and especially with the Rossi family.

Michael was busily engaged with school and new friends and also working with Papa, and Alice juggled her time among school, playtime with new friends and her cousin-best friend Meghan, and helping with household duties. Alfred was, well, Alfred, and had acquired a small friend who came to play during the week.

Papa's business was doing extremely well, even with the ready availability of factory-made watches, and his clock business was expanding too. As the growth of the Bronx pushed every northward, more customers found their way to Woodlawn Heights and to Papa's business and to those of his fellow tradesmen. The village was prospering and growing.

But everybody missed Stella.

And so as Alfred's fourth birthday approached, Mama came up with a plan, and she and Papa worked to put it in place. Dashing off a note to Stella, she proposed a weekend in Woodlawn Heights at the end of Stella's fourth week of classes so that the family could spend some time with her and they could all celebrate Alfred's birthday.

Colin volunteered to bring Stella home on Friday night and return her to the city on Sunday night. Papa decided to invite Tom Kane and his father, which Mama duly reported in her note to Stella, and all hoped Tom's schedule would be free on Saturday and Sunday. Uncle Nicholas' home had ample guest space now that his two older children had grown and moved away, so the accommodations were easily available.

Papa was pretty sure Stella would love the Kane family to join them, based on reports from Colin, who was also now friends with the Kanes. The whole plan was shaping up nicely.

Stella received the note from Mama and was immediately joyful and excited about going home for the weekend to see everyone and celebrate Alfred's birthday, and she was especially animated about possible time with Tom. She so hoped he might be free! He had been working such long hours. And she also had a great idea. She wanted to invite Jessie to come along too and meet her family. She had told them in letters about Jessie, and she had spent a fair amount of time telling Jessie about them, so it seemed a meeting would be highly appropriate.

She let Mama know she would love to come home and that she would bring Jessie, which she knew would be just fine with Mama. She could hardly wait for Jessie to meet her family, and as an added bonus, Jessie would likely have some time with Colin, which was good news to Jessie. She immediately asked her father if he would permit the visit, and he did.

Stella asked rather drolly, "Did he investigate us, Jessie?"

To which Jessie replied, "Oh, I'm sure he did right after we became roommates. That's what he does! And, Stella, he's given the thumbs up on Colin too."

The girls had little time to think about the forthcoming weekend because the fourth-week curriculum was exhausting and arduous. They were working even deeper in the heart of the syllabus now, which focused on tone and voice training, having gained reasonable skills in poise, pivoting, walking, gestures, and breathing. The week's work focused on training in loudness, distinctness, difficult sentences, flexibility of the voice, and speed of speaking.

After early morning floor exercises, which had continued throughout the course, the Delacourtes worked all of them each day through a fatiguing and repetitive series of elocution exercises and sample recitations that trained the full range of tone and voice.

"This is the heart of your training, and the most difficult part," said Mr. Delacourte, after one particularly strenuous session which found a couple of the girls in tears. "But be encouraged because with your mastery of these exercises, you are well on your way to high elocution skills," he promised. He also reassured them that all were doing well, and that the last two weeks would be less tiring, pulling together all their skills and putting them to work in satisfying and uplifting recitations in more public settings. Jessie and Stella looked at each other quizzically when he made this statement, wondering if they would actually go on the stage and where that might be.

Sitting out on the front steps together late in the week after supper, wrapped in warm capes and sipping hot cider, Stella and Jessie commiserated about their vigorous schedule, but each felt she had made progress. The warm electric light glow from the parlors cast a relaxing mood onto their sitting place as they watched early evening theatergoers rumble by in elaborate carriages. They had found this early evening time was a good opportunity to enjoy the cool night air after being so busy inside all day.

"Stella," said Jessie, "don't look up now, but it seems there are two men standing near the corner watching us, and they don't look friendly, not the usual people we see on Fifth Avenue. These two look pretty rough."

"We are safe here by the house, Jessie, but do you want to go inside now?" asked Stella as she casually glanced toward the corner.

"Let's finish our cider and keep an eye on them. If they move toward us, we'll go inside straightaway," said Jessie.

The men made no move toward them, but they didn't leave either. Stella and Jessie went back into the house a few minutes later. Once inside and upstairs in their darkened room, they parted the shade to see if the men were still there, but they had left. Stella said, "Do you think you should tell your father so that he can put a watch on the house for suspicious characters?"

"I might mention it to him, Stella, but unless we see them again, I don't think we should be concerned," Jessie answered. "But they were a little disturbing, just standing there watching us while trying to be inconspicuous. Of course, it could just be my sensitivity to sinister people because my father deals with so many of them."

"We'll keep a watch, Jessie," said Stella.

Friday finally arrived, and Stella and Jessie were ready when Colin came to escort them to Woodlawn Heights. This time, he said they would walk the four blocks to the Third Avenue El, ride to the Bronx, and pick up the horse and carriage at his trusted livery there for the rest of the journey. Bundled in warm capes, gloves, and hats, and with a satchel each, Jessie and Stella each took one of Colin's arms, and he escorted them to the El. They were off for their grand weekend in a high state of excitement.

Two men watched them as Stella and Jessie headed through the crowded streets with Colin, laughing and exclaiming.

"Nae, we caint snatch em t'night, not wit so many aroun', and that big lummox toting 'em," said the one.

"Best follo 'em, tho', an' see whot they're up to. Mebbe we'll have a chanc'," said the second.

Keeping far back, the men saw them climb the stairs to the El and disappear in the crowd to take the next car heading north. Clambering up the steps, the car pulled away before they could get through the crowd to get aboard.

"They'll be comin' back 'dis ways, an' we'll tell da boss man they'r on the move."

Arriving at the livery, Stella and Jessie discovered a fine five-glass landau carriage and the two Cleveland Bays waiting. This carriage was perfect for cooler weather travel and carried a large carriage lantern for nighttime use. But the biggest surprise was yet to come because inside the carriage sat the two Thomas Kanes.

"Tom!" cried out Stella as he reached out to pull her into the carriage. "What an amazing surprise, and Mr. Kane, you are here too."

"Dear Miss Manning, how lovely to see you again, and we are so pleased with the invitation to join your family in Woodlawn Heights," said the elder Mr. Kane.

Stella introduced Jessie to Mr. Kane, and Tom greeted her heartily. "And, Stella," said Tom, "I have the entire weekend off after working four sixteen-hour days this week. I'm tired but happy."

"Oh, Tom, I was so afraid you'd have to work and not be able to join us," said Stella, so relieved and so very happy as she folded her hand in his. Jessie sat next to Mr. Kane and immediately began engaging him in conversation, as was her friendly style.

"Let's be off," said a bundled-up Colin as he checked the horses, closed the doors, and climbed into the high driver's seat.

"I shall have to thank Uncle Nicholas profusely for this fine carriage," said Stella as she snuggled close to Tom for warmth, she assured herself.

The trip was fairly long because of the extra caution needed for nighttime driving, but the horses knew the way and Colin was a fine driver, so the party reached the Manning home well before the evening grew too late. Stella's family received her with joyous hugs and kisses, and everyone fell completely in love with Jessie at first meeting.

The Mannings greeted the Kanes, and Stella wished Tom and his father a restful night before parting. Colin smiled a good night to Jessie and then whisked the Kanes off to their guest quarters at his home, as planned.

With Alfred already asleep, Alice and Michael soon said goodnight, and Mama suggested Stella and Jessie might want to get into their nighttime wraps, unpack anything that might be wrinkled, and then join her, Papa, and Jo in the parlor for a nighttime snack. A small bed had been placed in Stella and Jo's room for Jessie, and both declared a good night's sleep was needed after such a busy week and travel.

Stella's favorite evening snack, rice pudding, soon appeared as they gathered in the parlor, reminding Stella of how wonderful it was to be home again. After a short time of easy conversation amid plans for the weekend, plus an extra hug for Stella from Papa, Stella and Jessie climbed the stairs with Jo to seek that good night's sleep, and Papa and Mama followed not long after.

Stella stole a quick visit to the boys' room to kiss a sleeping Alfred, and then she and Jessie and Jo settled in. It was strange being back in her and Jo's shared bed after she had had her own for the past four weeks, but being home was so wonderful, it didn't matter at all. She whispered a short thank you to God for a safe journey and for the blessings of home and family — and Tom.

Jo was up early in the morning to help Mama prepare for the day, and all agreed that Stella and Jessie should be allowed to sleep in, but that plan lasted until Alfred heard that Stella was home.

Bounding into her room, he yelled, "Stella, Stella, you're home!"

Stella was actually awake but not up yet, so when Alfred charged in, she quickly exited the bed and scooped him up, smothering him with kisses. "Alfred! Look how you've grown in four weeks. How is my big boy?"

"I am well, Stella, and I'm wondering if you've brought Mr. Kane with you?"

"As a matter of fact, I did," answered Stella, "and you will see him today. Tell me what you've been doing while I was away."

Alfred laughed and said, "Mostly playing trains, and I also have a new friend who comes to play, and I go to his house too. He's my best friend, and his name is Liam. Just wait until you meet him."

"I will look forward to that, Alfred. And you may call Mr. Kane *Tom* now. He and I are best friends too, and he's come to Woodlawn Heights with his father to visit our family and celebrate your birthday. And I want you to meet another best friend of mine, Miss Jessie."

"Good day, miss," Alfred said, suddenly remembering his manners.

"And good day to you too, Alfred," said Jessie. "I have heard many stories about you, and I'm hoping you will show me your trains after a while."

"You can even run them, Miss Jessie. They are absolutely excellent trains."

"I'm sure," Jessie replied.

"Alfred, please tell Mama we will be downstairs shortly for breakfast, will you?" asked Stella.

"I'll go and set your places," said Alfred as he charged out of the room.

"Delightful," laughed Jessie.

The day started with Mama preparing a big breakfast of potato pancakes with eggs, with the Kane men invited to join. Since Colin brought them over, he was invited to stay too, to Jessie's delight. Alfred ran to Tom the moment he entered the room, exclaiming, "Mr. Kane, Mr. Kane, Stella said I could call you Tom, and you are her best friend. Come and run the train for me, and I'll show you the tunnel I've built for it."

Tom laughed, greeting everyone with a special smile for Stella, and soon was playing with Alfred, teaching him more whistle signals, and showing him how trains backed up ever so carefully. Michael and Alice soon joined in, and Alfred, as promised, showed Jessie the train, and she ran the train too under Alfred's direction.

Mama announced breakfast, and all came to the extended table. Papa asked Tom to say a blessing, and Tom said, "Thank you, dear Lord, for safe travels, for the Manning family, and all gathered here today. Please bless our food and time together, and also please bless Alfred on his birthday." Stella was amazed at how easily Tom talked to God, like He was a friend. She resolved to ask him how he and God got to be on such easy speaking terms.

Papa asked Tom how his watch was keeping time and how his job was going and inquired about the elder Mr. Kane's health. Conversation was relaxed and easy. After breakfast, Mama announced Alice would help with the dishes, and the others could go for a walkabout on such a fine cool day in Woodlawn Heights. The only one not happy with this plan was Alice, who pouted momentarily but then cheered up.

Jo said, "And we'll stop at Luca's shop so that you can see all his new fall merchandise, and, oh, Stella and Jessie, you should see the new ladies' boots."

And so the day trundled on, with ramblings about the small village, a lively game of baseball organized by Luca and enjoyed by Colin, Tom, and some local boys and men while the girls cheered the best hitters, and a casual and relaxing lunch in the park.

But far south in the Upper West Side of Manhattan at the northwest corner of Seventy-Second Street and Central Park West sat two men who were not enjoying a relaxing

Saturday. Tapping his cane as he walked across the room to gaze out one of the high dormer windows set in the impossibly high gables and deep roofs of the Dakota, the better-dressed man said, "Enough of your two lackeys watching and tracking the girl. We need more information on her plans so that we can set up a time to snatch her and hold her as ransom. Her very famous 'pater' will do just as we demand once we have her."

"She is always accompanied by another girl, sir, and the both often are with young men."

"Who is this other girl?"

"We're not sure, sir, but she seems to be a student at the same school on Fifth Avenue at the Delacourte home."

"Then her father likely has money, so we'll grab her too and increase our demand."

"'Tis more trouble with two, sir. Twice as difficult to make it work."

"That's what I'm paying you for, you idiot, to figure out how to do this. Here's what I want you to do: snoop around and find out about any outings these students might be making. Find the when and the where. Once we know that, we can lay a plot."

"Yes, sir. I'll find a way. I'll find an opportunity."

"And be quick about it too. I'm getting tired of waiting."

Alfred's birthday party was a smash hit. Mama, Jo, and Alice had been cooking for a couple of days and served shepherd's pie, Irish beef stew, and seafood chowder with Irish soda bread. Luca's family insisted on bringing dessert from the bakery and treated the guests to a lavish "black cake" made of almonds, peanuts, coffee, and dark chocolate.

Both Manning families, the Rossi clan, Alfred's new friend Liam and his family, the Kanes, and Jessie—who had fallen in love with Stella's family—wished Alfred the best of birthdays and gave him a variety of little-boy gifts. But the most amazing gift of all to Alfred was Tom's gift: a train engineer's cap of narrow blue-and-white stripes and a printed red neck scarf. Alfred proudly and promptly put both items on and announced that now he was a "real engineer," to everyone's delight.

After bedtime for Alfred, the Mannings, Rossis, and Kanes remained in the large parlor relishing a memory of the good food and chance to relax into the evening. Stella had not had any one-on-one time with Tom and was hoping to sit on the front steps with him to enjoy the cool night air when Papa rose to speak and asked for quiet.

Stella immediately had a flashback to the night in Dublin when Papa rose to speak to tell them all about leaving for America and remembered how devastated she had felt. Surely no news of that kind was about to happen, she thought. She hoped.

Papa smiled and said, "We have been in America for almost six months now, and we've seen so many wonderful blessings come our way: everyone is in fine health, we have a comfortable home, our business is prospering, the younger children are doing well in school, Alfred is growing into a fine young boy, Stella is pursuing her dream of studying elocution, and Mama and I are happy and settled in our new life."

"That leaves Jo," said Papa, smiling while looking at Jo, who looked a little nervous at these words. Papa paused. "This week, Luca Rossi came to me to ask me for Jo's hand in marriage, and... I have granted it."

At that point, great exclamations arose from all, with everyone rushing forward to hug Jo and Luca. Stella was crying, and Jessie joined in too. Papa called for order. "Mr. Luca Rossi, please come forward and tell us the plans."

Luca grabbed Jo's hand and pulled her to the center of the room. He produced a beautiful small pearl ring from his waistcoat pocket, placed it on Jo's ring finger, pulled her close to kiss her on the forehead and, holding her hand, said, "Ladies and gentlemen, I am the luckiest man alive because Josephine Manning has agreed to be my wife, and her papa has given his consent. We are still deciding on a wedding date, but for now, we are content to be betrothed and share this wonderful news with our family and friends."

Applause and more hugs followed, and Papa proposed a toast with some fine wine he had set aside for special occasions.

Stella rushed to Jo to embrace her and tell her how elated she was for her. Jo's eyes were shining with happiness and excitement, and Stella had never seen her so animated. "Jo, dear Jo," she exclaimed, "I wish you all the joy in the world."

The end of the evening did find Stella and Tom sitting on the front steps, officially chaperoned by others nearby in the house, but quite alone together in the cool night air, as Stella has envisioned.

"I'm so happy for Jo," Stella said. "Her dream has always been to have a home of her own, and Luca is a fine man. They seem to truly love each other."

"And I'm happy for them too, Stella. Luca is an outstanding fella, smart and ambitious, with a great sense of humor, and kind too."

"Much like you, Tom," Stella teased.

"I'm probably more serious, Stella," he joked, "but feeling as happy as Luca to have a lovely Manning daughter in my life."

"Oh, Tom, what a dear thing to say," said Stella. "You know, I've never had a beau, or any man I cared to have a close friendship with, so having you in my life has been both remarkable and wonderful."

Tom paused to take a deep breath and then said, "Do you think, Stella, that with time, our friendship might be something more? I'm asking this question because I'd like to ask your father if I may court you, not rushing you in any way, but perhaps allowing our friendship to grow more into whatever direction the Lord might have for us."

Stella heard these words and asked God how she should answer. She had had no dreams of romance or love so far in her life; it was always poetry and literature, and elocution, and setting personal goals for herself. Was there room in her heart for this kind and loving man too? What if God had intended him for her? Had He? She should find out. But could she find time to nurture a relationship in the midst of her schooling and planning her future on the stage?

As always with Tom, she wanted to speak her heart. "Tom, dear Tom, I am so drawn to you. We each have our dreams, but do we have time in these busy days of our lives to invest in each other?" she answered.

"All things require a balance, Stella, dear. You have a family and dreams, and I have the same. Time will tell if our lives are meant to be together if we give it a chance in the midst of our busy days. I am ready to invest. What do you say?"

Stella paused a moment, then answered, "I say yes, let's go on the journey, and see where it leads."

"Stella, I am the second happiest man alive then, right behind Luca," announced Tom. With that, he turned toward her on the steps, turned her face to his, and gently caressed her face as he kissed her ever so sweetly on the lips. Stella closed her eyes and returned the kiss tenderly, feeling like she was melting. They held each other's gaze and hands and then laughed lightly in the sparkling cool air.

"Amazing," said Tom.

"Yes, quite," said Stella.

Sunday seemed to fly by, with more Irish food, more time to enjoy the family, more time with Tom, and more time to congratulate Jo and Luca. Neighbors had heard the news and had come to call. Stella spent time with Mama and her younger siblings, and especially with Jo, rebonding with her sister after several weeks' absence. Jessie fit right into the circle too because she had ample experience relating to her four sisters.

"But I never had a brother, Stella, and I love your two charming ones," laughed Jessie.

Stella observed Tom and Papa going down to Papa's shop for some privacy and returning somewhat later in a relaxed and friendly mood. Papa called her into the parlor to sit with him and Tom, and Mama and Mr. Kane joined them.

"I've been speaking with Tom," started Papa, "and it seems he would like to court you, Stella, and I'm not at all surprised by this request. Seeing you two these past weeks start a good friendship has made me happy because I have the utmost respect for Tom and for his father."

Tom beamed to hear these words, and Mr. Kane smiled expectantly.

"And so, Stella," Papa asked, "is it your desire to be courted by Tom, or, as he put it, to explore slowly how your friendship might develop into a deeper relationship to see where God might lead?"

"Yes, Papa, I would be in favor of that plan," agreed Stella happily, looking at Papa but smiling in her heart at Tom. "We have much to learn of each other in the middle of our very busy lives, and I highly value spending time with him."

"Then do invest your time wisely, both of you," challenged Papa lightly but seriously, and Mama and Mr. Kane heartily agreed. Stella smiled broadly at Tom, and he returned the smile with an even broader one.

Before long goodbyes were said, Mama packed some late-night snacks for the travelers, and soon Colin came to collect everyone for the long trek back to the city. He would leave the carriage and horses at the livery near the Bronx's Third Avenue El, they would all ride into the city together, the three gentlemen would see Stella and Jessie safely back to the Delacourtes', and Colin would spend the night again with the Kanes before reporting to work in the morning. Tom had an early morning run, so he would be off to Jersey City on the ferry.

The weekend was over, and Stella and Jessie prepared for another busy week, reminiscing on all the special events they had shared in the past two days and anticipating the last two demanding weeks of elocution training.

Stella had shared her happy news about Papa's permission for Tom to court her, and Jessie was ecstatic for her and also starting to hope that Colin might make such a request of her father in the near future. But for now, they decided they had to place their energies in completing their training successfully and see what opportunities might be in store to actually perform elocution. They remembered the Delacourtes' mention that they would appear in public settings during these two weeks and wondered how that might happen.

"Yes," said Jessie, "I do believe we will have some great adventures coming up, Stella, before we're finished with this season of our lives."

"I'm sure we will," said Stella.

How very true that would prove to be.

CHAPTER 16

New York City
November 1892

"These two weeks will see the culmination of your training in elocution," said Mr. Delacourte. "You have studied the Delsarte Method in great depth and with much dedication. We will be polishing all your skills through a final round of exercises each day and helping you seek the first opportunities for careers in elocution, if you wish to go on the stage."

"Of course," continued Mrs. Delacourte, "not all of you may wish to go on the stage. You may find satisfaction in many other speaking situations, such as religious establishments, business locations, schools and community organizations, or even within your own families. Good elocution skills transfer to a wide variety of settings and venues."

The girls listened attentively, each considering how she might wish to apply the training of the past four weeks and how to best use her time during these remaining two weeks. Stella and Jessie had already resolved that they would try for the stage, so their decision was easy. Others were not as sure.

"Tomorrow, however, we offer you a unique opportunity to have your photographic portraits done for promotional purposes," said Mr. Delacourte. A well-known local theater and society photographer, a Mr. Joseph Byron, will be here to pose you in various postures, all modest but dramatic, so that you will have a portfolio to show to prospective clients for elocution performances."

Numerous oohs and aahs arose from the girls, and one of the Miss Billinghams asked, "But what shall we wear for our portraits?"

"Good question," said Mrs. Delacourte. "We have hired theatrical gowns that will be ideal for the portraits, and you can choose two each this afternoon after they are delivered. We think these gowns will present you at your best for possible stage engagements. However, if any of you believe you do not wish to consider performing on stage, you may wish to forego the gowns and simply pose for a beautiful headshot, a lovely photograph of yourself to keep. Just let us know your preference.

"You will nonetheless be part of our public presentations during the next two weeks, gaining further skills in speaking in front of others, a final confidence-building step in elocution training," Mrs. Delacourte concluded.

As it turned out, two of the girls had no plans to go on the stage and, therefore, did not need their promotional portraits done. But each had a plan to use her new elocution skills.

Rachel Polonsky, whose father was a buyer at A. T. Stewart Department Store, said she would use her speaking abilities as a representative to the store's female customers in planned presentations of new fashions and fashion trends. Such events required careful preparation and the ability to enthusiastically and dramatically promote the store's expanding product line, and she was motivated about taking on this task with her new elocution skills.

Anne-Marie Cariveau, of the bakery family in midtown Manhattan, planned to use her speaking skills in helping her family open and publicize two new locations and promoting their growing line of bakery goods to a new audience of commercial customers at some of the fine hotels, so she too did not need the portraits.

But the other six girls readily accepted the invitation for promotional portraits gifted by the Delacourtes and enjoyed the fun of selecting their portrait outfits from the theatrical gowns that arrived that afternoon.

Stella selected two outfits that she just loved. One was a sophisticated black lace gown with lace ruffles at the somewhat lower neckline, open lace work on the long sleeves, and a deep lace hem. The other was purely fanciful, a sort of gypsy gown, as she called it, in ivory and deep purple with a dropped waist and long puffed sleeves on an attached fitted bolero with short fringes. The bolero connected in the middle of the gown's lowered bodice, above a stitched flower motif that ran from the bodice to the low waist. The hip area was decorated with a braided loop design, below which the skirt's colorful embroidered panels dropped to the floor.

It was not immodest, Stella thought, but very exotic and quite different from the rest of her wardrobe, and the other gowns, actually. The other girls selected their favorite gowns, and as all modeled their picks, great enthusiasm grew for the events of the next few days.

Mr. Byron, the photographer, was a delight to work with. He teased and cajoled and posed each girl in numerous settings against the background screens he brought, using his large box camera on a rolling tripod stand to create the best perspectives in the large parlor. Some of the poses were done sitting serenely, some standing in perfect posture, and some in a dramatic stance as if in the middle of a recitation. He also posed each girl in a classic head-and-shoulders shot, with tulle around her shoulders to project a soft feminine look. For some of the shots, the girls wore their hair up, and in others they were asked to take it down.

"A real experience it was," declared Jessie. Stella agreed and could hardly wait to see her portraits, which would be ready in a couple of days for viewing.

During all the excitement about the promotional photographs, the Delacourtes announced another salon event, this one for a larger audience, in the parlor on Friday with musical interludes, and again the girls were asked to select recitations from Mr. Delacourte's compendium. He chose the theme of "adventure" for this presentation, and Stella selected a dramatic reading called "The Lightkeeper's Daughter," which told a compelling story of a young lightkeeper's daughter who rescued sailors from a storm.

Jessie chose "The Burning Ship," an equally dramatic story of a family saved from a burning ship. Because these two selections had a similar theme, Mr. Delacourte said Stella and Jessie could recite them one after the other to set a vigorous tone for the event, right after the opening musical selection, a lively Vivaldi piece played by the string quartet they had engaged.

Stella and Jessie were inspired by their dual role in creating excitement at the beginning of the planned event, and they worked day by day on their recitations, challenging each other to do a superlative job in interpreting the material. And in the meantime, exercises, reviews, practice recitations, more exercises, and fine tuning of all the elocution skills they had learned continued at a brisk pace. It was an energizing but exhausting week, all agreed.

But the activity that garnered the most excitement was the quick return of the proofs of the promotional photographs. Everyone gathered in the big parlor as the photographer proudly displayed the results of his efforts on easel stands placed around the room.

The photographs were, as Stella said to Jessie, "quite extraordinary." The students, who had seen each other all through the classes in everyday outfits, now appeared to each other as glamorous luminaries in the proofs.

Stella was delighted with her photographs. The head-shot with the tulle around her shoulders, her hair up but with tendrils framing her brow, and a pensive look on her uptilted face, made her look quite grown and wise. The two shots in the so-called gypsy outfit were alluring, she thought; in one, she held her arms up and titled her head back, with her hands behind her neck, and in the other one, she stood straight with her arms toward her back and her hands behind her. She had been asked to wear her hair down for these shots, and she looked straight at the camera in a very forthright way.

In the final of her four poses, she was sitting properly in a straight-back chair in the black lacy gown, with her hair up again, holding a bunch of flowers, and looking straight at the camera with a studied pose. No smiles showed in any of the poses, but rather, she decided, her face projected a serene, confident look.

Jessie's photos were just as astonishing, both girls agreed, and Jessie commented, "How grown-up and professional we look, Stella."

"Indeed, so true, Jessie." And to herself, she thought, *Are these really me? I look nothing like the young Irish girl I was just last fall in Miss D's parlor.*

Tom was having an exhausting week too. During a busy week with double-shift work on the Pennsy freights, bundled against the early winter air, his thoughts strayed to Stella constantly while keeping track of his routes and responsibilities. How best might he court her? How could he honor her desire to achieve her goals in elocution, support her efforts to go on the stage, and fit into her life at a time when she was embarking on a dream-fulfilling adventure?

He respected her so much, and, yes, he was in love with her, and he believed she was beginning to fall in love with him. But he had not expected to find a woman to court as his future wife at this stage of his life. He was only in his midtwenties and working hard to build his railroad career, and it would be a number of years before he could truly afford to take care of a family. Stella was not from a wealthy family, but she was comfortable and secure within her father's protection, and her father had done well in his trade. He knew he would do well too, but what about in the meantime? Did he offer her enough?

Would their dreams collide or mesh together as each of them pursued the course they were on?

He had promised not to rush her, and he would honor that promise, of course. He had told her and her father that he was willing to let God lead them into a deeper relationship, if it was His will.

And of course, that was the answer. Let God lead.

Letting Jessie lead the opening recitation after the Vivaldi piece, Stella smiled at the substantial gathering in the large parlor. The Delacourtes had said that many influential people were attending tonight, people associated with opera and classical musical performances, art and culture leaders, talent managers who booked elocution engagements at private soirees among New York's Four Hundred, and others who were keenly interested — as were the Delacourtes — in promoting genteel entertainment in the city.

Some of the girls had felt somewhat intimidated by this description of the intended audience, but the Delacourtes assured them that the attendees were benevolent and trustworthy people, and that any and all potential opportunities that might come about after the evening would involve contracts and formal arrangements approved by the girls' parents.

"Besides," Mrs. Delacourte said, "they are all here to relax and have an enjoyable evening with music and recitations and libations, not here to judge a contest. It will be a jubilant evening and an excellent chance for you to gain more confidence."

Stella couldn't agree more. Everyone had been kind and friendly, and she felt at ease. She wished Tom were here, but she would see him tomorrow at ten o'clock for a picnic in the park and some time together. Thinking about Tom always energized her, and she felt that was a good thing.

Tom, dear Tom. Was she in love with him? Did love mean you respected and cared deeply for the other person's dreams as well as your own? Did it mean you felt comfortable sharing your heart and wanting him to share his? What about that feeling that you wanted to be held and caressed and, yes, even kissed? She told herself she must stop thinking about the moment when Tom kissed her last Sunday ever so sweetly and tenderly, and concentrate on her recitation.

Tom had said he was willing to let God lead them on the journey she had agreed to take with him. She so admired his faith and resolved to ask him tomorrow about how it had grown and why he was able to talk to God so easily. Sure, she could do so a little, but it seemed so natural to Tom. Why was that? Could that happen in her life too? Could she have a personal relationship with the Creator, like it seemed Tom did?

"And now, Miss Stella Manning will recite 'The Lightkeeper's Daughter,'" said Mrs. Delacourte, and Stella stood in her best posture, relaxed, made eye contact with her audience, and began by saying,

The pale moon hid her face; the glittering stars retired
Above the blackness of the night.
The wild winds moaned as if some human soul
In fetters bound was struggling to be free...

She was an elocutionist, savoring the living of her dream, all other thoughts put aside, at least for the moment.

With a good night's sleep, even after some late-night talking with Jessie and the others about their exciting but exhausting week and salon event, Stella was up and ready to enjoy a picnic in the park with Tom Saturday morning, but the weather proved a hindrance. Not only was it cold, but a dreary drizzle interspersed with rain showers dominated the day.

"Not to worry," said Tom as he arrived. "I've another plan for our time together today, and it's about time my family returned some of the Manning hospitality that has been so generously extended."

"Tell me the plan," said Stella, holding his hands and looking into his eyes and not really caring what they did as long as they were together.

"I've a hack waiting outside to take us to the Kane residence on Ninth Avenue, where Miss Stella Manning is cordially invited to attend 'the famous Saturday morning breakfast' prepared by an elderly gentleman of note, Mr. Thomas Kane."

"Ooh," said Stella, going along with the fun, "my cousin Colin has highly recommended this event, so I accept the invitation."

Snuggled inside the enclosed hack with the driver making his way through the crowded and rain-splashed streets, Stella asked Tom about his week and told him about hers, especially about the pictures and the salon event. The dampness was inconsequential, she thought, next to the warmth of his very handsome self.

The elder Kane greeted her heartily and welcomed her to his and Tom's home. The second-floor flat was cozy and redolent of fresh-baked bread and other savory aromas, and quite in order, Stella thought, for the home of two single men with no lady to care for it. A small reception area led in one direction to three sleeping rooms and a bath, and down a narrow hall in the opposite direction was a small kitchen that opened to a comfortable dining area, and a parlor with an overstuffed couch and matching armchair.

Stella could see a woman's touch in the homey furnishings, pleasant art on the walls, and small decorative objects. Scattered here and there on the various small tables and the sideboard were photographs of the Kane family, some taken, it seemed, many years ago when Tom and his lost sister were children. Despite the missing family members, the home had a cheerful air, was well-lighted on such a dreary day, and she felt quite at home.

The host served juices and fruits to start their meal at the nicely set table, and lively conversation began on a variety of subjects. Mr. Kane, who followed politics with great interest, remarked about the coming presidential election, which might put Grover Cleveland back in office if he defeated the incumbent Benjamin Harrison and, thus, become the first former president to be restored to office. Tom told about the growth of the Pennsylvania Railroad's Panhandle Route, opening up more opportunity for future expansion, and Stella told of her latest adventures at the Delacourte School of Elocution.

The three enjoyed Mr. Kane's fresh-baked bread and delicious egg and ham soufflé, topped off by fresh brewed coffee, which Stella had learned to drink now that she was in America.

"How ever did you become such a good cook, Mr. Kane?" asked Stella.

"I have always enjoyed helping in the kitchen, Stella, and when Tom and I began keeping house together and I retired, I determined to study cooking books and learn recipes and take over the food preparation for our household. I quite enjoy it!"

Although Stella offered to help with the dishes, Mr. Kane insisted she and Tom enjoy a second cup of coffee in the parlor while he tidied up. Before they sat, Stella asked Tom to show her the family pictures scattered about, and he took her on a brief tour of the family's photographic memories.

"Your mother was a beautiful woman, Tom," said Stella as she picked up a frame showing an elegant lady with upswept hair and the very same dark eyes as Tom.

"She was indeed, Stella, and my sister captured her looks too," said Tom as he showed Stella a picture of the two women together.

"And this picture, of the four of you when you and your sister were quite small is so precious, Tom," remarked Stella, holding another frame.

"Yes, those were happy days, and we have such wonderful memories of those years."

"Tom," said Stella pensively, "you told me when we were just getting to know each other that day of the picnic in the park in Woodlawn Heights, about your mother and sister, and I'll never forget your words. You said, 'We know our dear ladies are safe in heaven, and we shall see them again someday.'"

"Yes, Stella, I did tell you that, and I believe it with all my heart."

"Then tell me, Tom," said Stella, "how are you so sure of this?"

"Come sit with me, Stella, and I'll tell you." And they sat close to each other on the couch, with Tom looking right at Stella and holding her hands.

"God has promised us that we have an eternal home with Him in heaven if we believe in His son, Jesus, who came to suffer and die and grant us a right relationship with God, which we could never gain on our own. My mother Sarah and little sister Sallie believed this truth from the

Bible, as do Father and I, so we trust this promise and keep it close to our hearts when we miss our dear ladies.

"And because we have this trust and faith, we have drawn closer to God and have a personal relationship with Him through prayer and study of His Word. It's a wonderful thing, Stella, and I'm glad to share it with you."

"It sounds amazing, Tom. But can anyone have this relationship, or is it just reserved for a few?" asked Stella.

"It's for everyone, Stella, everyone who believes. It's a free gift."

Stella was quite amazed because she had gone to church most of her life, except for the last few months because there was no Catholic church available in Woodlawn Heights. And she knew a few Bible stories and had learned her catechism, and she had especially loved going to church with Tom recently. But this relationship that Tom talked about was above and beyond all her previous experience, and it was intriguing and very appealing to her.

"So I could have this too, Tom, this relationship with God? Just by asking?"

"And telling God you are sorry for all your sins and asking Him to help you live in His grace day by day."

Stella wondered if she was good enough for God, though, and wasn't sure if He would really accept her. She had tried to be good, but she had bitterly resented Papa for a long time, even though she had stopped feeling that way recently and felt more peaceful. But sometimes she was not so nice to Jo and entertained aggravated thoughts about her. And she didn't help Mama as much as she should because she was so interested in her own activities. And she was prideful about her elocution skills a lot.

And yet, maybe God was waiting for her to think all this new information through and make a decision. She would do that.

"Tom, you've given me much to think about," said Stella.

"I'm glad," said Tom, "and look outside now; it's clearing up. How about we spend some more time with my father then head back to the park for a walkabout?"

They finished their day later standing in the small parlor at the Delacourtes' as Tom held her loosely in his arms while pressing a tender kiss to her forehead and apologizing that he couldn't take her to church tomorrow because he had to work a double shift.

"It's fine, Tom," murmured Stella, wanting to throw her arms around his neck and reach up for more kissing while knowing that behavior was not proper and others were nearby, so instead, she said, "This last week of our formal classes will be a busy one, so I plan to rest tomorrow. And the Delacourtes said they will announce on Monday about our final public appearance, which I'm sure will take great preparation. I'll drop you a note as soon as I have details. Perhaps you can attend."

"I'd love to, Stella," said Tom as he gave her a tender kiss goodbye.

Later in bed in her room alone because Jessie was spending the weekend with her family, Stella savored Tom's parting kiss and then contemplated all that he had told her about God. She politely asked God to enlighten her on the subject of the free gift Tom had described, which sounded, quite frankly, too good to be true. Yet, she respected Tom and trusted his words. She wanted the assurance and the close relationship with God that he had.

She decided she would continue to think about it and maybe ask Jessie what she thought about such a free gift.

CHAPTER 17

New York City
November 1892

The students convened eagerly in the large parlor after morning exercises on Monday to hear the plan for the last week of classes. All were especially most curious about the public performance the Delacourtes had mentioned and were eager for details.

"I know you have been waiting for news of this week's schedule and the performance the school will present, and all is now in readiness," announced Mr. Delacourte. "We shall spend today doing summary instructions on all the critical skills you have learned, and the next four days preparing for our presentation to the art and culture community, and to your parents and friends, who are also invited."

"This Thursday, we will adjourn to the Lyceum Theater on Fourth Avenue, between Twenty-Third and Twenty-Fourth Streets, for rehearsals of our program, which will be held there on Friday, starting at eight in the evening," continued Mrs. Delacourte.

"This theater is well-known in the community and formerly hosted the American Academy of Dramatic Arts," she continued. "The actress Mrs. Helen Dauvray now manages the theater, and her associate Mr. Daniel Frohman is its producer. It's a beautiful theater because Mr. Tiffany of the

Tiffany Glass Company designed many of its elements. It seats more than seven hundred people and is the first New York theater to be lit entirely by electricity."

Amid the oohs and aahs from the students, Mr. Delacourte told them the Lyceum has a stock company with a troupe of actors performing several different plays each season, but the theater is "dark" now, between productions, and Mrs. Dauvray and Mr. Frohman have issued an invitation to host the students. "It's wonderful advertising for future elocution students and for the future of elocution," he said, "and an excellent opportunity to showcase your elocution skills to a wider audience."

"I doubt we will fill the theater," added Mrs. Delacourte, "but we should see an audience of more than two hundred now that these flyers are being distributed in genteel venues all over the city, starting today."

With that statement, she held up a beautifully lettered poster advertising the event. It read:

The Delacourte School of Elocution
Is Honored to Present
Elocutionary Performances
By Graduates of Its Inaugural Class
On Friday, November Fourth
Eighteen Hundred and Ninety-two
Lyceum Theater
Fourth Avenue between Twenty-third and Twenty-fourth Streets
Eight in the Evening
With Musical and Refreshment Interludes

And around these words were grouped pictures of eight lovely young ladies—all the students—each in an oval frame, with each one's first name beneath her picture. These pictures were the headshots the photographer had taken, and all the girls looked like elegant young women, ready to draw an audience of patrons of the arts and culture in New York City.

As the students looked at the poster in awe and commented on their pictures, Mr. Delacourte announced, "By the end of today, we'll give you the recitation pieces we are selecting for each of you, and our program will be off to the printer. You will each perform three times, and the recitations will show the full range of elocution skills, including narrative and descriptive readings; pathetic and humorous and dialectic pieces; religious and didactic selections; readings for children; dialogues and tableaux; quotations; and some Shakespeare—all of which you have studied and practiced."

"Oh my," marveled Stella to Jessie. "This is the real thing, Jessie. This is what we've been training for."

"Absolutely, Stella. We'll help each other, and we will have a wonderful time going on the stage, a real stage this time," replied Jessie.

One of the students asked how the class would officially end after the performance and when they would need to move out of their rooms, to which Mrs. Delacourte smiled broadly, and said, "In addition to the invitation your parents, relatives, and close friends will receive for the performance, they will also receive an invitation to attend a farewell dinner to be held the next day, Saturday, at the Fifth Avenue Hotel at Two Hundred Fifth Avenue.

"I suggest we all return here Friday night to relax after a busy week and an exhilarating evening, and then rest on Saturday and prepare for the farewell dinner. There will be no need to rush to return home. You may plan your move out and return to your families for later in the weekend or early next week, whenever convenient.

"We do expect that offers for elocution performances will start coming in after Friday night, and they will come here initially, so staying here through the weekend or into the early part of the week may actually be advantageous.

Of course, we know how to reach each one of you, so if you have returned home, we'll contact you about all opportunities that may arise."

Then Mrs. Delacourte said in a softer voice, "I'm going to miss each of you so much," as she looked around at all the girls. Mr. Delacourte repeated the sentiment and then added, "Our first class in the school will always hold the best memories, and I am so proud of each of you."

An emotional moment for all was observed. Then Mr. Delacourte said, "Now back to work."

Stella's mind was racing. She figured that her family might opt to stay in the city on Friday night, attend the Saturday evening dinner, also staying over, and then perhaps all would return to Woodlawn Heights together on Sunday. Or perhaps not. She needed to write to them immediately to confirm their plans, and also to Tom, because she so hoped he could be there, at least for Friday night.

So much to think about. What did her future hold, now that she would be a graduate of the school, gain public exposure this Friday, and possibly receive invitations to perform elocution? Would she stay at home? Live in the city, and if so, where? How would she be able to see Tom if she were busy on the stage?

One thing at a time, she told herself. First, write the notes, then work hard this week to get ready for the performance. She would actually be performing on the stage!

It was a jubilant morning at the Dakota on Tuesday. The well-known resident ushered in the man who had just come up the service elevator and steered him to the apartment's study, a tomblike room filled to the walls with banker boxes bulging with documents, a large desk, and two sturdy chairs.

"Look, take a look," said the host excitedly as he held out a poster showing pictures of young women and an announcement of some kind.

"This is the break we've been waiting for, and I had to find it for you. You couldn't come up with a plan on your own, you incompetent fool, but my vigilance led me to this poster today, on a stand down in the lobby. Happenstance, but lucky. Ha!"

"Lemme see it, sir," said the visitor, grabbing for the poster. "Ah, there she is, Jessie, our mark, and her lil' bosom frend. Seems her name is Stella," he said as he looked at the pictures, and his host sat down behind the desk.

"Yes, there she is, and we can see where she is going to be this Friday, can we not? Out of that house and away from home too. An elocution performance at the Lyceum, in plain view. Just excellent because I know this theater from many visits to, shall we say 'friends,' backstage, and it has a dark area perfect for snatching the girl."

"Will we be takin' the other un', this Stella, too?"

"Yes, as an insurance policy, if you get my meaning. Now, listen up. I will draw you a map of the back of the theater, the alley, the stage door that opens on to the alley, and backstage area, and you'll start to devise the taking plan."

"'Tis wot I do best, sir," said the visitor. "I'll git my boys into action an' we'll carry it off, no problin'."

"We'll need a copy of the performance program to see the best time for you to act," said the man behind the desk. "Look, here is the name of the printer on the poster. He'll be printing the program too, so go by his shop and pilfer a copy straightaway. Bring it here, and I'll work the whole plan with you."

"I'm off and on it, Gen'ral."

"Don't call me general. Just get the program and get yourself back here. And clean up your two goons and bring them too. Use the service elevator."

"Aye, sir!"

Assignments for the performance had been handed out, and all the new young elocutionists were buzzing with enthusiasm.

"Father will be so thrilled Charlotte and I will be doing a Brontë reading as one of our recitations," said Emily Billingham.

"And I just love my first Shakespeare piece," said Anna Bentley.

"Stella, what do you think of your three performances?" asked another student.

"I am quite pleased, and my final recitation is so very exciting," said Stella. "Jessie and I will do it together, as Mr. Delacourte has planned, and it's a poem I've always found fascinating, 'The Raven' by Edgar Allan Poe."

"And a real favorite of mine too," chimed in Jessie, "such a dark and mysterious poem. It will be such fun to dramatize it together."

Mr. and Mrs. Delacourte did a walkthrough of the program top to bottom in the large parlor, showing the students how to assemble and proceed one after another through their recitations, bows, and circulating back and forth between the "stage" and "backstage," which they designated in the parlor.

"We'll start with music from an ensemble in the orchestra pit, and the theater manager, Mrs. Dauvray, will welcome everyone. Then Mr. Frohman, the producer, will introduce my husband and me," said Mrs. Delacourte, "and we'll tell about the school and our vision for increasing the reach of genteel entertainment in the city through elocution training. Then we'll announce the start of the program, and you will be the stars of the evening.

"After the first round of performances," she continued, "we'll have an intermission, and you can briefly visit your families and friends in the vestibule while refreshments are served. Do drink some lemonade or water to keep your voices fresh before we all return for the next round, when you will recite your second pieces, as listed in the program. Oh, and we'll have copies of the program available later today for you to enjoy. Seeing your name in print in the program will make it all much more real.

"After the second round of performances, we'll have a musical interlude, and refreshments backstage for you, and then Mrs. Dauvray will tell the audience of coming performances the theater is sponsoring. She will then hand off to us again as you begin your final round of recitations. The whole evening should take about two-and-a-half hours, including the intermission and musical interlude. We'll have refreshments for the guests available all evening, so do not be distressed if you see a guest or two leaving during any performance to go to the vestibule," she added.

"To finish the evening," Mr. Delacourte said, "after the final two-person reading by Stella and Jessie, they will leave the stage and wait while each of you comes back for a bow, and then they will return to the stage last to join you to take a bow, and all will take a bow together."

"It all sounds complicated," one student announced.

"It sounds complicated when described," said Mr. Delacourte, "but it will all become clear and logical when we go to the theater Thursday to get familiar with the surroundings and start our rehearsals there. We'll walk through enough times, with the program in hand, to get you comfortable."

"And we'll give you much instruction about performing on a stage with lights, which is quite different than performing in our parlor," laughed Mrs. Delacourte. "You will learn so much, and you will be amazed how well your training will pay off."

The students said they had never worked so hard. Rehearsals at the Delacourte home proceeded apace, and Thursday morning, two carriages arrived to take everyone to the Lyceum. The three-story building had a perfectly symmetrical appearance, with a double-door lower central entrance and two broad flights of stairs leading from the street to other double doors to take guests to the first-floor auditorium level. In the center of the building was a large marquee with the words LYCEUM, and small central arches and fire escapes neatly framed the entire building. A motif of metal wreaths appeared at intervals, adding a decorative touch.

Mr. Daniel Frohman, the theater's producer, met the Delacourte party just inside the door and greeted the students, ushering them into the heart of the theater to have a look at the layout. He led them on a tour, and the girls stood in front of the 344 parquet or orchestra seats to turn their heads and take in the full view of the theater's seating: 727 seats in all, which also included 88 boxes, 172 seats in the dress circle, and 123 balcony seats. At seventy-five feet deep and forty-eight-and-a-half feet wide, the theater appeared immense yet had an intimate air.

The huge arched proscenium and stage were impressive, Stella thought, but she also concluded that the whole theater, while well decorated and appointed, was nowhere as beautiful and elegant as the Gaiety in Dublin. She kept that thought to herself, however.

To orient the students to stagecraft, Mr. Frohman explained how the huge velvet curtain, which comes down just behind the proscenium, hides the stage from view, and when the curtain is lifted or parted, those performing on the stage appear to be in a sort of frame, defined by the proscenium. Stella had not contemplated that prospect, although it was interesting to consider performing within a frame. She liked Mr. Frohman's flair and enthusiasm for the theater.

The producer took them on a tour backstage, which was discovered to be a bit of a dark labyrinth, with a curtained corridor traversing the entire length of the stage from one side to another, off of which were a couple of dressing rooms, each with a refreshment area, one for men and one for ladies. Entrances from both sides of the stage allowed a performer to wait quietly behind a small curtain out of the line of sight of the audience before emerging onto the stage.

Mr. Frohman laughingly showed them the stage door that led to the alley behind the theater, saying their many admirers would be there after the performance to greet them with flowers and seek their signatures on the program.

"Of course," he said, "they will also likely throw bouquets of flowers at you during your last bow, so do not hesitate to take an extra bow and enjoy the attention." And with that amiable comment and amid affable murmurs from the students, he said, "Mr. and Mrs. Delacourte, the theater is yours for rehearsals. Ladies, welcome to the Lyceum, and I know you will all do well tomorrow night."

Jessie whispered to Stella, giggling, "Quite dramatic, isn't he?" And Stella agreed.

Leading the students onto the stage, Mrs. Delacourte had them stand in a line and look outward, then said, "Look out at your audience, picture their faces smiling at you, remember your training, stand up, and recite. Remember our objective, which you learned and memorized the first day of classes:

We are training our bodies to make them
willing, graceful, and obedient servants
to our wills and emotions,

199

We are training our minds to abandon themselves to the spirit
of the selection in hand, forgetful of self and surroundings,
becoming for the time the real character
or the soul of the lines rendered.

"You have lived those words 'forgetful of self and surroundings,' and each of you will excel in your performance,"
she concluded by way of inspiration for all.

"So now," Mr. Delacourte stated, "we will get to
rehearsing our show, for it is a show of your hard-gained
elocution talents, and you will love being on the stage — this
beautiful stage," he concluded as he swept his arms out as if
to embrace the stage.

Others were also touring the theater for less benign reasons. Dressed as a cleaning crew, two men swept and dusted
the aisles, then went backstage with brooms and dust mops,
asking to be pardoned for any interruption by saying, "Jus'
doin' our jobs, we are," as they passed by.

Mr. Frohman had gone out, and the Delacourtes and
the students had the theater to themselves, so they figured
the cleaners were there at Mr. Frohman's behest to ensure
the theater was thoroughly cleaned before the performance
the next day. The cleaning men left via the backstage door
that led to the alley. Mr. Delacourte thought that was odd but
thought perhaps their cleaning cart was out back, so to do a
favor for Mr. Frohman after they left, he locked the door.

But Jessie had noticed something that seemed odd to
her. "Stella, look at those cleaning men. Do they look familiar
to you? Do they not look remarkably like the two men who
were staring at us as we sat on the front steps awhile back?"

"I don't know, Jessie," said Stella. "They might be the
same men, but so many common workers look a lot alike
with their slouch caps and baggy clothes."

"I guess I notice people more closely, Stella, maybe a trait I picked up from my father who has a genius for never forgetting a face."

"Do you think we should..." replied Stella.

Just then, Mrs. Delacourte called them to the stage for their rehearsal of "The Raven," so all was forgotten in the concentration of the moment. But high up in the Dakota, others were concentrating on a detailed plan, also being rehearsed until it was well learned.

Thursday night found the girls pretty well exhausted from the strenuous rehearsal but much more confident in the rollout of the program and their recitations.

"Now for a good night's sleep and one more short final rehearsal tomorrow in the costumes we shall wear," said Stella as she and Jessie turned out the lights.

Mrs. Delacourte had ordered long flowing gowns in each girl's size for the performance, which she said were in soft pastel colors, were lower cut than usual gowns but modest and would give them more fluid movement, while allowing their arms to express their gestures more freely. They would rehearse in the gowns tomorrow morning, leave them all neatly arranged in the ladies' dressing room, return to the house for a light lunch, have a rest, and then return to the theater at five o'clock to dress and begin final preparations for the program.

Refreshments, lemonade, water, and tea would be available in the dressing room before the show, as would chairs and chaises for relaxing. Hairstyles up or down, depending on the pieces being performed, would be the responsibility of each of the students, and each would keep track of her own copies of her readings. All was in readiness.

Excitement was high, and Stella had learned that Papa and Mama, and also Jo and Luca, would attend, brought to town by Colin, who would be there too. The younger children would stay at the Rossi home for the two nights the Mannings would stay in the city, and Colin would bring all home to Woodlawn Heights on Sunday, including Stella's belongings. Stella could not think beyond Sunday, but that was fine for now.

But the best news of all was that Tom did not have to work on the weekend and would be available to attend both the Friday performance and the Saturday farewell dinner. Stella could hardly wait to see him again and tell him how she believed she was ready to accept the free gift he had told her about last Saturday. She had discussed it with Jessie, who knew all about this free gift from God and had already accepted it herself.

"But why didn't you tell me about it, Jessie?" asked Stella, to which Jessie had replied, "I wasn't sure how you felt about such matters, Stella, and I did not presume to open a subject that might make you uncomfortable. My father and mother, who have always gone to church and believed in the Christian gospel, instructed all five of us girls in our early years. It's a private thing to some, Stella, and those who criticize my father's gruff manner would be surprised to know he is a true believer."

"I know Tom will be surprised, and so will Colin. Your father is a remarkable man, Jessie, in his important police work in the city and as the leader of your family."

"Yes, Stella, he has always been very respectful of family, very loving to all of us, and cared for his own mother for many years when she was ill. And tomorrow, he will be there for my performance in spite of all his responsibilities."

"Tomorrow will be a special, quite extraordinary day for us both," murmured Stella, and Jessie dreamily agreed as she fell asleep too.

CHAPTER 18

New York City
November 4, 1892

*T*he day was finally here.

Stella awoke a little earlier than usual and took a few minutes to remember the first elocution performance she had seen in Dublin with Miss D and her family, followed by her grave disappointment about losing her home and opportunities in Ireland, but followed then by gaining a new and even more wonderful home and life in America. How amazing it seemed, looking back over the time since her arrival in May, that she had found an entry point, a path forward, to pursue her dream of performing elocution on the stage in so short a time.

She remembered saying to Mama the night Papa had announced their plans to leave their Dublin home that she would be a nobody, just one of thousands in a new and foreign place, with all dreams cast aside. That hadn't happened, had it? No, Papa's words had proved true instead, that if her vision for the future were meant to be, it would happen in God's timing, no matter where she lived. She had even quoted it to him awhile back before school started. God's timing. It was perfect, wasn't it?

And so she had found the conference, gone to it and met the Delacourtes, and qualified for the very intense and thorough training she had just completed. Although the next steps were not clear, tonight she would be performing on the stage, on a genuine New York theater stage as an elocutionist, with an opportunity to perhaps find a place in the world of elocution. Had God arranged all this? He must have! How many people actually got to step into their dream? And so quickly.

And she had met Tom, someone like her, with a dream to fulfill, and like her, someone who loved family and valued hard work and honesty. And she had found Jessie, her new best friend and dear companion. How blessed she was.

Time to get up and get going.

The Delacourtes assumed serene, confident looks, aspiring to pass their attitude onto all the students, for whom tonight would be a signal day in their lives. Their leadership worked because the students, though excited, were calm and composed. The rehearsal in the gowns on stage went exceedingly well, further building confidence in all the girls. Mrs. Dauvray, the theater's manager, stopped by for a few minutes to observe and commented favorably on the dress rehearsal. As one of the first women theatrical executives in America, her opinion was highly valued, Mrs. Delacourte told the girls. A further confidence builder.

Evening was here now, all were dressed, and the theater guests were arriving. Stella wanted to peek out from behind the small curtain out of the line of sight of the audience at stage right or left to catch a glimpse of her family and Tom, but the Delacourtes advised they should stay in their comfortable dressing room, relax, take refreshments, and review their presentations. Mrs. Delacourte reminded them that right before their entrance onto the stage, according to the program, there would be some introductory remarks, and they could gather behind the small curtains to hear those remarks.

"You'll know when the introductory remarks will begin by listening for the end of the music," said Mrs. Delacourte. "That's the time to gather just offstage in the order of performance, some of you to stage right and stage left, as we've rehearsed, and after all the introductory remarks, the elocutions will begin."

The music had just ended.

"A very good evening, ladies and gentlemen," said an elegantly dressed Mrs. Dauvray to the nearly three hundred people in the parquet and balcony seating. "It is my great pleasure to welcome you to the Lyceum Theater to an evening of elocution, brought to you by the inaugural class of the new Delacourte School of Elocution. These young ladies have worked hard to showcase the skills they have gained during the past six weeks, and I am quite sure you will find the performance stimulating and delightful.

"I am pleased to introduce to you Mr. Daniel Frohman, my associate and producer here at the Lyceum, to present Mr. and Mrs. Delacourte, who will have a few words to say before the program begins."

With a flourishing hand gesture to welcome Mr. Frohman to the stage, she stepped aside, and Mr. Frohman, impeccably attired, took the stage. "And a hearty welcome, indeed, dear guests," he began. "The Lyceum is dedicated to presenting high-quality modern plays that reflect our nation's traditional melodrama style and also the newer, more naturalistic or realistic style. But we always desire to offer our patrons classical and time-honored experiences, and elocution — or the art of dramatic and expressive public speaking — is a powerful communicative and entertainment medium we share in our public life together.

"As I see it — and these young ladies who will turn an imaginative phrase or compelling anecdote will convince you — the art and science of elocution must prosper because the drama of communication, the words and gestures, speak beauty to all of us, and that beauty must continue amidst new forms of public entertainment."

Behind the small curtain at stage left, Jessie looked at Stella with raised eyebrows and a grimace, and Stella put her hand over her mouth to stifle a giggle at the flamboyant words of someone who seemingly liked to hear himself speak.

But mercifully, Mr. Frohman finished his monologue and ceded the stage to Mr. and Mrs. Delacourte, introducing them with a grand flourish and saying, "And now, ladies and gentlemen, Mr. Bernard Delacourte and Mrs. Sophie Delacourte, renowned and well-known practitioners and performers of the Delsarte method of elocution, will introduce our program."

Mr. and Mrs. Delacourte, both attired in fine evening clothes, thanked Mrs. Dauvray and Mr. Frohman for their introductions and for the kind use of the theater for the performance. They took turns speaking, in their very elocutionary manner, everyone observed, but cast a friendly and easy mood into the gathering.

Mr. Delacourte started by saying he was pleased so many were present to honor his students in their first stage appearance. He then stated, "When my wife and I decided to start the Delacourte School of Elocution, our purpose was to advance the art and science of elocution as a contribution to society. Our goal was to train new adherents to populate our city venues with this genteel form of entertainment. We wished to offer a sheer contrast to the rising tide of, shall we say, more common forms of performance seen all over the city. This is still our goal, to enrich our audiences' minds and hearts with classical works of merit."

"However," Mrs. Delacourte said, "in pursuing this goal, we have come to realize another wonderful aspect of the school, our joy in training these lovely young ladies. Each came to us with good speaking skills and a sociable personality, and each has worked exceedingly hard to develop her elocution skills. Seeing each one engage enthusiastically with the training and improve week by week, overcoming difficulties encountered, has been far and away our greatest delight."

"So without further ado," Mr. Delacourte said, "we present to you the recitations of the students of the inaugural class of the Delacourte School of Elocution."

At those words, the audience applauded heartily, the house lights dimmed, the stage lights came up, and the program began.

The first round of recitations went well, with some slight trepidation from the students, but each remembered Mrs. Delacourte's direction "to look out at your audience, picture their faces smiling at you, remember your training, stand up and recite."

Stella read a humorous piece called "The Drummer," a droll story about a traveling salesman who rides trains from place to place in the country selling wares and enlightening his customers with anecdotes. She especially liked the piece because much of the story involved his travel on trains, and she knew Tom would find it amusing.

She felt she had presented the five-minute piece well, enjoyed the laughter from the audience at some of the most amusing parts, and appreciated the applause afterward. She could hardly wait for the break to find her family and Tom in the vestibule.

"Well done, Stella!" said Tom, whose sentiments were echoed by Papa and Mama and Jo and Luca, plus Colin, as hugs were traded all around, even with Tom, which Papa seemed to approve.

"Really, Stella," said Jo, "you were amazing. You had everyone on the edge of their seats enjoying the humor." Stella was happy that Jo's "really, Stella" phrase now had a praiseworthy context as opposed to the "reallys" of their past life together.

Papa said, "Stella, elocution is truly your calling. You have done well, and we are all so proud of you." Mama echoed the sentiment and beamed broadly. Stella felt so elated with their praise. The Mannings were all dressed in their Sunday best, and she too was proud, proud of her family.

"Thank you, Papa," said Stella, especially relishing his commendation, and turning to Tom to pull him slightly aside to say, "I'm so glad you could be here, Tom, and I have so much to tell you. Remember that free gift we talked about..." But then she was interrupted by Jessie, who said, "Stella, I'd like you to meet my family, and oh, hello, Mrs. and Mrs. Manning, so good to see you again," as she moved closer, her arm linked to her father's.

"May I present my dear friend Stella Manning to you, Father? Stella, please meet my father, Superintendent Byrnes, and my mother and two of my sisters, Amy and May."

"I am so pleased to meet you, all of you, and may I present my family and my special friend, Mr. Thomas Kane," answered Stella. Introductions were made all around, and Stella had her first close-up look at the very famous Thomas Byrnes, a tall, well-built man, even burly, she thought, with big, broad shoulders. His bushy handlebar mustache was quite distinctive when paired with his high forehead and prominent cheekbones. She had heard he always had a cigar in his mouth, but tonight that item was absent, probably in deference to the genteel company, Stella surmised.

"Miss Manning, a great pleasure to meet you," said Mr. Byrnes, "and your family," he said, nodding to the others. "I also understand you have a fine young cousin, Miss Manning, Mr. Colin Manning, I believe," at which point Colin, who had been nearby, stepped up and said, "Yes, sir."

Jessie, a little flustered, introduced Colin to her father, who gave him a serious but not menacing look. "Mr. Manning," Mr. Byrnes said, as he met Colin, and Colin grinned a little nervously. "Sir."

Just then, the chime sounded, reminding them that all needed to return to their seats for the second round of performances, and the students needed to proceed backstage. Stella touched Tom's hand and said, "'Til later, my dear Tom," and he squeezed her hand with a deep smile and repeated, "'Til later, my amazing Stella."

The second part of the program was equally successful, with the slight nervousness of the first part completely absent. The students not only did well: they excelled in their presentations, and the audience warmed to the program.

Stella's recitation was "The Bridge," a melancholy poem by Henry W. Longfellow, in which he meditated on his life while standing on the bridge between Boston and Cambridge at midnight. In contrast to the humorous piece she had recited in the first part of the program, this dramatic poem showed yet more skills she had developed and the range of emotions she was able to portray.

It was Jessie's turn to be humorous, in the second of her readings, so she performed "Reverie in Church," a humorous tale by a Mr. George A. Baker, Jr., that told of a young girl's fanciful observations of all those around her, instead of observing the true purpose of attending church. The audience roared with laughter at the entertaining lines, and Jessie received loud applause. As did the others. Stella was so happy for each one of them. Whatever their future might be in or out of the elocution world, each of her classmates had worked hard to achieve striking personal success. She wanted to hug them all, and she was so thankful for all the tireless training the Delacourtes had given them.

After the second round of elocutions ended, and the musical interlude began, Mrs. Dauvray came back to the girls' dressing room to report she had seldom seen an audience so engaged with the performers. Mrs. Delacourte, sitting with the girls during the intermission, said she was highly gratified to hear this news. Refreshments were served, and everyone anticipated the final and third round with renewed enthusiasm.

Mrs. Dauvray opened the third group of recitations with a brief announcement of the Lyceum's next performance, starting December 5, a play entitled *Americans Abroad* by the French dramatist Victorien Sardou, whom she said was highly skilled in creating a well-made play. She thanked the audience for their warmth and conviviality and asked Mr. Delacourte to introduce the final segment of the show.

"This round of performances, dear audience," he said, "will showcase more of the variety of elocutionary genres and will conclude with a dramatic reading by two of our students, which will be a fitting conclusion to our presentation tonight. Thank you, and let's proceed."

Everyone again excelled, and Stella and Jessie waited backstage as the Billingham sisters delivered their Brontë recitation together, having such a wonderful time with their favorite author. Stella imagined how delighted their father, the Brontë enthusiast and English professor, must be to see his daughters on the stage performing such a piece.

As they finished and took a bow, she and Jessie came out together to announce the final piece, "The Raven," by Edgar Allan Poe. Mr. Delacourte had told them that this poem was considered by many elocutionists to be the most remarkable example of a harmony of sentiment with rhythmical expression to be found in any language. He had enthusiastically related how it had been widely translated and more universally recited than any other selection in all literature. How exciting it was, Stella thought, to be allowed to read this poem, and to do it with her dearest new female friend Jessie.

Once upon a midnight dreary, while I pondered, weak and weary,
Over many a quaint and curious volume of forgotten lore —
While I nodded, nearly napping, suddenly there came a tapping,
As of some one gently rapping, rapping at my chamber door,

The suspenseful poem built in intensity and mystery, and the symbol of despair, the raven, spoke just one word: "nevermore!" As Stella and Jessie read the heartbreaking and anguished words of the poet, creating the hopelessness and desolation Poe was portraying with such skill, the audience was completely entranced.

And the lamp-light o'er him streaming
throws his shadow on the floor;
And my soul from out that shadow that lies floating on the floor
Shall be lifted — nevermore!

They finished the final lines in almost a breathless attitude of gloom so real that the audience was stunned and silent for a moment before breaking into wild applause, standing and applauding more, and cheering. Stella could see Tom's face shining with love and admiration, standing just a few feet away from her in the second row.

She knew at that moment that she was passionately in love with him. A formal bow followed before she and Jessie exited to stage left, where the Billingham sisters waited behind the curtain for the call for the final bow. The other four students were waiting behind the curtain at stage right, and they would be called out to line up across the stage, by twos, with Stella and Jessie to go last. They lined up behind the Billingham girls, who were nearly undone with excitement and glee now that the performance was over.

Mr. and Mrs. Delacourte came up to the stage and called out the first pair of performers, waiting behind the curtain at stage right, "Miss Anne-Marie Cariveau and Miss Gianna Ricci, please step out and take a bow." And they did to loud applause. Then, "Miss Emily and Miss Charlotte Billingham, please greet your audience." And the Billingham girls stepped out, leaving just Stella and Jessie remaining at stage left. As applause finished for the sisters, Mrs. Delacourte called for "Miss Rachel Polonsky and Miss Anna Bentley" for their bows, and both of them came out from stage right.

Mr. Delacourte said, "And now to present our last two performers, after which all will take a final bow. Miss Stella Manning and Miss Jessie Byrnes, please step out." The audience began to clap, all on their feet now, and Tom looked eagerly to see Stella's face appear.

But it didn't. Nor did Jessie's. Mr. Delacourte said again in a louder tone, "Miss Stella Manning and Miss Jessie Byrnes, come out to greet your admirers."

The Billingham girls left their place on the stage to fetch Stella and Jessie, whom they surmised were just a little slow in coming out, but momentarily, both sisters came rushing back to the stage, shouting, "They're gone! They're simply gone! They're not backstage!"

The Delacourtes rushed backstage too and found not a trace of Stella and Jessie. By that time, Superintendent Byrnes had leapt onto the stage, and there was a general outcry from the audience. Mr. Delacourte went back to center stage and asked everyone to stay calm and take their seats, assuring the audience that "all is well, perhaps one student has fallen ill, and the other has helped her, do not worry, all will be well..."

The students stood together near the Delacourtes, and the audience continued to murmur ever more loudly. Mr.

Manning, Tom Kane, and Colin Manning came running up to the stage in deep concern, and soon Superintendent Byrnes pulled them into a huddle backstage and said, "I am so sorry, gentlemen, but it looks like foul play has occurred. The stage door is open to the alley, and it appears our girls have been taken."

CHAPTER 19

New York City
November 4, 1892

These words were almost heart-stopping for the Manning men and Tom Kane. Incredulous, breathtaking, devastating words. Mr. Manning gripped Superintendent Byrnes' arms and rasped out the words, "No, no, it can't be. They're just young girls. Who would want to take them? Why? Where? They are our daughters..." He fell back as if in a swoon, and Colin and Tom caught him, both saying at once, "We must find them, stop this thing from happening..."

Mrs. Dauvray and Mr. Frohman came running into the backstage area, crying out urgently, "What has happened?" And Superintendent Byrnes told them the appalling news.

Byrnes sprang into action, even his police-hardened steely face showing high emotion. "Lock down the theater, madame. No one may leave until all guests are accounted for on a list. I want everyone's name who was at the performance."

"Yes, right away," she answered and scurried off. "Daniel, come help me."

"I always have my men nearby, Mr. Manning, and look, here are two of them. Officers, quickly, muster every man on duty and rouse those coming on duty later tonight.

I want a citywide dragnet for two young girls who may be moving through the city against their will, likely in some kind of conveyance. Fan out immediately in all directions from the theater.

"Both are dressed in theater gowns. One is a redhead and the other one has brown hair. Mr. Manning, give the officer a more detailed description of your daughter and take a seat before you fall over.

"Bring the Delacourtes to me, Mr. Kane, and all the girls who performed tonight. Someone may have noticed something, someone unusual in the audience, or a comment or a gesture. We will question everyone who was onstage, and the police across the entire city will round up all known ruffians and troublemakers, and believe me, I know them all."

"Mr. Manning," Byrnes said as he turned to Papa, "I am quite convinced this kidnapping was a strike against me, and unfortunately, your daughter was involved as my daughter's friend. I will do all in my power to see they are both safely returned."

Papa croaked out weakly, "I know you will, sir."

"Superintendent, how may I help?" said Colin.

"Stay with Mr. Manning, see he gives the description of Miss Manning to the officer, gather your family and ensure they are safe, and bring all of them to the Delacourte residence where we will convene in a short while after I give further detailed orders to my men. But first tell my wife and daughters what has happened, then reassure them I am in action, and stay with them until I send a police escort to hasten them home and guard them."

At that point, a shaken Papa and Colin returned to Mama and Jo and Luca, who by now were trembling with fear and uncertainty and needed information and comfort. They were huddled with the Byrnes women, Jessie's mother Ophelia and two Byrnes daughters, also very upset. Papa put his arms around Mama and Jo, and Colin immediately began to carry out Byrnes' orders.

And Tom ushered the Delacourtes and all the students backstage, and Mrs. Delacourte suggested they meet in the dressing room with the superintendent, who appeared shortly and began his questioning, towering over them as he spoke while they sat nervously, some crying. "What did you see tonight that was unusual? Did anyone approach you at the intermission? Did you see anyone watching Miss Byrnes and Miss Manning at the intermission? Did you see anyone get up and leave during their last performance?"

The questions went on and on, and the girls, most of them now crying, were not helpful at all. Mr. and Mrs. Delacourte tried to keep them all calm, while they were also trying to remain calm themselves to answer questions. Mr. Frohman returned with the list of attendees and asked if all might be dismissed from the theater now. "Yes, yes," said Byrnes after he read the list, then turned to the Delacourtes and the students. "I want you to tell me about your last two times here at the theater for the rehearsals. Did you see anything unusual yesterday or this morning?"

"Nothing, sir," said Emily Billingham. "We met Mr. Frohman, had a tour of the theater and backstage, and then he left. We did our rehearsals, and oh, the cleaning crew came in for a little while..."

Mr. Frohman, who had been listening intently, raised his head abruptly, and said, "Cleaning crew? I authorized no cleaning yesterday. There were no cleaners in the building. The theater had been thoroughly cleaned earlier this week."

"But there were two men here," said Mr. Delacourte. "They cleaned the theater and then cleaned backstage and actually asked our pardon for disturbing us. And after they left, I found the stage door to the alley unlocked, which I thought was unusual. I locked it, though, and thought little of it with the rehearsals on my mind."

"Can you describe them?" asked Byrnes. "Tell me everything you remember about them, all of you who saw them. Age, size, facial or physical characteristics? Quickly, now."

"Well, they were just cleaning men," sighed Mrs. Delacourte, "and they were wearing baggy street clothes, slouch hats, with sweepers and mops..."

"One of them had a sultry look," said Miss Polonsky. "He had a, I guess I would call it, a smirk, but I didn't pay much attention to him."

"Oh dear," prompted Anna Bentley, suddenly on her feet, "I just remembered something. When the cleaning men were here, I heard Jessie asked Stella if those two men looked familiar. She said something like, 'Do they look like the two men who were watching us when we sat on the steps out in front of the house awhile back?'"

"Miss, this is very important," prodded Byrnes. "Tell us everything you can remember about them." And looking around, he said, "All of you, think, remember, help me here. Two lives may depend on your memory. Close your eyes, picture them, tell me what you saw and heard."

They all did exactly that, but no one could remember anything more specific about the men. Mrs. Delacourte said, "One of them said something like, 'pardon us, just doing our job, we are.'"

"Any kind of an accent?" asked Byrnes.

"No, just the usual inarticulation of the common man, no accent that I could discern."

At that moment, a runner from 300 Mulberry Street Police Headquarters dashed into the room. "Superintendent Byrnes! A note was just delivered to Mulberry for you, sir," as he handed Byrnes an envelope with the words written in a very tidy script:

Superintendent Byrnes, For His Eyes Only

Byrnes tore open the envelope, being careful not to destroy it, and read the words written in the same very tidy script, then sat down to read the words again.

> *You are such a fine detective and police superintendent, Mr. Byrnes. You can solve any crime. Well, you will not find your daughter and her friend in the city, and you will not see them alive again unless you pay me $500,000 cash within 48 hours. I will send instructions. You have ruined my life and reputation, and now I seek payback. Surely your very wealthy friends will lend you the funds. Goodnight, Mr. Byrnes.*

Stunned but already planning his next moves, Byrnes asked the Delacourtes and the girls to return to the Delacourte home, where he would join them shortly. "Let the young ladies go to their rooms, and we will convene in your home with the family members and several of my detectives," he announced to the Delacourtes.

"No one, and I mean no one, will breathe a word that I have received a note. Is that understood?"

Nods all around as everyone sat in stunned silence.

Colin took the Mannings quickly to their hotel to gather their belongings and check out, taking them to the Delacourte home, where the Delacourtes lent them Stella and Jessie's room, with a cot for Jo and a place on the second floor for Luca. Tom stayed with the Delacourtes and helped escort and calm the students, who by now were near hysteria.

The Mannings could not rest. Papa paced nervously, and Mama and Jo sat together, holding hands, and trying not to cry. Tom and Luca got them comfortable in the large parlor and went to find the maid to brew a calming tea for them. The parents of the other students came to the house, wishing to take their daughters home, fearing danger for all, but Byrnes would not allow it until he had questioned them further, so the girls were sequestered in their rooms for now with a police guard all around the house.

The press had gotten wind of the crime, of course, and they had converged on the theater as all were leaving, shouting out: "Superintendent! News is that your daughter and another girl have been taken! Tell us more!"

Byrnes, in his usual way of handling the press by feeding them just enough information, but not enough to satisfy them, said, "There will be a statement later. Let us pass."

Stella heard the lapping of the waves and felt the motion before she was fully conscious. She reached out in the dark and found another person beside her. "Jessie?" she asked. No response. She pushed against whoever it was, and the other person stirred and moaned. "Jessie, is that you?"

The motion of *yes, it was a boat*, Stella decided, made her nauseous in the dark, and the remnants of the thick sweet smell she remembered encasing her contributed to her nausea. She tried not to scream, but fear won her heart. Just then, the other person moved and began to speak.

"Stella?" the other person said. "Is that you? Where are we? What happened?"

"Oh, Jessie, yes, it's Stella. Thank God you are speaking. It seems we have been captured and taken away from the theater. The last I remember was waiting for our last bow, and then an arm around me, and a cloth over my face with a sweet, sickening smell, and then, as it seemed I slept, I remember horses clopping in the street, and now we are out on the water, I think."

"Oh, Stella, I remember the arm and the cloth and the sweet smell too," said Jessie. "But nothing else. There must have been two men who came in through the alley backstage and crept up on us. But why? What do they want with us? Are you harmed?"

"No, not harmed, just tied up, and very frightened," Stella replied.

"Yes, I am tied, too, and I think, unharmed, but oh, Stella, I think I am going to be sick," Jessie said as she turned her head and retched, causing Stella to do the same.

After a minute, Stella said, "Enough of that. We must be very brave and find out what is going on and how we can help ourselves."

"Yes, we must be brave. But perhaps we should scream for help and someone will rescue us."

"Yes, let's try that," agreed Stella, and they both cried out "help! help us!" for a few minutes. At last, someone opened a door, stuck a head in, and Stella could see moonlight through an open hatch door, but the face was shrouded in the night. "Shut yerselfs up, you twae, or it's goin' ta be worse fer ye," barked a man's voice.

"Who are you?" asked Stella. "And what do you want with us?"

"Eh, you'll be findin' ut in due time, missy. Fer now, shut yer trap." With that, he slammed the door shut, obscuring the moonlight and casting them into total darkness again. Stella thought they might be in a cabin on a small boat.

"Oh, Stella," said Jessie. "I think this is about my father. Someone bad has taken us to get back at my father for something, or maybe for money. He arrests criminals and testifies against them in the courts all the time. Maybe someone is angry at him and is trying to take it out on us. It's all my fault for getting you into this fix."

"It's not your fault, Jessie. It's not your father's fault. There are bad people everywhere, and we've fallen into their hands. Your father will track them down and rescue us."

"I hope he can do it in time, Stella, but maybe there's nothing he can do if they plan to k...k...kill us and dump us in the river."

"Jessie, if they wanted to kill us, they could have done so backstage, like Jack the Ripper did with his victims. I think they captured us for ransom. And if they plan to exchange us for money, they have to keep us alive."

"I pray you're right, Stella, but what will they do to us in the meantime?"

"Let's not think about that, Jessie, but let's just pray."

And so that is what they did as the winds picked up on the water and they were tossed about and carried off over the dark waters of the Hudson River into the night.

Byrnes flew past the members of several newspapers who had now gathered outside the Delacourte home, saying not a word in answer to their repeated and loud inquiries.

Mr. Delacourte let him in, slamming the door shut behind him and led him into the large parlor where the Manning party waited anxiously.

"Is there any news?" asked Mr. Manning. "Please tell us you have found them and they are safe."

"There is no news yet," Mr. Manning, "except that the entire police force is working the case, and we will succeed. My men are not called 'immortals' for nothing. They are highly trained and able. I have brought several detectives with me to search the premises for any clue and to continue to interview the young ladies. I am convinced someone saw something that will be useful. Now that a little time has passed and some calmness may have occurred, we may get more information."

"I understand from Mrs. Delacourte that you received a note," said Mama nervously, stifling a sob. "Please tell us what it says."

"Mrs. Manning, I do not wish to upset you, but you do have a right to know what was in the note, I suppose. Mr.

Manning, please take your wife aside to read the note to her," he said, handing the note to Papa.

Papa did so, which resulted in more suffering and anxiety as he and Mama shared the note with the rest of the family and with Tom. "Please, oh please, Superintendent Byrnes, find my daughter," Mama cried, collapsing into Papa's arms.

"Madame, my daughter is as precious to me as yours is to you," said Byrnes. "We will find them and end this insanity. Now we all must work together. The note left several clues, which my men are following up on now at my direction.

"First, we think the girls have been taken out of the city, and that leads us to search in several directions, with the Jersey Shore and Brooklyn as prime areas for criminal endeavors, making the Hudson and the East Bay escape routes. We are working the entire waterfront, and believe me, we know the waterfront."

"Could they not have headed north, uptown, to the Bronx?" asked Tom.

"Possible, but not likely," said Byrnes. "Too many crowds to get through, slow going on a Friday evening. I'm thinking running to the waterfront would be quicker. And the second clue is important. The writer of the note is someone I've helped convict, but he is not in prison. He is suffering a loss of reputation, so he is likely someone who was high up in society, was well thought of, and has fallen in the public eye, especially among his peers. He is likely still in the city but in reduced circumstances, or perceives himself to be and needs funds to recover.

"That profile fits only a relatively small population of criminals I've arrested and built cases against." Byrnes continued, "Most are low-life people with no reputations to lose. So the mastermind behind this treachery is someone who was important in the world and is not so now. I have two or three individuals in mind who fit that profile, and my men are locating them now and putting a tail on any who are on the loose."

"Why would you not bring them in and question them right away?" asked Mr. Manning.

"Ah, good question," said Byrnes. "We do not know what orders the individual has given his minions who captured the girls. He is seeking money, so he has very likely instructed that the girls be unharmed as ransom for the funds, but if a flaw should happen in the plan, say if he is captured, he may have given orders otherwise."

"Otherwise, Mr. Byrnes?" said Mama. "You mean to hurt the girls if he cannot use them for ransom?"

"I am sorry to say that might be possible, Mrs. Manning, so we must not take any chances. Please know, dear madame, that the safety of our daughters while they are out of our arms is my prime concern." Byrnes continued, "This man has chosen to mock me and play on the rumors that fly about corruption, mentioning my wealthy friends, so we are dealing with a man who is not only malevolent, but also jealous and vindictive. We must proceed carefully with such a mind."

"What about the funds, sir? Will you raise the money and be prepared to follow his instructions to return our ladies?" asked Tom.

"Absolutely, Mr. Kane. We will pay the ransom, ensure our girls are safely back to us, and then we'll track the criminal to see he gets his just rewards, if you know what I mean. Right now, we are waiting for the 'instructions' he promised and the way in which those instructions are delivered may lead us to him or to the girls. But again, we must be careful in approaching him. The criminal mind is devious, although not as clever as the detective mind," Byrnes added.

"How can we all help?" asked Mr. Manning.

"Stay here, stay together, be prepared to welcome your daughter back. And right now, I need all the young ladies in the dining room to speak one-on-one with my detectives, who will question them gently but thoroughly, seeking any additional information we might glean. I will make a statement to the press in a few minutes, telling the culprit that I accept his terms and to send the instructions. That is my next step." Saying that, Superintendent Byrnes stepped outside, raised his hand for silence to the waiting reporters, who numbered more than a dozen by now, and said, "Gentlemen, I have a statement. Are you ready?" Amid shouts of affirmation, Byrnes said, "There has been a kidnapping. I am ready to accept the terms the kidnapper has stated and await further word at 300 Mulberry." Then he turned on his heels and marched back into the house, avoiding and ignoring the frenzied shouts and clamor for more information.

As the detectives questioned the girls in the dining room, Mrs. Delacourte herself served tea, coffee, and light refreshments. She saw to the Manning family, and Luca and Tom too and offered any hospitality and comfort they could possibly need. She sat with them and told them how highly she valued Stella and assured them Superintendent Byrnes would solve the case.

Tom, falling apart himself for fear of Stella's situation, nevertheless took a leadership role with the distraught family, speaking quietly with each one and leading a quiet prayer in the small group to ask God to work mightily. With Colin's help, he sent a telegram to his father and Reverend Houghton for support and prayer too.

An hour later, with no new information gathered from the students, they were sent to bed, and Superintendent Byrnes, who had gone to police headquarters, returned with news that leads were developing at the waterfront in lower Manhattan, and his three primary candidates for the mastermind had been located and were being watched.

As he was leaving, suddenly running down from upstairs, Charlotte Billingham appeared in her nightwrap, exclaiming, "I just remembered something I saw, sir. I don't know if it's significant or not because Mrs. Delacourte told us people might be leaving from time to time for refreshment during the program and not to be dismayed if we saw someone walking out, not to take it personally."

"Yes, yes, I did say that," said Mrs. Delacourte. "But what did you see?"

Superintendent Byrnes leaned in closer as Charlotte began to speak and said, "Miss, tell us exactly what you saw."

"Well, there was this gentleman in the balcony to stage right. I noticed him because so few people sat in the balcony, and he was there during the whole show. After Emily and I finished our piece, we waited backstage to stage left while Stella and Jessie took the stage to do the last elocution. I noticed, as they finished and took their first bow, that he abruptly got up and left, hurrying toward the part of the theater where the exits to downstairs are.

"I thought it was strange that he left so quickly after their performance, not waiting for the final bows, but I figured he had to go somewhere, so—"

"Miss," interrupted Byrnes, "can you describe this man?"

"As he stood up, I saw that he was tall, and he walked with a cane. He had a lean, narrow face, and he strode out with a... I guess I would call it a military bearing, sir. And I am so sorry I did not recall this observation earlier. I was so upset."

"It's good you remembered now. Anything else?"

"He seemed in a terrible hurry, sir," said Charlotte, "like he needed to get out of the theater fast."

Colin, who had listened intently, added, "I saw such a man as he came in earlier in the evening, sitting up in the balcony, and I can verify this description. I am thinking, if he is our man, he might have guessed you would lock down the theater, sir, and make a list of all the occupants, were a crime committed, and wanted to escape so as not to be among those tallied."

"Precisely, Mr. Manning, that could very likely be the case," said Byrnes. "And I am quite sure now who the man is, and this information is highly useful. Thank you, miss."

The Mannings and Tom all looked at each other with rising hopes.

CHAPTER 20

New York City
November 5–6, 1892

"Hurry it up, now, ya twa, befor' it gits busy here. Mov' along!" said the man who had spoken to them on the boat. Stella knew his voice now, and he and the other man pushed her and Jessie along the narrow dock leading to a carriage, standing where the dock touched land. They were hustled inside, still bound, and their two captors jumped to the driver's seat, with one driving and the other one keeping him company.

Inside was another man. Stella assessed him as a common man but dressed up a bit. *He isn't as rough as the two thugs who kidnapped us, but not a whole lot better,* she thought.

He quipped, "Ah, my pretties, so nice to meet you this fine early morning."

Jessie said pertly, "It's not so nice for us, if you please, and who are you?"

"I'm an employee of a very important man who has some business with your father, and you don't need to know my name."

"What business is this, if I may ask?" said Jessie snidely, leaning forward.

The man reached out and slapped her across the face, and she drew back, and Stella reeled from the blow too, sitting so close to Jessie.

"You'll show some respect!" he bellowed. "You don't need to know nothin', but as it happens, your father helped put my employer in a bad light. In fact, he ruined him in the eyes of all who matter, and now it's payback time, ye see. He'll pay a bundle to get you and your little friend back, and my employer will be able to improve his situation – and mine, to boot."

Hoping to engage the man to get more information and thus perhaps to plot an escape, Stella asked politely to avoid a slap, "May I know what happened? Perhaps there is a way to undo what has been done, right any wrong, and avoid all this trouble."

"Not likely, missy, because it's five years past now, water under the bridge, so to speak."

"But," Jessie replied, "it seems wrong to involve us."

"Ah, but that's the point, ain't it? How else to get your father's attention and snatch some considerable ransom money to, as your friend says, 'right the wrong.'"

"What do you intend to do with us, if may ask?" said Stella nervously while trying to appear nonchalant.

"You'll be held in a place they'll never find you until we have the cash. We're not monsters, ye see, just businessmen. Of course, if you give us any trouble, there's no telling what will happen to you." Looking at Jessie, he sneered, "And if your father does not come up with the money on time, there will be worse consequences for you both."

At that moment, the carriage lurched to a stop, and the two men hastened down to open the door to pull Stella and Jessie out. Stella smelled cinder, and there was steel under her feet. *Train tracks*, she thought. *We are in a train yard.*

The two unkempt captors and the so-called employee pushed and led them, all stumbling in the very early morning light across a series of tracks, well into a deep labyrinth of boxcars until they came to an especially dark and dirty one. One of the thugs jumped up to open its sliding door, reached down to get Jessie, who was boosted up by the other thug and found herself in the car. Stella's turn was next.

The one ruffian took the ropes off the girls' wrists, hopped down to the ground, and stood beside the other one. Then the man they met in the carriage spoke: "You'll find water, some bread, and a blanket inside. Make yourselves comfortable, ladies. The door will be closed all but for six inches to let some air in. You're in the far corner of the freight yard where no one will hear you, so don't bother screaming. And remember what I said about not making trouble if you want it to go easy on you."

The two men slid the wooden door—which hung on a top runner and seated on a track on a bottom runner—almost all the way closed and then jammed a railroad spike in the lower door runner so that the door could not be opened.

Stella and Jessie did not answer as the men walked away.

At about the same time, the door was jammed shut across the Hudson in Jersey City, the *New York Times* Saturday morning edition hit the streets, and New Yorkers woke up to the shocking news of the kidnapping.

BYRNES' DAUGHTER KIDNAPPED IN
DARING RAID AT THEATER
KIDNAPPERS LEAVE A NOTE AND
BYRNES ACCEPTS THEIR OFFER
ANOTHER GIRL TAKEN, TOO

The scene at the Lyceum Theater
was pure chaos as Superintendent Byrnes
sprang into action at the daring kidnapping

of his daughter, Miss Jessie Byrnes, and her
fellow student, a Miss Stella Manning…

The Mannings and Tom, now joined by the elder Mr. Kane, read the headlines and the rest of the story with heart-piercing agony after a nearly sleepless and tearful night at the Delacourtes'. It was decided that Jo and Luca would return to Woodlawn Heights to retrieve the younger Manning children from their stay at the Rossi home and muster all the neighbors for a vigil and prayer service. After a sobbing goodbye in a carriage arranged by Colin, and Colin's promise to send news as quickly as possible when there was news, the pair left. Colin stayed close, ready to help in any way.

In midmorning, an exhausted Byrnes came in, reporting his men at the Hudson River waterfront had a strong lead they were pursuing, and within the hour he expected to question two men caught bragging by his undercover police in a seedy riverside eatery, that they had pulled off a "steal" overnight.

"Does this mean they will lead us to the girls?" asked Mr. Manning.

"They will receive the third degree of questioning and will likely squeal on whoever masterminded this kidnapping," said Byrnes. Everyone knew about Byrnes' harsh interrogation techniques, which he had perfected over the years, and the record showed that during his twelve years as head of the New York City Detective Bureau, he and his men had been responsible for ten thousand years of criminal sentences for those he and his men had apprehended, questioned, and then seen indicted and prosecuted through the courts.

Byrnes' meticulous method of gathering evidence, keeping records and photographs of criminals, shadowing suspects, surveilling the criminal underworld, working his extensive network of snitches, doing random roundups, tracking down those who tried to hide, and other techniques had led to a substantial record of solving cases. Yet, these techniques sometimes took time, even weeks, and the deadline he now faced to meet the kidnapper's terms was extremely short.

Byrnes knew he had to act quickly and decisively.

At that moment, a detective arrived from the Mulberry Street headquarters with a critical message. "Superintendent Byrnes, we have the note from the kidnapper, as he promised."

"Did you not apprehend the messenger who brought it?" demanded Byrnes.

"No, sir, it was sent by telegram."

As Byrnes read the note, the family and the others gathered round closely with murmurs of apprehension. Byrnes read the note silently and then read it out loud:

> *You shall meet me on the Hudson 300 yards off Pier 40 Sunday night at 11 pm with the cash I have demanded, and you will be given instructions where to retrieve your daughter and her friend. Come alone by boat. Look for a slowly blinking red light to find me. Do not be late.*

"Mr. Byrnes, how can we trust him? Can you do this? Will the girls be safe?" asked Mr. Manning all at once, with Mama beside him shaking and crying.

"There is no honor among thieves, Mr. Manning, but my plan is to find our daughters first, meet him with the funds he requires, and capture him."

"Can you find them in time? How can you capture him out on the river?" said Mr. Delacourte. "How can you do that alone?"

"I will find a way, and I will not be alone, although he will think I am. We have today and tomorrow to find our girls, and that is my mission. Believe me, Mrs. Manning, my wife is as distraught as you are. We will find them, and we will find them quickly. Please stay here and stay together. I will be in touch with news."

Stella and Jessie watched the men go and tried the door several times, but it was jammed shut except for about six inches of air space. They began to explore their surroundings in the chill early morning November air.

"Stella, let's wrap this pathetic thin blanket around our shoulders and walk about this car to see what we might find," said Jessie.

"Good idea," replied Stella, "and we need to drink some water to stay well. But let's ration it because we don't know how long it will be before we're rescued, or if there will be more."

"Oh, Stella," exclaimed Jessie, now starting to tear up, "I do hope we will be rescued. What if nobody finds us, and we are left here to die?"

"We are being ransomed, Jessie. We are valuable. They will keep us alive to get whatever money or favor they are trying to extract from your father. In the meantime, let's see what we can find out about this horrid boxcar."

They found dirt and dust, and droppings from some kind of small animal, and cast off over in a far corner were a few pieces of chalk, and nothing else. "We'll hold onto the chalk and maybe figure out if we can use it in some way to help us get out of here," said Stella.

They sat together on the dirty floor of the boxcar to keep warm, leaning against one of its walls. They ate a bit of the stale bread for nourishment and kept watch through the slit in the door in case anyone entered the far corner of the yard whom they could call to for help.

"Jessie," said Stella, "we need to rest and keep up our strength. We should take turns sleeping, with one of us keeping watch and one of us sleeping. I'll take the first shift of watching, and you try to sleep."

"I am exhausted, Stella, with no sleep last night and all the miserable events we've been through. Wake me before long, though, so that you can get some rest too."

"I will, Jessie, and I'm absolutely convinced that God knows our plight and will help us. Let's pray first, and then you nap."

As they did, a light drizzle started, and a gray day got under way, with the sounds of the railroad coming to life faraway from the freight yard. Stella could hear train whistles in the distance and thought of Tom and her family, and how worried they must be. "Lord, comfort them, and let Mr. Byrnes find us soon," she said.

Things were developing fast at Mulberry Street. Byrnes' detectives had brought in the two men found bragging down at the waterfront and had put them in a lineup. He was able to locate them so quickly because, as he explained, criminals love to brag about their "work." And he also knew the habits and hangouts of the worst of the waterfront thugs and had a revolving crew of undercover men who worked the sleazy bars and eateries, keeping tabs on these ruffians.

The Delacourtes and two of the girls had viewed them in the lineup and were fairly certain these two were the men who had been the so-called cleaning crew at the theater.

Byrnes took the men one at a time, using one of his standard techniques, telling each one that the other one had given him information about the kidnapping crime, and telling each one privately he would go easy on him—if he admitted the crime and told on the other one. He also used his well-honed psychological techniques to undermine their confidence that they could lie and get away with it. He finally had to resort to the third degree, which included some physical violence, an accepted part of police procedure in these days and perfected by him.

It took most of the day, but finally one man, and then the other, broke and confessed that they had been hired to break into the theater's alley entrance and kidnap the girls, but that they were just taking orders from a man who reported to another very important man who had masterminded the whole plot. They were locked up for booking, and Byrnes turned to the next tasks.

He wanted names, and he got them from the two men, now jailed. The middleman was a known criminal, and the mastermind was indeed the man Byrnes had selected from his list of candidates. Now he had two goals: to find the girls somewhere in the vast Pennsylvania Jersey City freight yard, as the men had confessed their holding location but admitted they couldn't find the exact place again. And then he had to lay a snare for the other criminals—the middleman and the mastermind.

He reported to the Mannings and the two Kane men at the Delacourtes', and Tom Kane immediately stepped up and said, "Superintendent Byrnes, I know that freight yard like the back of my hand. I am a Pennsylvania Railroad freight engineer. It's a large and complex yard, especially with the large amount of RIP equipment."

"RIP equipment, Mr. Kane?"

"Sorry, sir. It means repair in place, a word we call bad-order cars needing repairs. I will help you find your way through the yard, and we will find the girls."

"How very convenient, Mr. Kane. I will gather more of my men and some supplies, and we'll all be off to find them while we still have some daylight."

"And I will go along to help too, sir," said Colin, and Byrnes agreed.

Mama ran upstairs to find Stella's cape, and she found one for Jessie too and gave them to Tom and Colin "to keep them warm when you find them."

As the men left, the elder Mr. Kane said, "I will stay with the family, and we will pray for quick success and no problems. The minister from our church, Rev. Houghton, will be here shortly to hold a prayer vigil for us so that you will be covered in prayer while you search."

"Amen to that," Mr. Byrnes said. And so he and Tom Kane, Colin Manning, and a small group of detectives raced to the waterfront to take a boat to the Jersey shore in the fading light, amid threatening skies and a brewing storm.

"Stella, it's getting colder," Jessie said as they huddled in a corner of the filthy boxcar trying to keep warm, "and here we are in these lightweight elocution gowns. I wish I had my warm cape."

"I wish I had mine too," said Stella. "Let's get up and walk around and wave our arms and stamp our feet every few minutes to help warm our bodies."

They devised a plan to each walk fifteen times around the boxcar, then sit close together to preserve body heat. They had the rest of the day, remembering it was Saturday, and then perhaps the night to get through first before thinking about how long they really might be imprisoned.

"Let's take our predicament a day at a time, Jessie. Our captors will want their money quickly, and we'll be ransomed. Let's concentrate on keeping warm today and hoping tonight is not too cold. Surely, help will come before too long."

"Or those evil men will come back to do us harm," said Jessie.

"We can't think about that. We must trust God has a plan for our rescue. You told me, Jessie, that you had already accepted his free gift of our Savior, and last night on the boat, I accepted that gift too. So we are the Lord's daughters, and he will look out for us."

"Yes, Stella, I believe that," said Jessie. "So let's be at peace. And let's talk about our childhoods, our parents, our friends, anything to keep our minds occupied. Let's remember some cheerful and happy times and share them with each other."

And so they did. As the storm swept into New Jersey from the northwest, the air grew colder, the drizzle eventually increased and turned into rain, and then snow, just as the daylight was ending.

But before dark, Stella had an idea. "Where is that chalk?"

"Ye can't cross now, sir. It's not safe with the gale and the snow blowin' up a storm," said the sturdy and reliable boat captain Byrnes had tapped to take the rescue party across the Hudson to the Pennsylvania rail yards.

"It is critical we get there to rescue hostages, especially with the storm and the dropping temperatures," said Byrnes. "We cannot wait."

He had notified the Pennsylvania Railroad authorities of the situation, and they promised support, but not until the weather cleared somewhat. "Perhaps in the early morning," the yard superintendent had said.

Byrnes was furious, and he also understood the danger of crossing the Hudson in a violent storm. Danger not only to his party, but to the boat captain and his crew. But his protective-father feelings overrode all concerns, and he said, "We go. Now."

"Aye, sir. We'll do our best to get you there, but it will be rough going," said the captain.

So a treacherous journey was undertaken, trusting that God and the captain would carry them across safely. The waves increased as they moved into the river, and the wind tossed the strong craft about. The men stayed inside the cabin with the captain and crew, holding on to any stable surface and almost blinded by the scene through the windows of the snow swirling overhead and all around the boat. Heaving to and fro, the boat ploughed the Hudson, with waves washing over its bow as it heaved down into the water then rose up again.

"Steady as she goes," shouted the captain, holding tight to the wheel, "and give us more steam," he shouted through a pipe to the engineer far below in the hull of the boat as the storm raged.

Tom prayed like never before for the men onboard and for Stella and Jessie. And he knew the prayer team back at the Delacourtes' was lifting them up minute by minute. Surely God was listening. *He always does*, thought Tom.

CHAPTER 21

New York City and Jersey City
November 5–6, 1892

"Thank you, Lord, thank you so much," said Tom as the boat slammed hard but safely into the dock at the Pennsylvania Railroad yards on the Jersey shore. They had made it, all of them, and it was full dark now. The storm raged, and the temperature was below freezing, but at least they were closer to Stella and Jessie.

"Mr. Kane," said Byrnes, "draw us a map of the yards showing how the freight cars are stored and arranged, and we'll split up into teams to begin the search. The captain has foul weather gear onboard we can don, we've brought kerosene lamps, and we can't waste a minute because of the freezing temperatures."

"Yes, sir," said Tom and taking the scrap of offered paper began to draw the labyrinthine layout of the freight yards. Eight tracks formed parallel rows with walking space in between, with boxcars lining the tracks of each row end to end. Many of the tracks had a dozen or more cars. Some cars were open, and others closed up tight. Varying kinds of doors were to be found; some had trap doors on top, and others didn't.

"We will inspect every car systematically," said Byrnes, "and even though the wind is howling, we will call out their names in case they can hear us and let us know where they are."

They divided up the rows with two men to a row to provide the muscle power to open doors. Byrnes had thought to bring several crowbars and hammers, so they took them along. What miserable work this was in the freezing cold, with little visibility because of the blinding snow, plus the arduous work of getting into the boxcars and the emotional pressure of knowing every minute could make the difference between life and death for the girls in the freezing temperatures. The men knew there was some shelter inside the boxcars, but the bitter cold did not augur well for survival overnight.

They worked tirelessly through the night, though, driven by the hope that they could find Stella and Jessie in time, while some of them doubted that the kidnappers had told the truth about the location of the captives. But Byrnes had no doubt, and after they rendezvoused at the agreed-upon time of five o'clock in the morning, he allowed a thirty-minute rest for the exhausted men but then spurred them on. And they resumed the methodical search.

Tom, searching with Colin, was bone tired and freezing cold. He knew Colin was too. Still, each held onto the vision of the sweet faces of Stella and Jessie and pushed onward.

Just as the first glimmer of morning light appeared, with the storm finally abating and a fresh cover of snow under their feet, Tom looked in the direction of a boxcar a few cars distant and thought he saw something familiar. It wasn't a person, but a mark or a symbol, or something that resonated with him.

He stared and asked for recall and wisdom and guidance. He was a praying man, as Stella had said, and whatever it was, whatever he saw, warmed his heart in the cold morning air. He blinked, cleared his eyes, stared, and knew what it was. The outline of the Tara Brooch.

Chalked roughly but distinctly and fairly large into the wooden side of a boxcar, next to a door that had been jammed almost shut with a railroad spike, was the unmistakable image of the brooch. Grabbing Colin, he ran and called out to all the men in the other rows. He reached the boxcar, ripped away the spike, opened the door, and hurtled inside. The first thing he saw were two huddled figures in a corner with a red curl escaping out from under a thin blanket.

Hardly breathing, he ran to the corner and found Stella and Jessie, barely conscious and freezing cold but alive. Colin was right behind him, and together they each drew a girl to them to bring warmth and comfort.

"Stella, Stella darling, you are safe now," croaked Tom, barely able to speak from emotion and exhaustion, as she fell limply into his arms.

"Oh, Jessie, Jessie, you are found," murmured Colin, also overcome by emotion, and holding a semiconscious Jessie.

"Tom, Tom, oh, Tom. I knew you'd come," said Stella, barely able to speak.

"Colin!" said Jessie as she regained her senses and broke down in tears.

At that moment, Byrnes bounded into the car, followed by his detectives, and the big, strong, no-nonsense tower of a man tenderly took his daughter from Colin's arms and held her to his chest, burying his head in her thick red hair and kissing her all at once.

"Father, you have found us," murmured Jessie as capes were put around each girl, and plans were made to get them through the yards and back to the boat.

Stella just looked and looked at Tom as he carried her in his arms, cradling his face in her very cold hands, savoring those deep brown eyes and his wonderful face, and said, "Tom Kane, I love you, and I will do so forever. Not just because you rescued me, but because of who you are to me, the dearest soul in all the world."

After a fairly smooth boat ride across the Hudson, with both girls fast asleep in warm bunks covered with blankets, a quick carriage ride led to a joyous reunion for all, with many tears, at the Delacourte home, where Mrs. Byrnes had gone to be with the Kanes. Mama couldn't stop crying, and Papa couldn't stop shaking. The elder Mr. Kane, still there to add comfort, rejoiced to see the Mannings, and especially his son, so happy about Stella's safe return. Colin's telegram had gone to Woodlawn Heights as soon as they were back in New York, so Jo and the family and community knew by now that all was well.

After warm baths and fresh clothes, and nourishing food at the Delacourtes', Jessie and her mother were escorted home for rest by two burly policemen after hugs and, again, many tears between the girls and a promise to be together again soon. Colin promised to come see Jessie in a few days, which brought a weak but happy smile to her face, as she hugged him goodbye.

Knowing Stella needed to rest too, as did Mama and Papa, the Delacourtes insisted they stay overnight before making any plans to return home. Stella knew Tom was exhausted too, and she urged him and his father to return home and rest but not before she and Tom had "a few moments together," she announced.

So she sat with Tom in the small parlor alone for the first time since the rescue, wrapping her arms around him and remembering their first kiss. She needed another one now, she knew, and she needed to know if he loved her too. Too shy to ask, she rested her forehead against his forehead and then heard the words, "Stella, I am so thankful you are safe, and I promise to be sure you are safe the rest of your life, if you'll let me, because I truly love you. I'll not rush you because you are so young and have many things you want to accomplish..."

"We'll reach our goals together, Tom, supporting each other with love and all our energies. We'll put it together day by day, and we can get started on our plans after we both have rested."

"Yes, Stella, we shall," said Tom and gave her that sweet, tender kiss she so longed for.

Superintendent Byrnes had plans to make too, and two criminals to catch, and after resting for a few hours from the long day and night following the kidnapping and rescue, he went to work. He sent two detectives to find and bring in the man he knew was working for the man behind the kidnapping, the "employee" Stella and Jessie had met in the carriage.

His name was Joseph Hartley, and he was known to Byrnes as a former midlevel bureaucrat, now a criminal for hire, who had lost his city job through the corruption trials of the scheme's mastermind, a former Union Army general named Alexander Wiley. When the two thugs who snatched the girls had given up the names of these two higher-ups, Byrnes had hatched a plan to catch them, but his first priority had been the rescue. Now he could lay the trap.

Hartley arrived at 300 Mulberry Street all huffing and puffing about why he was being arrested and confronted Byrnes with the same attitude.

"Not arrested, Mr. Hartley. You're just here for a friendly chat," said Byrnes, smiling.

"About what?" he responded.

"Step into my office, Mr. Hartley, and take a seat. I'll be in shortly," answered Byrnes.

As Hartley sat down on an oxblood wingback chair in the windowless office, he noticed that three of the four walls contained tall locked glass cases with an assortment of crime paraphernalia such as crowbars, hooks, brass knuckles, pistols, derringers, knives, and other items. He spied a series of black hoods, each with a date and label indicating the criminal who was hanged in it.

Hartley shivered, crossed his legs, and tried to assume a casual air as Byrnes arrived to take a seat across from him at his heavy oak desk. Byrnes picked up a cigar and lit it. His face was pleasant but inscrutable.

"So, Mr. Hartley," Byrnes said, "I understand you've been keeping company with an old friend of mine, a certain Mr. Alexander Wiley, or should I say General Wiley?"

"Sure, I know him," answered Hartley. "So what?"

"There are individuals in this city who can testify to your helping the good General commit a serious crime recently," said Byrnes, smiling.

"Preposterous!" said Hartley.

"Do you know the punishment for accessory to kidnapping, Mr. Hartley?" said Byrnes, casually picking up another nearby sample of the black hoods and running it through his fingers.

Hartley twisted in his seat and didn't answer. So Byrnes continued having a friendly chat with him as the afternoon wore on.

The storm had passed, although the sky was still leaden, and no moon could be seen. It was a quiet late Sunday night on the Hudson as a lone man with powerful arms rowed out from Pier Forty in a small boat. He soon picked up a boat with a blinking red light, as predicted, about three hundred yards offshore. As he came nearer, he hailed the boat, saying, "Thomas Byrnes approaches alone with a package."

At the railing, two men appeared, their faces in shadow in the moonless night.

"Ah, Byrnes, we meet again," said a gruff voice.

"And whom do I have the pleasure of meeting again?" asked Byrnes as he held the oars steady in their gunwales.

"An old friend. Do tie the boat and climb aboard on the ladder you'll find, Mr. Byrnes, so that we can speak face-to-face, and you can give me what you've brought me."

Byrnes climbed aboard, sliding easily down to the boat's deck, his package in a sack slung on his back, and followed the two men into the lighted cabin at their invitation. "Indeed, if it isn't General Alexander Wiley," said Byrnes, extending his hand while also looking steadily at both men in turn.

Not extending his hand, the general said, "Good to see you again, Mr. Byrnes, or should I say Superintendent Byrnes now? But no time for small talk, right? Give me the package." Byrnes slowly removed the sack and handed Wiley the package. He watched as Wiley greedily counted the five hundred thousand dollars in hundred-dollar bills.

"This will do nicely, Mr. Byrnes," he said, "to compensate me for losing my reputation and good name because of the bribery charges you conspired to bring against me in 1885. Although my two subsequent trials resulted in deadlocked juries and I was set free in '87, my political career was over, as you know, and now I have run out of my family money to continue my lifestyle."

"General Wiley, I did not bring those charges. I merely arrested you when your acts were discovered by others."

"But you humiliated me, Mr. Byrnes, serving me a warrant in front of my family, whom I have now lost, booking me as a common criminal, and not being willing to work out a gentlemen's agreement with me to release the charges."

"I had no authority to release you," Byrnes said. "In spite of your heroism as a Union officer in the war and your service to the city, it was my duty to serve the warrant and bring you to justice. I would have done the same for anyone."

"We could have worked out something, Mr. Byrnes," whined Wiley, "but, as you see now, we are working together — this time — as gentlemen to resolve the issue. The funds seem to be here, Mr. Byrnes, and I'll be leaving town straightaway, so here is a note telling you where to find your daughter and her friend."

"Do you really think, General," said Byrnes, slowly standing up and not taking the note, "that I would have handed you five hundred thousand dollars if I did not have my daughter and her friend safe already?"

Wiley stood abruptly and exclaimed, "What? You cannot. Mr. Hartley, what is the meaning of this? You have assured me the girls are locked away."

"I'm sorry, General," said Hartley. "Mr. Byrnes broke your kidnapping scheme yesterday, the young ladies are home, and I will face reduced charges in this case because, you see, I myself reached a gentlemen's agreement with Mr. Byrnes earlier today."

"You dastardly traitor!" shouted the general, drawing a small derringer from his inner pocket. But Byrnes was faster, knocking the weapon out of the general's hand and drawing his own weapon, while tossing a pair of hand-cuffs from his pocket to Hartley. "Put these on him, Mr. Hartley, and we shall both join my men waiting in another boat next to the one I tied up. And bring the bundle of money too."

"You have committed a heinous and cowardly crime, General Wiley," rasped Byrnes menacingly, "terrorizing and risking the lives of two young women, and this time you will pay for your crime. Let's go."

Once again, Superintendent Byrnes made headlines in the *New York Times* in the morning paper:

BYRNES' DAUGHTER RESCUED
AND THE KIDNAPPER CAPTURED
BYRNES SOLVES ANOTHER CASE IN SHORT ORDER
GENERAL ALEXANDER WILEY OF RECENT FAME
IS ARRAIGNED AS MASTERMIND OF PLOT

> Superintendent Byrnes' daughter, Miss Jessie Byrnes, and her friend, Miss Stella Manning, were rescued early Sunday morning by Byrnes, his "immortals," and two other men, and Byrnes captured the criminal mastermind himself out on the Hudson at midnight...

And this headline caused no cringing and agony, except on the part of General Wiley. It did cause great thankfulness and a happy celebration on the part of the Manning, Kane, Delacourte, and of course, the Byrnes families.

CHAPTER 22

New York City
November 1892

Papa awoke first, as was his habit, from the cot at the Delacourtes' to find his two dear ladies dreaming still, Stella in her bed, and Mama in Jessie's bed, all tucked safely away in Stella and Jessie's room. Papa knelt down by his cot and thanked the Lord again that Stella was safe—that both girls were safe—and returned to their families.

Today would be a joyous day, returning home on a bright but cold Monday morning. He was eager to know if Byrnes had caught the mastermind of the kidnapping plot last night and dressed quickly to go downstairs to see if the morning paper told the story.

And it did. *Amazing,* thought Papa. Although Byrnes' detective skills were well-known and awe-inspiring, only God alone could have orchestrated the splendid timing of finding the girls before they suffered more, and quickly discovering the trail of the instigator.

Mrs. Delacourte agreed as she poured coffee for Papa, saying without prompting that God surely had a hand in the safe and rapid return of Stella and Jessie and the tracking down of the architect of the crime. Mr. Delacourte soon joined them, and all three read the details of the story with great interest.

As Stella awakened in her own bed at the Delacourtes', she was happy to see Mama up and about, gathering her belongings. Mama came and sat on Stella's bed, hugged her, and said, "Stella, dear, I never dreamed last Friday what these past days would have been like. Papa and I are ever thankful for your safe return, and for Jessie's too, and we will have a proper celebration with the family and all our Woodlawn Heights friends later this week after you have rested and recuperated from your ordeal."

"I am ever so thankful too, Mama," said Stella as she sat up and gave Mama a hug. "It will be wonderful to go home and rest a bit before thinking about the future."

"We've much talking to do, Stella, because we want to be sure you will not be endangered in the future if you continue your work on the stage."

"I understand," said Stella, "and we will work through all the concerns. Right now, let's get ready for the day!"

As the two ladies came downstairs, dressed and coiffed, Papa and the Delacourtes greeted them and told them the details of the capture, and they all marveled together about the rapid detective work that finished the sordid tale.

"But who is this General Wiley?" asked Stella. "Why would an important man commit such a crime?"

"Ah, Stella," said Mr. Delacourte, "therein lies a tale. Back in 1885, then-detective Byrnes arrested General Alexander Wiley at his home on bribery charges. Wiley had been a Union Army hero at the Battle of Gettysburg and was at the time commander of the First Division of New York's National Guard and president of the board of health. He was, shall we say, well-connected and enjoyed a luxurious lifestyle and high social status.

"But the warrant for his arrest stated he had taken bribes in connection with the purchase of sites throughout the city for armories. Our Mayor Grace took one look at the evidence and filed charges with the district attorney. Hence, Byrnes was sent to serve the warrant and take him to police headquarters to question him, which he did. The mayor was not willing to set bail, and although General Wiley's friends tried to use their influence to free him from jail, Byrnes upheld the mayor's wishes, and Wiley faced not only the charges but disgrace in the eyes of his influential friends."

Mr. Delacourte continued by saying, "The general had two trials, with the juries deadlocked, resulting in neither a conviction nor an acquittal. Eventually, the district attorney dropped the charges against Wiley, and the indictment was dismissed. But although he was never convicted of taking a bribe, his political career ended, and in 1886, the governor honored his resignation as commander of the National Guard. Then in 1887, he was removed as president of the city's board of health.

"So, you see, he was 'ruined,' so to speak, socially and politically, and he withdrew to a quiet life, living at The Dakota, a very expensive and elegant building at Seventy-Second Street and Central Park West. The rumor was that he had family money to sustain himself, but according to the news article, he was obsessed with Superintendent Byrnes, was running out of funds to continue his lifestyle, and sought to both pay back Byrnes for his arrest and gain a substantial sum by the kidnapping."

"But," Stella commented, "Mr. Byrnes had nothing to do with his crime or bribery case. He merely arrested him. Why did he wish to strike back at Byrnes, and especially his family, in such a way?"

"Good question," said Mrs. Delacourte, "and who can probe the depths of the criminal mind? His wife and family left him after the trials, and perhaps he was bitter, and saw Superintendent Byrnes prospering and his family intact. I also suspect that in his rage and distorted mind, he was careless in choosing the men he used to carry out his plan—criminals known to Byrnes—and did not have the wherewithal to pull off such a crime."

"So very sad," said Stella, ever looking at the human side of things.

Just then, the door chime rang, and the maid brought Jessie and Superintendent Byrnes into the dining room. "Jessie!" called Stella as she jumped up to hug her dearest friend. "How are you feeling today?"

"So much better, Stella, and you are looking rested and well."

"Yes, and I am so grateful you and I are all in one piece, and the criminal has been caught. Thank you, Superintendent Byrnes," she said as she turned to him and gave him a heart-felt smile.

"No need to thank me, Miss Manning. Just doing my job," said Byrnes. "And I've stopped by to ask you a question and give you some information. And, of course, we'll need your statement and, later on, a testimony at the trial for the general and his co-conspirators."

"Yes, of course," said Stella. "But what is your question, sir?"

"I was curious," said Byrnes, "how you were able to draw the search party to the boxcar you were imprisoned in. In the excitement of finding you and Jessie, and seeing you safe, I did not ask that question of Mr. Kane and Mr. Manning."

"Ah, a good question, sir," said Stella. "You see," she said, pointing to the Tara Brooch she wore at her neck, "my gentleman friend Mr. Kane had recently inquired about this brooch and its significance and history. I had told him about it, and he had been quite interested in the design.

"Jessie and I found some pieces of chalk in the boxcar, and the door was secured with just enough open space to enable me to reach my arm through to draw the brooch's design, as large as I could, on the wooden side of the boxcar.

I thought Mr. Kane might be in the search party because we were in the railroad yards, and I knew he would recognize the symbol — that it would lead him straight to us."

"Very clever, Miss Manning," said Byrnes. "You were very clear thinking even in the midst of your troubles, the freezing weather, and the nighttime hour."

"Well, sir," said Stella, "Jessie and I had prayed very hard together, and I believe the inspiration was from God, whom we know was looking after us."

"Amen," said everyone at once, even the superintendent.

"Now to give you some information," said Byrnes. "My men and I searched the general's home late last night after he and his companion were secure, and we found a whole room filled with banker boxes, overflowing with paper. He had copies of every newspaper article written about me and the detective bureau, copies of many of the transcripts from court cases where I've had to testify, and other documents detailing my career. He was truly obsessed with me, a very sick thing indeed. And we also found samples of the writing paper he used to write the original note and other implicating evidence. He will be convicted."

"Such a terrible man," said Jessie.

But Stella commented, "A very mentally disturbed man too, and I shall pray for him to have some peace someday."

"Please, Inspector Byrnes, do have some breakfast," said Mrs. Delacourte. "You have put in some very long hours since Friday evening."

"Thank you, but I did catch a few hours' sleep, and I must be on my way. Jessie can stay, though, and I'll send a policeman to escort her home in a little while."

"Thank you, Father," said Jessie, giving the very burly policeman a big hug as they all walked him to the door and returned to enjoy some nourishment to start the day before the Manning family had to leave for home.

As they sat, chatting amiably, the door chime rang again, and this time it was the telegraph delivery man and the postman. "Several missives for the Misses Byrnes and Manning, if they are still here," said the delivery people.

Stella and Jessie opened the telegrams and letters at the table in front of the Delacourtes and Mama and Papa, and both looked at each other in wonder, eyes growing wider at each opening.

"Why, these are offers to perform elocutions at several venues and private functions all over the city in the coming weeks," said Stella.

"Yes, it seems many people want to see both of us again," laughed Jessie.

The Mannings and the Delacourtes looked at each other, and Mrs. Delacourte spoke first: "I am not surprised. Your readings at the Lyceum were outstanding, and now with the recent sad escapade, you have also become, shall I say, famous?"

"Oh my," responded Stella and Jessie all at once. "These invitations are the reason we worked so hard on our skills," said Stella, "and now I'm not sure what to say."

Papa said, "We need to consider your future very carefully, Stella. I will not have you endangered again, and I'm sure Superintendent Byrnes and his wife will have the same concern for you, Jessie."

"Yes, yes, I can well understand," said Mr. Delacourte. "I propose a plan. Let us respond to these invitations, and others that may arrive, saying the young ladies need a respite after their ordeal, and they will respond later this month about accepting any invitations. We'll all have time to rest, think, and decide what is best. We'll get advice from Superintendent Byrnes about safety, and we'll take some time to sort all this out."

"An excellent plan," replied Papa, "and now I must take my wife and daughter home. I believe my nephew Colin has arranged transport, which should arrive soon."

"I will help Stella pack her trunk," said Jessie, "and we have to pack my trunk too. Let's go, Stella."

"One moment before you leave, young ladies," announced Mrs. Delacourte. "I want to let you know that we have rescheduled the banquet planned for the completion of your class, which we had to postpone, of course. It is scheduled for Saturday night, November 19, and I'll be sending out invitations today."

"We will still have the banquet?" asked Jessie.

"Of course," answered Mrs. Delacourte. "We still need to celebrate our new elocution graduates from the inaugural session of the school."

"Wonderful idea," said Papa, "and we shall plan to be there. But for now, let's push through this miserable melting snow toward home."

And so they did in a beautiful enclosed landau carriage Colin pulled up a short while later for a well-deserved comfortable ride homeward in the chill but bright winter air.

How good it felt to be home, thought Stella. With all the glamour and excitement of the city, being back in her peaceful village and familiar home was just heaven. Jo, Michael, and Alice greeted her heartily, and little Alfred came bounding into her arms, smothering her face with kisses.

"Really, Stella," said Jo, "we were all so distraught. No one could sleep, and neighbors kept coming by for news. Luca organized a prayer vigil for the entire neighborhood on Saturday evening, the priest came, and you should have seen the candles and prayers offered for you and Jessie. It was powerful."

"And as the night ended, we were found," said Stella. "God is so good, and he honors the prayers of the faithful, as Tom has told me."

"He does indeed," added Mama. "Now let's get you settled and filled up with some good Irish food."

And so the day progressed with many neighbors and friends stopping by to greet Stella and welcome her home. Small celebrations seemed to happen every hour. She felt so treasured and valued within the circle of her family and friends. The only one missing was Tom, but she knew he had to work and would come to see her on his first day off.

Falling asleep in her own bed, the one she shared with Jo again, Stella whispered a thankful prayer to God, now her special friend she knew, because she had accepted His free gift during her ordeal. How special it felt to be His, and she couldn't wait to tell Tom and get some advice on growing her new relationship with her Savior.

Family life in Woodlawn Heights fell into its usual pattern, and the cold continued to grow. Winter seemed much colder in New York, thought Stella, and another snowfall seemed to deepen the cold. She and Jo and Mama spent time each day sewing, she helped Alice with her lessons, they cooked warm and satisfying meals, and Stella helped Papa in the shop. Both Michael and Alice had made more friends now, and each divided time among school, home responsibilities for Alice and watchmaking duties for Michael, and outings with friends, especially to enjoy the snow.

Alfred spent time with his special little friend Liam and was also learning phonics and gaining early reading skills. And Jo and Luca began planning their wedding. They were thinking a Christmas wedding would be so wonderful, and when their parents agreed, they began active planning. They would marry in the front parlor among family and close friends and would celebrate at Uncle Nicholas' larger home with a grand feast that Mama and Mrs. Rossi would prepare. Stella would stand up with Jo, of course, and Vittoria and Alice would be bridesmaids.

Jo wanted a simple wedding dress, a soft cream color with a lacy high neck, puffy sleeves, and six-inch deep cuffs with lace edging. Mama talked her into four small rows of lace going down the bodice to the waist, with a repeat of the lace in another four horizontal small rows at the hem. A short shoulder-length poufy veil would crown her hair. The three Manning women got to work on the dress and veil as soon as all the details were decided, and Alice helped too.

Luca's shoe business was in a building with an apartment upstairs, and he had been busy readying it with fresh paint, some clever built-ins, and good buys on used furniture. Luca was excellent at trading services for supplies for their home, so the residence was fast taking shape. They would be neighbors.

During these busy but serene first few days back in her family, Stella began pondering her future in the elocution world, and with Tom. She was absolutely sure she wanted to spend the rest of her life with Tom. She loved him so. And she also wanted to be on the stage. Not forever, but for a time, to explore her potential and live out her dream. Could she do both? Tom had said he wouldn't rush her, and she knew he meant it. He also had goals to work on in his railroad career. She knew they needed to start talking about their future.

And she needed to explore with Papa and Mama, with the Delacourtes, and with Tom about the safety issue. New York was a wide-open city, growing rapidly in all directions, with many cultural opportunities but also with an increasingly coarse population and an intensive criminal element. She had heard about city government corruption and crime-fighting activities, and even with Superintendent Byrnes on the job, the city could be a dangerous place. She wanted to be safe but not isolated from the world. What were the best options to consider? Were there even any options?

In the midst of this dilemma, a long letter arrived from the Delacourtes, which offered a unique solution. They proposed an amazing offer if the Mannings and Stella were willing to consider it. Essentially, they would hire Stella to be a resident counselor to the new elocution class starting in January at the Delacourte home and school. Stella, as a successful recent graduate of the initial program, would live with the new girls, encourage them, help in their training, and also be free to accept elocution assignments at carefully selected and safe locations in the city.

They had received a deluge of applicants, they reported, and were in the process of selecting students for the next class. And the next class would be larger because, as it turned out, the Delacourtes were excited to report they had had an opportunity to buy the townhouse next to theirs, and they would be combining the two residences/school areas for more space for students. Classes would resume in January.

But the opportunity grew better as Stella read the offer. Jessie would also be asked to be a resident counselor, playing the same role as Stella, and they would fulfill elocution assignments together under the watchful protection of a police escort that Superintendent Byrnes would provide for each outing.

The Delacourtes said they had been fielding numerous requests for not only Stella and Jessie, but for the other graduates too, and with safety always in mind, their mission to offer elocution as an antidote to the vulgarity and coarseness of New York's many forms of mass entertainment seemed to be catching on. They were elated their graduates were so well-received, many others were seeking training in the Delsarte method, and elocution was growing as an art form in the city.

This news was immensely joyful to Stella, to see the Delacourtes' dream flourishing. She realized the dreams of others had become as important as her own. And the offer was intriguing to Stella and her parents. She would realize her dream of performing elocution, would be able to study the art continuously and help new students, could live in the city in a familiar and secure home, have safety concerns covered, and, she added, live closer to Tom so that they could see each other often.

An offer well worth considering, Papa said, but he also said he would like to learn more about Byrnes' offer of security for the girls. He would be traveling into the city early in the following week to attend a watchmaker's guild meeting and would plan to visit the superintendent and the Delacourtes.

Stella was elated and dashed off a note to Tom with some of the details and to get his thoughts and ask for prayers too. She also remembered dear Miss D, who told her to pray about how God would like her to use her gift to His glory and to help others, and the Delacourtes' offer seemed to be a fit with this wisdom.

But she would pray about it.

CHAPTER 23

New York City
November and December 1892

*T*om could hardly wait to see Stella again. He had started the week fairly well-exhausted, physically and emotionally, from the events of the preceding weekend, and even though he worked long hours all week, he had slept well and felt refreshed. He and his father had had some good meals together and some relaxing time a couple of evenings when he had arrived home in time for supper.

He was concerned about his father, though not for his health but for his relative isolation. The elder Kane had agreed to minimize his University Settlement Society work during the cold winter months but missed the contact with his "students," young immigrants in the squalid Lower East Side eager to learn English and improve their opportunity to not only survive but thrive. His father was such a giving soul, Tom knew, and although he enjoyed cooking, visiting with a few friends occasionally, and following politics, he led a relatively isolated life, especially now with the cold weather.

The note from Stella about her possible move back into the Delacourte residence and a start to her elocution performances gave him an idea for some outings together that might help get his father through the winter before the easier days of spring arrived. And with Sella closer by too, they could all share some meals together.

And he was thrilled about Stella's offer for all the reasons she was elated. It seemed God was at work in her life, and in theirs too. They had much talking and planning to do, and she had hinted the day of the rescue at some special news she had to tell him, something about God that he would be happy about. He was eager to know that news.

Work on the railroad was going well. He had received several kudos from his supervisors, not only for his diligent and careful work on the freights, but also for a few ideas for improved operations in service that he had offered, which were well-received and implemented.

And this weekend, he would visit Stella, and perhaps take his father along too.

"Superintendent, thanks for seeing me," said Mr. Manning, "and please tell me your ideas and proposed actions for keeping our girls safe if they decide to pursue their elocution careers this winter through the Delacourtes' offer, which I'm sure you've heard about by now."

"Yes, indeed, Mr. Manning," said Byrnes, chewing on a cigar. "My Jessie is so determined to have a career in elocution, as I think your daughter is, and the plans the Delacourtes have put forth seem quite excellent. They are fine people, as you know, Mr. Manning, and I admire their determination to elevate our city, while so many others are intent on tearing it down.

"Of course, Mr. Manning, our two girls will eventually marry fine young men and settle down, and I've already seen two examples of fine young men in Mr. Kane and your nephew. But in the meantime, we must encourage them to fulfill their dream of being on the stage while keeping them safe, eh?"

"We should indeed, Superintendent," said Mr. Manning. "And what are your plans?"

Byrnes continued, "Sadly, I did not realize until this latest terrible affair how vulnerable my family might be because of my work. I have five daughters, Mr. Manning, and while two are married and in their husbands' care, my youngest three are still at home and under my care. I am determined Jessie, Amy, and May will remain safe at all times, but I cannot restrict their lives to the point they have no freedom.

"So I have decided to retain private guardians, my own agents, to be with my girls whenever they leave the house. They will always be nearby, though not intruding in their lives, and they will be armed. If Jessie and your daughter go for a walk along Fifth Avenue, for example, my man will be nearby, keeping an eye on them. If they are performing on a stage — and only in an acceptable venue, of course — my man will be close by in the audience, and another one will be backstage. They will secure any facilities ahead of time to ensure no bad elements are present.

"I shall also have police patrols frequent my home and the Delacourtes', and I've asked Jessie to report to me any suspicions she may have. I don't know if you know this or not, Mr. Manning, but the two men who took our girls had been watching them for a while, and Jessie had observed their watching. She did not report it to me, but if any such incidents occur in the future, she definitely will."

"You seem to have a good plan, Superintendent," said Mr. Manning.

"Always my job to think ahead, Mr. Manning, and now I am on high alert about the extra measures I need to protect my own family, which, regrettably, I had not considered earlier."

Satisfied, Papa shook the superintendent's hand and thanked him again for his amazingly swift resolution of the kidnapping and safe return of Stella.

Another visit with the Delacourtes to understand details of the arrangements for Stella and Jessie to be in residence again—and for vetting all elocution opportunities—went well, and Papa returned home to report a positive outcome on his mission, which gave Stella a lot of reasons to rejoice.

The days of the next week flew by, with Mama, Jo, and Stella sewing Jo's wedding dress, Jo trying to stand still for fittings as the beautiful dress took shape, and all the family busy at their various pursuits. Papa was extraordinarily busy with new orders with Christmas coming up, and they all reminisced how they had worked together this previous season in Dublin with the Guinness watch order. This year, Michael's skills had grown considerably, so he was able to take some of the time pressure off Papa. They laughed together how quickly the year had gone by and how many changes they had seen, all good except one, but that blessedly resolved.

Alfred had a whole village set up now for his train set in the room he shared with Michael, who complained constantly about "trains, trains, everywhere..." but enjoyed playing with the set and the wooden village he had helped Alfred build. Alice, becoming more ladylike every day, was starting to enjoy poetry and literature, and she eagerly shared this new and growing interest with Stella.

But Stella's mind was on Tom increasingly as the week lengthened because she knew he would come to visit on Saturday, and she couldn't wait to see him.

And he did, arriving midmorning, along with the elder Mr. Kane, whom everyone was also delighted to see. After a special hug with Stella and greetings all around, plus a tour of the new train village upstairs with Alfred, Tom and his father went downstairs to greet Papa and Michael, both working in the shop, and then returned to visit with the ladies. Knowing Stella likely wanted time alone with Tom, Mr. Kane suggested he help with any food preparations. Mama reluctantly agreed, laughing that having a man in the kitchen was a bit odd, but she believed she could put his culinary skills to work on a couple of projects.

Stella and Tom adjourned to the nearby but somewhat private, big parlor to hear each other's news of the week and sit close, looking at each other with hands clasped. In the sunny parlor with the rays of the winter sun striking Tom's deep brown eyes, Stella remembered that moment on the stage after her final recitation when she had looked out at Tom and knew that she was in love with him. She had not told him of that moment, so did so tenderly now. He caressed her face with his hand and said, "I will treasure that moment and your telling of it," then paused and said, "but I was way ahead of you, Stella, darling. I knew that feeling in the few weeks after we had met and had spent some time together, and I had hoped you would share the same sentiment before long."

"And I do," said Stella, laughing and squeezing his hands, "and I also want to tell you about accepting that free gift you told me about."

"Yes, that's a story I want to especially hear today," answered Tom.

"I had been thinking about our conversation that day at your home, and I talked to Jessie about the gift, and, lo and behold, she had accepted it earlier in her life. I thought and prayed some more, thinking I was just not good enough for the Lord to accept me into His family, but then I remembered your words. You said that He loves us and offers us a free gift we cannot earn, through His grace, and that we just need to ask Him to forgive our sins and believe in Him, and the gift of life forever is ours."

"Yes," said Tom, "it's a wonderful and amazing offer, isn't it?"

"To be sure, and I was ready to accept it but then got caught up in all the excitement of the performance, all wrapped up in myself and not wanting to slow down and take that important step. Then, as you know, the kidnapping happened, and I was thrust into a bad situation. Yet, even then, Tom, I knew God was with me, and that Jesus was right there in the night on the water, and in the boxcar…" Stella began to cry softly as Tom held her hands and brought them to his heart, and said, "Yes, my darling, go on if you can."

Stella, tears streaming down her face, continued, "So I asked Him to come into my heart, I accepted His gift, and although the situation was still dire, I had a sense of peace come over me, a warmth in the cold cabin of the boat. I can't explain it, Tom. It was a peace in the midst of chaos and uncertainty."

"Ah, Stella, that's what He does," said Tom as he dried her tears with his pocket handkerchief. "He gives us peace we cannot understand and comfort when we need it."

"He did, and He continued comforting Jessie and me throughout the whole ordeal and even gave me the idea and the chalk to draw the Tara Brooch sign so that you could find us in the bitter cold. God is so good!"

"He is good all the time. I'm so happy for you, Stella, and I'm rejoicing because now we share an even more remarkable closeness because of our walk with the Lord together. He has given us to each other, and He is part of us. Here's a mental picture, dear one. Think of a threesome: you, I, and Jesus, in a circle holding hands, a loving, secure, unbroken circle shared together."

"What a beautiful image, Tom," whispered Stella.

As they sat with each other, their family nearby, sharing tender moments, Stella remembered the Delacourtes' offer and asked Tom what he thought of it.

"It sounds ideal from every point of view, Stella, and when Father and I visited with your Papa in the shop, he told me of his conversation with Superintendent Byrnes about safety, which was a big concern I had. But it seems that factor is well accounted for, so if the Delacourtes' offer is one you favor, I say it's serendipitous and well-earned."

"I know it will be a wonderful opportunity for me to pursue elocution and help new students. You can work hard to reach your goals, and with me in the city, we can plan our times together, Tom, and look at our future. We'll include your Father too and start to become our own little family..."

"Stella, you are so thoughtful to think of him. He's becoming increasingly isolated, I think, so including him in some of our activities will be good. And you can enjoy his cooking when you come to visit."

"Then we have a plan!" laughed Stella, planting a kiss on his cheek.

The day progressed with family talk, a fine midday meal together, and Tom and Mr. Kane heading back into the city in late afternoon. The two families planned to be together again at the Delacourtes' farewell dinner on next Saturday the nineteenth and then would attend church together the next morning at St. Patrick's Cathedral. And Stella and Tom would also try to see each other the Friday before the dinner.

As part of their recent correspondence, the Delacourtes had invited the entire Manning family, plus Luca, to spend the weekend at their home, starting on Friday night, and Colin had already invited Jessie out for that evening, he had told Stella, so a foursome looked a possibility for Friday, and if Jo and Luca wished to join them, a six-some was even better. *What a wonderful weekend to look forward to*, thought Stella.

And the week flew by quickly, with sewing for Jo's wedding and all the usual Manning family routines, and before long, they had bundled up and were heading into the city with great anticipation. Friday turned out to be a snow day, and the city looked very handsome with its white frosty covering. Central Park's trees glistened with a shiny ice coating, "looking like a fairyland," Alice commented, with the ice kept in place by the below-freezing temperatures.

The Delacourtes were delighted to meet the rest of the Manning clan and welcomed them to their home heartily, this time under happy circumstances. Mama said, "Mrs. Delacourte, we are overwhelmed by your kind hospitality, and we have given young Alfred strict orders to be on his best behavior."

"He has already discovered our telephone, and my husband is showing him how to make a call."

"Oh, dear, he will want to see every new device you may have," replied Mama. "He is intensely curious."

As the older people settled into a relaxing evening, Tom arrived with Colin, who had already collected Jessie, to Stella's great delight, and the four of them, plus Jo and Luca, set off for ice skating in Central Park, which was Colin's suggestion for the perfect way to spend a late-winter afternoon and early evening in the city.

Colin had actually acquired a sleigh, which were hard to come by and very expensive to rent, but his father's carriage business connection paid off again, so they had the great good fun of sleighing in the park before skating. Stella held on to Tom tightly as they encountered many other sleighs, going much too fast and quite close together, it seemed. But mounted policemen were on duty, and Colin told them they all had horses fast enough to catch runaways and speeders. As they glided along West Drive, Stella noticed the impressive statue of Daniel Webster and also the hugely impressive Dakota apartments in the background. She remembered for a fleeting moment that the mastermind of the kidnapping had lived there, but she quickly pushed such eerie thoughts aside amidst the laughter and fun of the sleighride.

Tucked in with blankets and wrapped in warm cloaks, gloves, hats, and keeping their hands warm in furry muffs — which Jessie had brought for the girls to enjoy — Stella, Jessie, and Jo were almost giddy with fun, while Tom, Colin, and Luca, also warmly wrapped, concentrated on the traffic and keeping the sleigh safe.

As they arrived at the lake, they found a place to rent skates for twenty-five cents an hour. Skate chairs were also available for young children or older people who wanted to go out on the ice but could not skate. Stella saw that several men were engaged in a raucous game of curling in one section of the lake. *So many people of all ages, loving life and winter*, thought Stella, and she fell a little more in love with her new home, this city of New York she had not wanted to live in just a few short months ago.

They all dared to try skating, urged on by Colin, and soon found their footing. Wobbly at first, Stella and Jessie discovered their elocution training in balance and body control helped them gain a nice glide, and they showed the others some of the tricks they had learned. They all skated in a line, holding hands, then the couples skated together. The three men held a short race with the girls cheering them on, and Luca, who was used to running the bases in baseball, won easily.

Keeping warm was not a problem at first with such activity, but their cheeks soon glowed rosy red from the cold. Stella blushed further when Tom asked her to dance with him on the ice, and she marveled at his strength as he guided her through a slow dance. It seemed as if they were the only two people on the lake, alone in the world, looking into each other's eyes.

Finally feeling the cold, they returned the skates and climbed aboard the sleigh for another busy and exhilarating ride through the park, which was getting more and more congested by the hour. Colin remarked there were other places to skate in the city, but Central Park was the most beloved of all and would always be crowded on a snow day.

Waiting for them at the Delacourtes' home were a warm beef soup and a hearty bread, which they devoured gratefully, telling all about their great sleighing and skating adventure. Even Jo, who was usually reticent, described her excitement in great detail. Stella thought how happy Jo was in America, and now almost a bride, and she was, once again, so grateful that Papa had brought them all here. Surely God was truly in charge of their lives and blessing them. Why had she ever doubted?

A wonderful morning was planned for Saturday. Tom had invited Alfred to be his guest for a tour of Grand Central Depot, where he had discovered his love for trains as a young boy. Alfred was beside himself with joy, not only to see the trains and the depot, but to ride the El and have a day of adventure in the city with Tom's mindful care. Jo and Alice were allowed to accompany Mama and Mrs. Delacourte for a visit to A. T. Stewart's Department Store, their own special adventure. Papa and Mr. Delacourte went over to the Fifth Avenue Hotel to ensure that all was in readiness for the banquet.

Stella and Jessie spent some time together at the house, back in their old room, ensuring their outfits for the evening were in order, but mostly to just be together again and talk about the future.

"First of all, Stella, tell me about you and Tom," said Jessie.

"We are in love and plan to be together forever," sighed Stella. "And we're not rushing into the future but looking at it together in light of our goals and timing. He has many things to accomplish in his railroad career, and I have my elocution work to get started. We're supporting each other in these endeavors and in the meantime hope to spend a lot of time together."

"Very sensible and logical, Stella, but don't you yearn to be with him, really with him, as his wife? Are you not tempted to push aside goals and strivings and just melt into his arms?"

"Oh yes, Jessie, but we want to put our life together bit by bit, and yet sometimes, I do want to just rush ahead to marry him. Frankly, I'm not sure we can both be sensible and give ourselves some time to grow in our careers before tying the knot, but we've vowed to try."

"So are you engaged?" asked Jessie.

"Well, I guess not officially, but I hope we will be soon. And what about you and Colin?"

"I'm terribly fond of him, Stella, and I'm hoping he'll ask my father if he may court me, and I think the answer will be yes."

"Your father spoke well of him to my father after our rescue," said Stella, "and I think he respects him and likes him."

"It seems we have both found wonderful men, and now we also have a chance to establish our elocution careers with the Delacourtes' offer," said Jessie. "And I don't see any conflict between the two wonderful options. Do you, Stella?"

"No. I think we are blessed to be asked to serve as resident teaching assistants, perform when we choose to, and also nurture our relationships with our fine gentlemen. I'm so excited about living in the city and all these amazing things that are happening in our lives. And since I've come to know the Lord, as you do, Jessie, I plan to ask Him to guide me each step of the way."

"Yes, Stella! We will do that, and we will have some great times together. Amen!"

"But right now," Jessie continued, "we need to bathe and start on our hair arranging to prepare for our banquet.

Think of it, Stella, we are the first graduates of the Delacourte School of Elocution and have a real opportunity to be on the stage, help new students, and foster the increase of this fine form of entertainment in the city. We are pioneers in a sense."

CHAPTER 24

New York City
November and December 1892

And the banquet was a wonderful celebration of the young pioneers.

Held in a private dining room of the Fifth Avenue Hotel at Two Hundred Fifth Avenue, which filled Fifth Avenue between Twenty-Third and Twenty-Fourth Streets, at the southwest corner of elegant Madison Square, it was a pure delight. The hotel's sober exterior of plain Italianate palazzo-style in brick and white marble revealed a richly appointed interior. The banquet was held in a beautiful high-ceilinged room with deep crown molding and paneled wall murals between evenly spaced Corinthian columns and lighted by large brass and glass chandeliers.

Considered by many the most exclusive hotel in the city, the Fifth Avenue Hotel featured the first passenger elevator installed in an American hotel and advertised private bathrooms and fireplaces in every guest room. Its gilt wood, crimson-and-green curtains, rosewood, and rich carpet seemed to complete its offering of grandeur and comfort. It had hosted numerous famous guests over the years, including members of the British royal family and American Presidents Grant and Arthur.

But tonight, it hosted some very excited young ladies and their families and close friends. The new elocutionists, dressed in the flowing gowns of elocution performance, each hosted a table, and the Delacourtes sat at their own table encircled by the others. The gentlemen and ladies were attired in their best, and Stella was delighted to see Tom wearing his very handsome "Sunday clothes," as he called them. The Delacourtes had graciously invited the elder Mr. Kane, whom they had gotten to know during the recent calamity with Stella and Jessie, and Stella glowed to see all her dear loved ones surrounding her on this special night, save an exhausted Alfred, who was tended by the Delacourtes' cook back at the house.

The menu was extraordinary, served in five courses over the evening, and placards at each table listed the courses, which started with asparagus soup, followed by a lettuce salad with cheese fingers. The main course consisted of two entrees: baked salmon with hollandaise sauce and roast chicken with potato balls. Ham timbales with cucumber sauce and green peas accompanied the entrees. Dessert was chocolate mousse with pastries and lemon sherbet ice cream, followed by coffee and a selection of liqueurs.

The evening, it seemed to Stella, was set in slow motion, with easy ambiance and time for the students to visit other tables between courses to meet friends and family. Stella was delighted to see Colin's friend from the Columbia University, Clarence, who had helped her attend the elocution conference, and who was obviously smitten with one — or perhaps both — of the Billingham girls and had been invited as their special guest.

Superintendent Byrnes, who rushed in late as everyone was getting seated, was well-received, and Stella concluded his quick thinking and heroic deeds in the kidnapping had earned him some new respect and admiration among the parents of the students.

Mr. and Mrs. Delacourte spoke briefly, thanking all the families for supporting their daughters' efforts to train in elocution, and then giving a brief summary of the class and all the students had learned. Mr. Delacourte spoke of their plans to enlarge the school in January and his excitement at seeing the growth of elocution as a genteel form of entertainment in the city, and Mrs. Delacourte spoke of the hard work of the girls and how much she valued each of them.

As each student stepped forward to receive a certificate and handshake, the families clapped and cheered. Then, with the Delacourtes sitting on chairs and the students surrounding them, their picture was taken by the same gentleman who had taken the professional pictures during the last weeks of class. The evening ended with many hugs and promises to keep in touch and a hearty round of applause from the attendees to thank the Delacourtes for the excellent evening and for their very successful work with the graduates.

A sweet goodnight kiss from Tom before he and his father left for home, and a brief conversation to coordinate details for the next day, left Stella mellow and happy. Back at the Delacourtes with her family surrounding her, she fell asleep with all her world in order, she thought, thanks be to God.

After early-morning coffee, a warm goodbye, and extra thanks to the Delacourtes, the Manning party left for church services at St. Patrick's Cathedral, a visit the senior Mannings had long anticipated since coming to New York City. Papa excitedly told the family about the construction of the magnificent edifice, which he had put to memory.

"Work to build the cathedral was begun in 1858, but the American Civil War halted work. Its building resumed in 1865, it was completed in 1878, and dedicated in May of

1879. It's made of brick and clad in marble, but not just any old marble, but pure white tuckahoe marble from a famous quarry up in the Bronx."

Papa's enthusiasm continued, "The beautiful spires you'll see were added not too long ago, in 1888, and they are the tallest structures in New York City and the second highest in America right now. They soar an amazing 330 feet, and the church absolutely dominates Midtown Manhattan with its beauty and neo-Gothic grandeur."

"Papa," said Jo, "I'm thinking the cathedral is named after our Irish saint because there are so many Irish in New York, and it's wonderful for us Dubliner-New Yorkers that it shares its name with our beloved St. Patrick's cathedral in Dublin."

"Yes, wonderful, Jo, but, ah, our Dublin cathedral dates back to medieval times. Everything in America is so much newer!"

Then Papa continued, "And do you know, children, here's an interesting story of two cathedrals named for St. Patrick: Our Dublin St. Patrick's had fallen into a state of complete disrepair early in this century and was about to be torn down. But when I was a young man, a member of the Guinness family, Benjamin Lee Guinness, paid for a full-scale restoration of the building, between 1860 and 1865, at the same time our New York St. Patrick's was waiting to be built while the Civil War waged here."

"That's very remarkable, Papa," said Michael, "that the two cathedrals we know have their coming-to-life stories in common."

"God is always at work, building and refreshing His church, Michael," said Papa.

"And refreshing hearts and mind too," said Stella as she watched the breathtaking cathedral come into view, taking up a whole city block between Fifty and Fifty-First Streets, Madison Avenue, and Fifth Avenue. Even more breathtaking was meeting up with Tom and walking hand in hand with him, and with her family, into the huge and ornate nave, surrounded by tall stained-glass windows reaching upward to the enormous, elaborately decorated ceiling.

As Tom whispered, "Stella, three thousand people can worship here..." one of the cathedral's two pipe organs burst into life, bringing the church alive with sonorous sacred music that almost overwhelmed the senses.

Seated together, the Mannings, Luca, and Tom filled nearly a whole row of the highly polished pews. Stella could see how moved Mama and Papa were by the beauty and sacred surroundings, the ambient light floating in the tall windows and casting sparkles of color throughout, and the sweet smell of incense. Even Alfred looked about in silent awe. The service was equally inspiring, and Stella felt the same closeness to Tom at communion as she had at The Little Church Around the Corner. Comparing the two in her mind as they walked back out into the bright winter sunshine, however, she decided she preferred the intimacy of the Little Church over the grandeur of the cathedral, but it was truly amazing to worship in such a beautiful place.

The whole family traveled to Tom's home to accept Mr. Kane's previous invitation to sample some of his cuisine, which had won praise from Stella and Colin on earlier visits. He greeted them heartily and made them feel right at home with some warm cider in the cozy flat he shared with Tom. The compelling aroma of fresh-baked bread and the friendly ambience soon had everyone talking and relaxing, while Mr. Kane brought out some mementoes from his railroad days for Alfred to enjoy. This activity was great good fun for Alfred following his exhilarating day at the Grand Central Depot with Tom.

Dinner was announced, and Mr. Kane said he had decided to serve a typical English boiled dinner consisting of slow-cooked beef, carrots, potatoes, leeks, rutabaga with parsley sauce, and, of course, fresh bread. This feast he served on a side table buffet style, and the many guests found comfortable seating here and there around the dining room and parlor to share the meal. Tom said a blessing, and the feast was on. Mr. Kane had prepared a delicious caraway seed and lemon cake for dessert, which he served with a light lemon sauce.

"You are an excellent cook," said Mama, "and Tom tells me you have perfected many recipes in the past few years as the Kane family chef."

"He likely exaggerates, but I do find it stimulating and challenging to keep us both well-fed, and I usually send Tom off with a nutritious meal or two to sustain him through his long work hours.

"And Mrs. Manning, dear Esther, if I may be so bold to call you, this small offering cannot compare to the many times of excellent hospitality and delicious Irish cuisine at your home. Tom and I are indebted to your kindness."

The afternoon ended all too soon, and the Mannings wanted to get on the road to home with some daylight remaining, so goodbyes were said, and Stella promised Tom she would drop him a note with all the family plans for the rest of the month and December, and they would figure out times to be together.

"It's the Christmas season, Stella darling, a blessed time of year, and we will celebrate it together for the first time," said Tom.

"Yes, dear Tom, and to think that last Christmas I had no idea I would be here in New York and surrounded by so many new and wonderful happenings and people. And that I would meet you. You are truly a gift to me."

"And you to me, Stella."

The rest of November flew by, and as December's first days began, all were busy focusing on preparations for Jo's wedding on Christmas Eve morning, decorating the house for Christmas, and freeing up Papa's time to fulfill his Christmas orders.

Early in the month, Stella received a letter from the Delacourtes asking if she would consider partnering with Jessie to participate in a Christmas pageant by presenting four Christmas elocutions for the congregation and neighborhood of the Little Church Around the Corner, which delighted Stella in every way. The date requested was Sunday evening, December 14, and everyone in the family agreed Stella should take this opportunity because all activities were on schedule in Woodlawn Heights.

"A Christmas elocution! How very exciting," Stella commented, "and to be held in such a beautiful place." And she knew Tom would be there.

The Delacourtes had chosen two pieces for each of the girls, and they asked if Stella could come to town for practice early in the weekend with Jessie and to tour the church to plan their presentation's movements. In addition, the Delacourtes were in heavy planning mode for the January class and would like to consult on a myriad of details. The girls could stay at the house, of course, and perhaps have time for a little Christmas shopping.

So Stella rode into the city with Colin on Friday, December 12, and she and Jessie spent some planning time with the Delacourtes for the new class then got right to work on their elocutions. The pageant included music and songs, scripture reading, and a festive reception afterward, with the elocutions spaced throughout the evening service. Stella would do the first elocution early in the program, presenting "In the Bleak Midwinter" by Christina Rossetti, which Miss Rossetti had written in 1872. Then midway through the celebration, both would recite John Milton's "On the Morning of Christ's Nativity," a somewhat longer piece Milton had composed in 1629 when he was in his early twenties.

Finally, two shorter pieces would round out the end of the program, again interspersed with music and scripture and a short homily by Reverend Houghton. Jessie would read "The Christmas of 1888" by John Greenleaf Whittier, and Stella's final presentation would be "Now Let the Angel Song Break Forth" by the Reverend M. D. Conway written in December 1863 during the Civil War.

Both girls were excited about their readings and so happy to be performing together again, so Saturday was busy practicing and perfecting their presentations. The Delacourtes invited Tom and Colin to join them for supper on Saturday, and Stella and Jessie performed a rehearsal of their pieces for them, with Tom and Colin beaming and applauding. Some good rest and a long sleep were next on the agenda.

The evening of the pageant was a cold one with snow threatening, but attendees began filling the courtyard and streaming into the Little Church, and it was filled to near capacity with parishioners and neighborhood friends about an hour before the program started. Tom and his father arrived early to wish Stella and Jessie well and to find a seat up close to the altar area where the program was staged. Boughs of greenery brought the pungent scent of the forest into the church, and tall flickering candles highlighted the beautiful altar. The atmosphere, while electric with excitement about the pageant, held a peaceful, sacred aura.

Stella and Jessie walked through their elocutions silently and unobtrusively near the altar for a final time while the audience gathered when suddenly a nearby voice cried out, and Stella saw a woman running up the center aisle toward her.

"Stella! Stella Manning! Oh my goodness, I can't believe it."

Stella stared incredulously as Miss Dowling, her very own Miss D, embraced her with tears streaming down her face. Amazed and stunned, and completely overjoyed, Stella returned her embrace and found her own tears. "Miss D, you are here, in New York..."

Then more hugs and tears. Finally, both recovered enough to speak, as Stella introduced Jessie and pulled Miss D to a corner to find out what fate had brought them together again.

"You just won't believe it, Stella. My father's elder sister, dear aunt Mary, whom I'm named after, passed away last summer and left her entire New York estate to me. She was a widow with no children and no heirs on her wealthy husband's side, and only my father's family on her side. Her home is a lovely townhome, small by comparison to some of the others, but near Central Park just off Fifth Avenue, and it seems I have inherited it and a bequest to enjoy it for the rest of my life."

"Quite amazing, and you came alone to New York in winter?" said Stella.

"Father said it was time I found my way in the world, Stella, and he booked a first-class passage for me and my maid Kitty on a swift steamboat just before the Atlantic weather closed in, with orders to the estate solicitor to see me safely and well-settled. So here I am, recently arrived and just getting situated. My first mission was to find you in Woodlawn Heights, but I had seen the Little Church's program listed when I visited here last Sunday, and I thought it would be a wonderful thing to go to the pageant and hear the elocutions. And then when I received tonight's program, saw your name, and then saw you, I nearly fainted with surprise and delight. Oh my goodness, I do need to sit down..."

"I know just where you can sit," said Stella. And she took Miss D to meet Tom and his father, who made room in their nearby pew for Miss D to join them. "Miss Dowling, please meet my very special friend, Mr. Thomas Kane, and his father, also Mr. Thomas Kane. Gentlemen, this lovely lady is my precious Miss D, my dear friend and mentor from Dublin, newly arrived in New York to live."

"The same Miss D you have spoken of so warmly, Stella?" asked Tom as he graciously bowed to Miss D, as did his father.

"The very same, Tom, and I can hardly believe it. We'll have time to talk after the service, and believe me, there is quite a story here."

"Miss Dowling," said the elder Mr. Kane, "it is a delight to meet you, and Tom and I will be honored to have your company for the program. Do make yourself comfortable," as he held out his hand to help Miss D into the pew, looking down at her as if she were a Christmas present given just to him.

"Thank you, Mr. Kane," murmured Miss D, blushing slightly, and she was cordially engaged with him in pleasant conversation within a few seconds.

Stella and Tom looked at each other and grinned, and Jessie rolled her eyes.

The pageant was a huge success, and of course, the Delacourtes were there. Stella noticed the undercover men that Superintendent Byrnes had stationed in two locations in the church only because Jessie pointed them out surreptitiously to her. She felt safe knowing the two big men were nearby and relaxed into the performances. She and Jessie received many kudos afterward at the reception. And Miss D was practically speechless after seeing Stella perform her elocutions. The only words she could utter were "extraordinary, completely exceptional."

The Delacourtes were elated to meet Miss D because they had heard of her early work with Stella, and Miss D was amazed to learn of Stella's progress in elocution and completion of the first class at the Delacourte School of Elocution. Mr. and Mrs. Delacourte invited everyone back to the house for dessert, giving all a chance to relax after the vigorous and exciting evening.

"What an unexpected, amazing turn of events," Stella exclaimed as Miss D finished her Coming to America story for all, and the Delacourtes promptly said, "And we'll be neighbors."

Stella could hardly wait to tell her family about Miss D's arrival, but before she drove home with Colin on Monday afternoon, she and Jessie did spend some time Monday shopping at A. T. Stewart's — with their Byrnes-provided "guardians" nearby — for some Christmas gifts with the honorarium each had received from the performance. Miss D had asked them to visit her new home for tea, but Jessie had to return home for a family activity, so Superintendent Byrnes' men took Jessie home and let Stella off at Miss D's townhome, where Colin would collect her later for the trip back to Woodlawn Heights.

Stella found Miss D's townhome to be an ideal situation for her. Located just off Fifth Avenue at East Sixty-First Street, it was literally across from the park. Much smaller than the Delacourtes' townhome, yet just as elegant in a brownstone facade, she climbed curved steps that led to a small veranda that opened through a glass and wood door into a front hallway, courtesy of Kitty, who was delighted to see Stella again. With steps going upstairs on the left, and a parlor on the right, Miss D showed Stella the spacious parlor then walked Stella to the back of the house through an ample dining room, which led to the kitchen — the home offering a downstairs that was both comfortable and welcoming. Upstairs hosted three bedchambers off a long hallway with a luxurious bath and ample closets and built-in shelving for linens. A third floor held four small bedrooms and one more bath.

"I have no idea what to do with all these bedrooms," laughed Miss D.

Miss D's aunt had left beautiful furnishings, which Miss D was in the process of updating with cleaning and dusting and rearranging, plus adding special touches of her own from the several trunks she had brought with her from home in Dublin.

"I can hardly believe I'm here, Stella, in my own home in this new and welcoming city. Father was right; it was time I stepped out in the world. Who knows what adventures I'll have!"

Stella couldn't be more pleased for Miss D and spent some time asking about her family and the Poetry Society girls. It seemed Rose and Mavis both had gentlemen friends, and all the girls were prospering in their poetry study. "Alas," said Miss D, "the Poetry Society will not continue unless one of the young ladies steps up to lead it. My father will allow it to continue in our parlor if new leadership is found."

"Do you think you will start a new group here?" asked Stella.

"We shall see, come springtime, but right now, I want to get to know New York and find my place in the world of elocution and genteel company. I am so excited to meet your friends the Delacourtes and to learn about their mission. Their school is more than I could have ever dreamed possible in this very busy, modern, hectic city."

"I think you will grow to love New York, as I've done," said Stella, "although at times I still miss our serene life in Dublin." She related how she had spent the last few months, with many details about the Manning home, family news, Papa's business, Jo's coming wedding, the training and performing she had done, how she and Tom had met, and even the very terrifying story about the kidnapping and rescue. Miss D paled at the retelling of this latter story and hugged Stella again, as she caught her breath and regained some calm.

But as Stella told about her spiritual journey, which was related so closely to her close relationship with Tom and the kidnapping, Miss D became elated with joy and hugged Stella, calling her a "sister in the Lord."

"And, Miss D, I have truly remembered your advice to ask the Lord how best to use my gifts. He is showing me His purpose bit by bit. Reciting the joyous news of our Savior's birth at the church last night honored Him, I do believe, and inspired many to consider how they might follow Him more closely."

"It's such a blessing to hear, Stella, how you remembered my words and are seeing the truth about how to use the gifts we are given," said Miss D.

"And now tell me more about your Mr. Kanes, both of them."

And Stella did.

CHAPTER 25

New York City
Christmas and New Year's Eve, 1892

*J*o was a beautiful bride. As their guests and the wedding party waited downstairs, Mama and Stella adjusted Jo's veil while Papa stood proudly, ready to take her on his arm downstairs to meet her groom.

Mama kissed Jo and told her she loved her and walked down the stairs to the parlor, surrounded by the soft tones of the violinist Papa had hired for the morning wedding on this bright and sparkling Christmas Eve. Mama took her seat beside Michael, who was keeping track of Alfred, both dressed in their finest attire.

Stella held Jo's hands and said, "Jo, you will melt Luca's heart away when he sees you. You are gorgeous."

Jo, a little nervous but mostly just elated, said, "Really, Stella, do you think so?"

"Absolutely," said Stella, squeezing her hands and giving Jo's hand to Papa's arm, who beamed at Jo with just the slightest tears in his eyes. "My firstborn, a bride, and a beautiful one," said Papa.

Stella came down the steps slowly, carrying a small bouquet of fragrant dried flowers lovingly preserved from the summer. She smiled at the assembled family and close friends waiting eagerly in seats gathered for the event and stepped to the side, in front of the parlor window where the ceremony would take place, and where Alice and Vittoria, as bridesmaids, already stood. Luca stood beside his father, who was his best man, looking more handsome than ever in his tailored dark suit, starched collar, and highly polished shoes. Luca's mother sat close by, and the Manning cousins, Tom, and a few close friends gathered around the family.

The priest's garments, in the white and gold of the Christmas season to symbolize purity and joy, reflected the bright light of the morning, as Father O'Malley stood next to Luca waiting for his bride.

Stella smiled at Tom, who returned her smile warmly and seemed to be caught up in the beauty and solemnity of the moment, Stella observed, by the serene and pensive look on his face. The violin music slowed and increased in crescendo as Papa and Jo came down the stairs and into the parlor. Everyone noticed Jo's radiant face, it seemed, because of the breathless "oohs" and "aahs" around the room. Luca and Jo looked right at each other with such love, and Stella was never happier for her sister.

Uncle Nicholas and his family had volunteered their much-larger nearby home for the wedding feast and celebration, so after a marriage and Christmas blessing by the priest and initial congratulations to the newlyweds, the party moved there, and others from the neighborhood joined them. As planned, the elder Mr. Kane arrived from the city with Miss D for the celebration, and both had been invited as guests to stay over with Uncle Nicholas and his family. Tom would stay over too, spending the night with the Rossi family in Luca's old room. And Luca and Jo would be in their new home for their first night as husband and wife.

Tom found Stella right away after the ceremony, kissed her cheek, told her how happy he was for her sister and family and how beautiful she looked. They joined the celebrants for a feast that lasted all afternoon and into the evening and proved to be a perfect combination of Irish and Italian traditions and festive food. As it turned out, the classical violinist was also expert at Irish jigs and Italian tarantellas, so dancing was fun for all.

Colin had arranged for a special bridal carriage decorated with greens and ribbons to transport Luca and Jo to their nearby home, and Colin looked the perfect carriage driver in a tall hat and satin cape. All waved and shouted good wishes, and neighbors drifted off into the night. The Mannings and Kanes bid the newlyweds goodbye and settled down in Uncle Nicholas' large parlor to reminisce about the day, and Stella and Tom sat close, each lost in thought about the significance and joy of such a day in the lives of young people in love.

Uncle proposed a toast to the newly married couple and to all, and hot toddies were shared around. Mr. Kane clinked glasses with Miss D, saying "Sláinte!" in his best Gaelic, which caused Miss D to blush and squeeze his arm. Then Colin, acting as official carriage driver again, took Tom to the Rossi home with a fond farewell from Stella and then took the Mannings home. Helping Mama get a sleeping Alfred in his bed and kissing Alice goodnight, Stella sat with Mama and Papa and Michael to reminisce about their family life and how Jo would have a whole new chapter to share with them. All tired, they made their way to the sleeping rooms, and Stella shared her and Jo's bed with just her dreams that night.

As she drifted off to sleep, she murmured, "Give Jo and Luca a happy life, dear Lord, and let our family be blessed this Christmas Eve. Thank You letting me share this day with Tom too, and may our own special day be not too distant."

The morning brought more celebrations of glad Christmas tidings, and Father O'Malley returned to say a Christmas mass in one of the warehouses nearby in a chilly but jubilant room. Uncle Nicholas insisted all return to their home to finish the feast and enjoy more celebrations and holiday food. Mama made a turkey, ham, and leek pie with leavings from the wedding feast, and Mrs. Rossi presented a luscious plate of "ricciarelli," which she explained was a type of macaroon originating in fourteenth-century Siena and made from milled almonds, sugar, honey, and egg white, and then lightly sprinkled with confectioner's sugar. This perfect Christmas treat was welcomed by all.

Gifts were exchanged, and Alfred was enchanted with a roundhouse for his trains, lovingly made by the Kanes from an old hat box. Stella had bought a pretty shawl for Alice and a little wooden bridge for Alfred's train set, plus a hand-lettered Irish blessing plaque for the Manning home, which she proudly presented to Mama and Papa. She gave Michael a new set of leather braces, which he eagerly tried on and displayed. She had done well on her trip to A. T. Stewart's and had found selections even more abundant than in her previous shopping in Dublin's South City Market.

She in turn was surprised and delighted when Mama gifted her with a lovely evening dress, suitable for formal elocution programs, handmade by the three Manning women. Soft folds of pale green silk in the stylish but modest gown fell from the empire waist into a train in the back, and short puffy sleeves complemented the look.

"How beautiful," cried Stella, hugging Mama and Alice, and just then, as Jo and Luca appeared to share Christmas with the family, she hugged Jo too, noticing her new-wife radiance and happiness. Stella had bought Jo and Luca a beautiful porcelain plate for their new home, which they received with great delight.

But she wanted to give Tom his gift in private, so they held off until all were engaged in various conversations, and she could pull Tom away to a quiet corner in the large parlor. She had planned this gift early in December, and the Delacourtes had helped her achieve it, and she hoped it would be just right.

Tom received the prettily wrapped gift from Stella, leaning over to give her a kiss and saying, "I need no further gift than you, Stella, but thank you, dearest." As he opened the delicate box and discovered the pair of rugged but stylish metal cufflinks, and found his initials on them, he was overwhelmed.

"They are everyday cufflinks, Tom, not fancy ones for Sunday best, but ones you can wear with your uniform for work and think of me each time you see them as you drive your freights."

"Such a thoughtful and loving gift, Stella. I will treasure them and put them on right now to show them off, and I'm hoping you will have tender thoughts of me when you wear my gift." He then presented her with a box, which, when opened, revealed a small golden locket, a most precious heart-shaped pendant, which she immediately adored and put on.

"Oh, Tom, how beautiful and feminine. I shall wear it always, and we can put a small photograph of each of us inside the locket."

"Yes, my darling, and I wish you the most wonderful Christmas ever. Sharing it with you and your family has made it just perfect in every way."

"And it seems your father has had a lovely Christmas too," said Stella, glancing over at Mr. Kane and Miss D, who were in a deep, animated conversation.

"Truly wonderful, your Miss D is, and she is bringing father's once-vibrant personality back with her lively interest and friendship. I think they are very good for each other."

"You know, Miss D has considered herself a spinster, Tom, and has not had gentlemen friends for many years, so I can see she is delighting in your father's attentions. I'll be eager to see how their friendship develops."

"Well, I can tell you now that he is smitten with her. I've never seen him pay attention to any woman since we lost my mother, so I am hopeful there may be a future there for both."

"Like the one we are planning, perhaps?" said Stella, smiling at Tom, who smiled in return, and said, "Yes, my darling!" with a sweet kiss. "And I have some time off in the coming week, and knowing you are heading into the city tomorrow to get settled at the Delacourtes to plan for the early January class, let's plan some nice excursions around the city as you have time.

"And, Stella, I'd love for you to join me for the Little Church's New Year's Eve celebration. They have a dinner at 9:00 p.m., followed by a watchnight service until midnight, then a toast to the new year. I know it will be a late night, but Father has already secured a yes from Miss D, and we'll all be together. Do you think the Delacourtes will agree?"

"It sounds like a perfect way to bring in the new year," said Stella.

Remembering from past years that the week between Christmas and New Year's had always seemed a peculiar week to Stella, she was finding the opposite happening during that peculiar week now. This year, the days were especially busy, moving back into town into her old room at the Delacourtes' with Jessie, working long hours to help prepare for the new students, enjoying some time with Tom at the recently expanded Metropolitan Museum of Art at Fifth Avenue and Eighty-Second Street to view its growing collection of classical antiquities and the recently acquired Manet collection. They had found some time for a brisk stroll or two in Central Park, lunch at Miss D's with the elder Mr. Kane, and even a special "insiders" tour of the Grand Central Depot, which Stella had not visited yet.

The last day of the year soon arrived, and Stella reflected on the many changes in her life in 1892. It had been New Year's Day when Papa announced they would leave Dublin, a day followed by a season of great sadness for her, and yes, she still missed Dublin in some ways. But her new life in America, slowly embraced at first, had not been the end of her dream but the beginning of it. And so much more. How blessed she felt.

She dressed slowly and carefully, wanting to look her best for the celebration at the Little Church. A long-sleeved silky blouse with high lace collar, suitably adorned with the beautiful locket from Tom flowed into a deep green satin skirt with a small train and a wide belt of the same satin. As she floated down the broad staircase into her cape and Tom's arms, and greeted his father and Miss D, she felt that her life, like the new year, was just beginning. The Delacourtes wished them a happy new year and had been kind enough to supply their own carriage and driver for the evening. More blessings!

Tom seemed a little nervous, but Stella figured he felt extra responsibility for ensuring their safety through the milling city crowds and streets clogged with carriages, with many out to celebrate the new year. Arriving safely, they enjoyed an extravagant dinner prepared by the ladies of the church amidst the company of the kind and friendly parishioners, most of whom Tom and his father knew, and who welcomed Stella and Miss D most cordially.

After dinner, Miss D and Mr. Kane said they would step into the church to secure seats for all, and Tom suggested a walk in the peaceful garden churchyard that Stella had so admired on her two previous visits to the Little Church. They sat on a small stone bench, surrounded by the soft organ music inside the church, and Stella looked up to see a thousand stars in the winter sky, feeling total peace.

Tom shifted on the bench and said softly, "I found some time to speak with your father at Christmas, Stella, yet not wanting to take any time away from Jo and Luca at their special celebration, and he has given me permission to speak my heart to you."

Holding her hands and looking deep into her eyes, Tom knelt down in front of her gently but purposely and said the words she had longed to hear: "Stella Manning, my own true love, my darling, I love you so much. Will you spend the rest of your life with me as my wife?"

A million thoughts flashed through Stella's mind as she heard the welcome words Tom spoke: she remembered the self-centered, resentful, and driven girl so set on her own goals; her relentless desire for achievement and recognition; the slow awareness that God had a plan for her life that could include another's dreams too; the tender and stirring love she had grown to experience with this caring and giving man; the danger God had brought her through and how He had received her into His kingdom and given her His peace; and now the freedom to choose a new dream to add to her heart.

As Tom removed a velvet pouch — one of her own — from his watch pocket and held in his hands a small and delicate ruby ring, she said through tears, "Yes, yes, my dearest. Nothing could be better than a lifetime as your wife. We will share our dreams and build our lives together on the path the Lord will show us, day by day.

"Happy new year, my cherished Tom. Now let's go and tell the others!"

EPILOGUE

July 16, 1895

Stella and Tom sat on the small stone bench in the peaceful garden churchyard of the Little Church Around the Corner. What wonderful memories they shared of this welcoming space, and of their wedding exactly two years ago this day. They spoke softly and intimately of their remembrances of the joyful and sacred covenant they had celebrated inside the church by candlelight, surrounded by family and close friends.

"Two years, Stella. I can hardly believe it," said Tom, kissing his wife heartily.

"The time has flown by, Tom, and I have treasured every moment," said Stella, returning the kiss. "And to think of all that has happened since your proposal in this very spot in the closing hours of 1892."

"It's quite amazing, when you think about it, Stella. You have established a reputation as a fine elocutionist, loving what you do in various private and public venues around the city, often with Jessie, and you have helped several dozen students achieve success in the flourishing Delacourte School of Elocution."

"And you, Tom, have achieved well at the Pennsylvania Railroad, receiving promotions to more and more responsibility, with your goal of passenger service engineer coming closer and closer."

"We are so blessed, Stella, and not only us. Your dear Miss D, now a happily married Mrs. Kane, has flourished in her new role, while my father has reemerged into the vibrant man he used to be. And they made it to the altar before we did, remember?"

"Yes," said Stella, laughing. "Your father said they had no time to waste being engaged when they could start their new married life together.

"They are so delightful, Tom. They share so many interests in their domestic life, and I've loved their stories about cooking elaborate meals together. When Miss D first suggested they live in her townhouse, though, I remember your father was hesitant to do so, feeling he needed to provide a home for her, not the other way around. But she was most persuasive, and she has gladly handed him the role of master of the house."

"Which he has stepped up to well. And as a result of his moving, we were able to get happily and comfortably settled in the flat Father and I had shared, Stella. You've made it a wonderful home for us. Someday, we'll move to a larger place, but it's been just perfect as our first home together."

"Yes, it has. I love our little nest. But, Tom, the most exciting part of our past two years is the wonderful work the Lord has given all of us to do with the Settlement House. Who knew Miss D, now a glowing Mrs. K, had such a heart for helping young girls from poverty backgrounds to learn proper speaking skills, manners, and social graces, living in those four bedrooms on the top floor of their townhouse, while training to find useful employment?

"And that your father could continue and expand his teaching skills with the young immigrant men who meet in the parlor each day to study English?"

"And who knew, Stella," said Tom, "that you would work with the young girls week by week to refine their proper speaking skills so that they could take advantage of the opportunities opening up for young women as telephone operators?"

"It's been a blessing to work with these young ladies, Tom, to help them get out of the factories and sweatshops and help them come up in the world. After the first telephone exchange opened at Five Eighteen Broadway, this profession has become an entry point for young women with good speaking skills, and these girls are so eager to learn good diction and basic elocution. Many of 'Mary and Stella's Girls,' as they're called now, have found employment in this growing field, and in other situations throughout the city, especially with the Delacourtes' contacts."

"And we've seen many of them come to faith and welcomed them and their families into our congregation here at the church too," said Tom. "And let's not forget to count our blessings for your dear friend Jessie, newly married to your cousin Colin."

"And this happy event in her life has come along just when her father has gone through some difficult times, with the state government's Lexow Commission investigating corruption in the city and Mr. Roosevelt, as the new police commissioner, essentially forcing Mr. Byrnes to resign, even though no guilt was found. And yet, better times are coming now that he has formed the Byrnes Detective Agency, which is off to a running start. It seems God opens a new door, Tom, as He shuts other ones."

"Indeed, Stella. Look at all the doors He's opened for us, and the wonderful fellowship and friends we're enjoying at the Little Church. And your parents and brothers and sisters are doing well, Stella, with your Papa's business growing, and your family now expanding, with Jo and Luca's new son."

"Yes, my darling, there are so many blessings to count on this remembrance day," said Stella. "And today is the perfect day to tell you of another miraculous one, news that our little family will soon be expanding too."

Tom paused, blinked, and smiled, and then said, "Stella, am I hearing what I think I am hearing?"

"You are, indeed, Tom. With our Lord's blessing, we will be parents early in the new year."

"Oh, Stella..." and Tom enclosed his wife, Stella Manning Kane, in the warmest embrace she had ever experienced, sitting in that peaceful garden, and dreaming of the future they were blessed to share.

ACKNOWLEDGMENTS

*S*tella Manning Kane and Thomas Herbert Kane are my maternal grandparents. I am the daughter of their middle daughter, Estelle Nancy Kane Beck. I was fortunate to know Stella and Tom for many years of my life, and my last picture of Stella was taken in 1970, when she was ninety-four years old, holding my firstborn.

Stella and Tom moved to Perryville, Maryland, and raised their family there. Tom served fifty-two years on the Pennsylvania Railroad, rising to achieve his goal of passenger train engineer. One of my vivid childhood memories is seeing him bring in his train at Baltimore's Penn Station, waving to me from high up in his engineer's cab.

Stella was a busy mother of her and Tom's six children because he was often "on the rails" with his job. She remained engaged with the world and operated in the attic of her home—with the help of her three growing daughters—the telephone exchange for her community. She was active in the early growth of the telephone industry and later served as an agent of the Baltimore Suburban District of the then-existing telephone company.

Stella was my beloved "nana," my mentor and arbiter of all things profitable for a young girl to learn, growing up in the post-World War II world. Speaking well, exhibiting social graces, and attaining ladylike behavior were lessons

I learned early, reinforced by my mother, also trained by Stella. As a prolific communicator, nana would often send me two or three letters a week, even though we lived nearby most of her life. She was only about five feet two but lively and outgoing throughout her life, and Tom used to jokingly call her "captain" or "cap" for her leading role in the life of her family.

Although Stella spoke fondly of Ireland from time to time, she became a patriotic American, fervently supporting causes and organizations that embraced America's founding values, especially in the face of the rise of Communism in the twentieth century.

Key parts of Stella's story are based on accounts of her life she shared with me, but most of the story is highly fictionalized. She did emigrate from Dublin with her family; her father was a watchmaker; she had siblings of the same names (although I have changed their birth order); and she studied elocution and performed on the stage (sadly, I have no specific details). I knew her siblings Josephine and Alfred, as great aunt and uncle, respectively, and Jo did marry an Italian man named Rossi, providing my mother with a wonderful best-friend boy cousin. Alfred fought in World War I, returned whole, and eventually became a rancher in Arizona.

Stella did marry Tom Kane in the Little Church Around the Corner (I have their marriage certificate), but I never learned details of how they met and fell in love. I have precious pictures of Stella in the stage costumes described in the story. I also have a picture of her and Tom on their wedding day. A treasured possession is her mother's Bible passed down to me with many notations and family records. Another treasure is Tom's pocket watch and chain, which helped him keep time during his long Pennsylvania Railroad career. But my most precious item from Stella's life is her Tara Brooch, which I proudly wore while visiting Ireland a few years back.

Some of the other characters in the story lived actual lives in the New York of the 1890s. The very well-known detective and head of the New York Police Detective Bureau (later superintendent of the police department), Thomas Byrnes, appears in his police role, and his accomplishments and personality portrayed in the story are very true to his life, as reported by his biographers. He did have five daughters, one of whom was Jessie. The kidnapping story and his subsequent actions are fictionalized but true to his documented style of police work. The character of the mastermind criminal he captured is based on an actual Byrnes case, with the perpetrator's name and plot changed.

Helen Dauvray managed the Lyceum Theater, and Daniel Frohman was its producer in 1892. Joseph Byron was a society photographer of the era.

You can imagine my delight when I found the proceedings of the First National Convention of Public Readers and Teachers of Elocution, held in 1892, exactly as described in the story. The elocutionary art of public speaking became a powerful communicative and entertainment medium of the nineteenth century's public life, entertaining and teaching literary arts through dramatic gesture and speech. Sadly, other forms of public entertainment overcame the elocution movement as the new century turned, but the twentieth century saw a new rise of the art and science of oratory and public speaking in such organizations as Toastmasters International and in the development of the profession of speech therapy.

Another delight was finding "The New Popular Reciter and Book of Elocution," a turn-of-the-century compendium of instruction in the Delsarte Method of Elocution, including a complete curriculum for training in elocution and an extensive handbook of recitations. This book gave me the details I needed to tell the story of Stella's training and performance. Its pictures of elocution gestures and descriptions of instruction methods are priceless, and I drew heavily from this rare and beautiful book to bring the lost art of elocution alive.

The Delacourte School of Elocution is fictional, however, but the brief flourishing of elocution in the city at that time did occur, and other schools of elocution were founded in other American cities. Therefore, it is not impossible to imagine devotees of the art, including the well-documented Delsarte Method, wishing to train others to expand the cultural influence of the movement at this time in New York City.

Researching Dublin and New York City culture, neighborhoods, transportation, technology, infrastructure, housing, fashion, foodways, and the entertainment industry — and especially New York City's expanding environs in the 1890s — was pure delight. I have tried for accuracy through multiple sourcing, but all errors are mine.

In researching the Pennsylvania Railroad and the occupation of railroad engineer of the time period, I was blessed by the friendly and highly knowledgeable advice of my most excellent "all things railroad" friend, Mr. Bob Kessler of Reston, Virginia, to whom I owe hearty thanks.

Readers and critique reviewers, to whom I am highly indebted, are Amy Anderson, Bob Kessler, Rosemary Maziarz, and Deborah Barnes, and I am grateful for their feedback, suggestions, and corrections. I am also grateful for many friends who showed interest in my progress with kind queries as I wrote.

Special thanks go to Marilyn Turk, my wonderful writing mentor, who, in listening to my three ideas for this first fiction novel, wisely advised me to tell Stella's story when she said, "Only you can tell that story. It's your story to tell." And then she offered encouragement as I wrote. Another writing mentor, Lynn Austin, has offered friendly advice along the way too, and my original writing mentor, Brad Parks, has been an inspiration and an early encourager.

Working with the talented staff at Christian Faith Publishing to prepare this book for publication has been a delight.

My husband, Bob, has cheered me on from the beginning, while a small twenty-one-year-old cockatiel named Louie sat patiently on my wrist during many long writing sessions.

But to my Savior and Best Friend, the Lord Jesus, I give all the credit for letting me find the time and energy and inspiration to tell Stella's story. I was constantly amazed at how He filled my heart and mind with the stories the characters wanted me to tell, as I got to know them. To Him be all the glory.

ABOUT THE AUTHOR

$\mathcal{B}$arbara Beck Lovelace is a writer, publications manager, and business owner. She has written technical, academic, and business documents, but her real love has been researching and writing historic plays for performance, drawing on her MA in American history. Her first fiction novel builds on family history to tell the reimagined story of a cherished grandmother who emigrated from Ireland in the late nineteenth century. When not writing, Barbara's passions are enjoying time with her husband, Bob, interpreting the lives of women of the past in living history settings, reading American history, and spending time with the Lord. In her blended family, she is blessed to share her life and homes in Virginia and Florida with seven grown children and fourteen grandchildren.